PRAISE FOR *SIX*

'A complex and subtle mystery, unfolding like dark origami to reveal the black heart inside' Michael Marshall Smith

'Wonderfully horrifying … the suspense crackles' James Oswald

'Original, inventive and brilliantly clever' Fiona Cummins

'The literary equivalent of dark metal music – gritty, dark, often shocking, and always exciting. A masterful debut' Kati Hiekkapelto

'Wonderfully atmospheric. Matt Wesolowski is a skilled storyteller with a unique voice. Definitely one to watch' Mari Hannah

'A tight, claustrophobic mystery' David F. Ross

'A remarkable debut from a fine new fictional voice. Written as a series of six podcasts, which attempt to uncover the truth about the death of young Tom Jeffries, this compelling narrative pulls you in from the start and keeps you in its grip to the bitter twisted end. A great book!' Shelley Day

'A stunning piece of writing – chock full of atmosphere, human insight and beautiful writing. Take a note of this guy's name. He's going to be huge!' Michael J. Malone

'Following the success and major interest in podcasts such as *Serial* and *This American Life*, *Six Stories* draws its inspiration from the current digital age and relates it back to a two-decades-old murder in a very inventive and intriguing way. Dark, mysterious and definitely not without elements of horror, I was more than a little unsettled while I read it. A genre-bending book, with some hauntingly threatening prose … I could not put it down. Highly recommended!' Bibliophile Book Club

'*Six Stories* is a stunning literary thriller with a killer ending. This is going to be in my top ten books of the year, for sure' Liz Loves Books

'Pulsating with life, with characters who are so incredibly realistic and a plot that is both haunting and terrifying, *Six Stories* is bang up to the minute, relevant and fresh. This is a book that knocks the breath out of the reader. *Six Stories* is genre-busting: it's a crime story, a psychological thriller, a coming-of-age story. An absolute triumph and highly recommended' Random Things through My Letterbox

'My verdict? WOW! *Six Stories* is unlike anything else I've read. It's current, fresh and skilfully delivered. An eerie, spine-tingling read, it's unpredictable and chilling and kept me guessing all the way through. Matt Wesolowski has built up a dark, atmospheric setting with his vivid descriptive prose. The voices were so distinctive that I felt like I was listening to a podcast rather than simply reading the transcript. Everyone will want to read this book – and should. Outstanding' Off-the-Shelf Books

'A quirky, but extremely well-written thriller set around the imagined Scarclaw Fell in Northumberland. *Six Stories* scores extremely well in the dialogue and authenticity of the interviews – whether held in person, by Skype or by phone … you feel they are actually happening. Matt Wesolowski has created a very clever concept' Trip Fiction

SIX STORIES

Six Stories

MATT WESOLOWSKI

**ORENDA
BOOKS**

Orenda Books
16 Carson Road
West Dulwich
London SE21 8HU
www.orendabooks.co.uk

First published in the United Kingdom by Orenda Books 2017

The lines quoted on page 189 are taken from 'The Wendigo' by Algernon Blackwood (1869–1951).

ISBN 978-1-910633-62-5

Typeset in Garamond by MacGuru Ltd
Printed and bound by CPI Group (UK) Ltd, Croydon CRO 4YY

SALES & DISTRIBUTION

In the UK and elsewhere in Europe:
Turnaround Publisher Services
Unit 3, Olympia Trading Estate
Coburg Road
Wood Green
London
N22 6TZ
www.turnaround-uk.com

In USA/Canada:
Trafalgar Square Publishing
Independent Publishers Group
814 North Franklin Street
Chicago, IL 60610
USA
www.ipgbook.com

In Australia/New Zealand:
Affirm Press
28 Thistlethwaite Street
South Melbourne VIC 3205
Australia
www.affirmpress.com.au

For Cobweb

—So do we pass the ghosts that haunt us later in our lives; they sit undramatically by the roadside like poor beggars and we see them only from the corners of our eyes, if we see them at all. The idea that they have been waiting there for us rarely crosses our minds. Yet they do wait, and when we have passed, they gather up their bundles of memory and fall in behind, treading in our footsteps and catching up, little by little.

Stephen King – *Wizard and Glass*

—Mountains overawe and oceans terrify, while the mystery of great forests exercises a spell peculiarly its own. But all these, at one point or another, somewhere link on intimately with human life and human experience.

Algernon Blackwood – *The Willows*

—Says milord to milady as he mounted his horse / Beware of Long Lankin that lives in the moss

Northumbrian/Scottish Murder Ballad

Scarclaw Fell
2017

I recognise this bit of woodland. This recognition ignites a little ember of joy inside me, a sense of accomplishment. The more I come out here, the more familiar with it I get. The trees glaring down with their familiar, pinched faces.

When I first met this land, it overawed me, just an unrelenting mass; disorder. There was no way of straightening it out. The woods just sort of jump at you from the dark; all those trees filled with croaking, fretting birds, the buckled heads of ferns that slap lazily at your shins as you pass through.

At first, I wondered if I should call in the bulldozers, get it swept away; just like Dad did with that Woodlands Centre. Now I'm glad I didn't. In a strange sort of way, these woods are starting to become beautiful. Thinking this fills me with a horrible, leaden feeling; it's the last thing that should enter my mind. It's not proper. Yet the tiny pockets of spiders' webs, each holding a single raindrop, and the peppering of gorse flowers on the fell-side tell me otherwise.

There's magic here between the trees.

In my own way, I am beginning to understand this land. Its utter indifference to those who dwell here. Like the rest of us, these woods crouch in the shadow of the fell, which rears up in the distance; a cloud-crested wave of blackened scree.

Scarclaw Fell. It sounds like something from *Game of Thrones.*

I stop in a natural sort of clearing in the trees. I've been walking for ten minutes, now, and I can barely see the building behind me.

Dad was overjoyed when he finally got that place built on the site of what was once the Scarclaw Fell Woodlands Centre. Outside its front door, there's a brass plaque. I fought tooth and nail with Dad about the new name: 'The Hunting Lodge'. It just sounds so … twee. I guess he wanted to sweep away everything that had happened here before.

Dad filled The Hunting Lodge's bookshelves with these tatty, leather-bound volumes. Something for the tourists to look at, though I doubt any of them ever read them. I've been looking through them recently. Their pages are thick, the yellow of old bones. The smell of pipe tobacco rises from them: like the ghosts of things past.

That's what I do when I'm out here: I chase old ghosts. Stir up shadows. Think.

Sometimes I wonder what I am, what part I play in this whole mess. Am I, Harry Saint Clement-Ramsay, just another Dr Frankenstein, grubbing the dead up out of their graves to try and heal some old wound?

Should I have even agreed to be interviewed at all? Should I have agreed to wake the dead? Will my words destroy the peace that has taken twenty years to fall on Scarclaw Fell?

He wore a mask.

Just a white thing, the features of which jutted out from beneath his hood. Cheeks and a nose in pale plastic. A forehead that curved like a skull.

It should have been comical. Like the masks that crusty lot wear when they're railing against the multinationals. But I was scared.

When he pulled up at the gate of the Mayberry Estate, we watched him from the security box. We had all his emails printed out; months of them – begging, pleading, promising. I was fully expecting a Hummer, blacked-out windows and all that. He was famous on the internet wasn't he?

So the Ford Ka with a rash of bugs across its bonnet was the last thing we imagined he drived. Tomo rang my phone. I answered and left the line open, slipped it in my pocket. Tomo put his on speaker. We'd practised this. The code line was, 'Did you try the farm shop on your way here?' Not very original, but it would take the lads less than a minute to get from the security box to the gate if I said it.

Wait till he gets close, I thought, wondering if I could go through with all this. If the other chaps hadn't been nearby, on guard, then I don't know what would have happened. Maybe I would have bottled it; bowed out.

He had warned me he was going to wear the mask. When I searched online for him, I read all about it, sort of understood why he wore it. Yet when he stepped out of that car, I nearly said fuck it, no way. Nearly turned around and closed the gate. If he wasn't even going to show his face … He could have been anyone.

I suppose that was the point.

I was scared. But I wasn't going to show him that, was I? Justin had a shotgun. I don't know if it was loaded. Tomo had a knife, still sharp from the packet. They were there to protect me. But in some way it was like they were defending the memory of that night twenty years earlier. The memory of what we saw. The memory of what we found.

The chap in the mask got out of his car and someone I didn't recognise as myself walked over and shook his hand; that same someone betrayed no fear. I thought I could hear a smile in his voice.

He could have been snarling, scowling, mouthing profanities, hating the bones of me behind that mask. I'll never know.

He thanked me. We got in my car. He clipped a microphone to my lapel and turned on the recording device.

Then we talked.

I stop in the clearing and pour tea into the cup of my flask. Everything is damp and I don't want to sit down. It's a cliché I know, but you never really stop and listen to silence, do you? I have started to listen when I'm here, beneath the branches. When I first started coming out, I used to wear headphones, one ear-bud in my right, my left empty.

The woods aren't silent, not really; if you stand and listen there's all sorts going on: rustlings and chattering; when it rains, the sound of the leaves is a cacophony of wagging green tongues; in the mornings the indignant back-and-forth clamour of the birds is almost comical.

I've not come out into these woods at night. Not for a long time, anyway.

The last time I walked here in darkness was nearly twenty years ago – it was me and Jus and Tomo. That was the night we found *him*. That boy. It was where the woods begin to thin, where they turn upward towards the bare back of the fell; where the path turns to marsh.

I think I don't like silence because, when it falls, that scene begins its loop.

Nearly twenty years, and what happened that night, what we found out there, still doesn't fade.

The man in the mask said he understood that; said he understood some ghosts never die. I think that's what finally got through to me, and to Dad. If anything, he said, telling him what happened might help.

Help.

That's not a word I'd have ever expected when it came to us. People didn't think the Saint Clement-Ramsays needed help. Of course we didn't; we had money, right? Who needs help when you're rich?

Twenty years ago, Scarclaw Fell Woodlands Centre was still standing. The Hunting Lodge wasn't even a concept; not yet. All of it – the woods, the fell itself, the Woodlands Centre – was Dad's though. And the toilets and the showers still worked, so we just thought 'sod it', me Tomo and Jus. We left our cars sitting in puddles on the track leading up to the centre.

The Woodlands Centre back then was an awful, seventies block, all MDF and lino. It had a smell: steam, soil, warm cagoules; and in the kitchen the reek of veggie sausages and fried eggs. There was a spattering of muddy boot prints around the doorways; fold-up chairs, cobwebs in the corners, painted metal radiators. Someone – the Scouts or the Guides, one of the groups that used the Woodlands Centre – had made a frieze on the far wall in crêpe-paper: *'Leave nothing but footprints – take your litter home.'* A smiling badger beneath it. One of its eyes had come off and there was a tight scribble of black biro in its place.

To be honest, that first day in August 1997 wasn't much fun. Me and Jus and Tomo were, what, all twenty-one or twenty-two-ish? It was chucking it down so the three of us sat in that long dining-room area, drank beers and played fucking *Monopoly* all afternoon. We ended up pretty trolleyed, just getting on each others' nerves. We were all hungry and no one wanted to start cooking; but Kettle Chips and dips don't fill you up. We were stupid, stupid city-boys. There were no takeaways around here and no one was sober enough to drive into the village or look for a petrol station. Jus pulled out some vintage whisky. That meant we'd drink till we were sick; be asleep by nine, with the rush and chatter of the trees haunting our dreams as we snored.

If only it'd ended like that

I finish my tea, scatter the dregs into the undergrowth. Dawn begins to swell, her light expanding over the woodland. I turn toward the cloak of branches and brambles, and press on. That's what we did back then – went off the beaten track. We were so wasted and it was so wet, we couldn't even see a track, beaten or not.

I take another look back and the light in The Hunting Lodge window is still visible. I try to imagine what the Woodlands Centre looked like to that boy back then. This is the way he came, back in 1996. Through the branches, I don't imagine it looked much different: a light in a window; the promise of warmth, four walls.

I keep going, plunging into the wood. You only have to be careful where you step when the ground starts sloping upward. There are signs now, but there weren't back then. This was the way they came back in '96, I'm sure of it: a couple of miles north-west of The Hunting Lodge (or the Woodlands Centre, as it was back then) there's a sort of natural path between the trees. I follow it.

As I walk, there's a little pull of nostalgia inside me: a longing. As if some little part of me, some thread, has caught on the memory.

Like I have become part of everything that happened here.

Which, in some ways, I suppose is true.

Episode 1: Rangers

—Dad bought up all the land round there just before ... before *it* happened. I mean, literally, it was a few weeks.

Then the shit-storm descended.

Oh, terribly sorry ... am I allowed to swear on this?

This is the voice of Harry Saint Clement-Ramsay; Harry's the son of Lord Ramsay, owner of the land around Scarclaw Fell. Owner of the fell itself.

Scarclaw Fell: For those old enough to remember, that name has a certain resonance.

These days, that resonance is largely silent.

Meeting Harry in person is somewhat of a breakthrough, to say the least. The Ramsay estate has not acknowledged my emails or letters for months. I actually thought we might fall at this first hurdle. Indeed, without Harry, this podcast would lose significant authenticity; become just more speculation about what happened that day in 1996. The teeth of a rake through the long-dry earth of an old grave.

It's been twenty years since the incident and the Ramsays have been consistent in their refusal to speak about it to anyone.

Until now.

Suited and booted, rosy-cheeked and athletic, Harry looks as if he's from fine stock. As a person, he's affable, but guarded. He reminds me of a politician visiting the proles in the lead up to an election. Every word is chosen with precision.

When it comes to Scarclaw Fell, Harry is evasive – careful with what he says. And to be honest, I don't blame him.

—I think Dad was going to get all the old tunnels – the mine-shafts and what have you – filled in. Then he was going to try selling it – to one of those developers, you know? For log cabins, fishing holidays or something? But … I guess it was too much of a job. And after what happened, the impetus just … wasn't there anymore. And it's like a bloody rabbit-warren under the fell – all the fissures and hidden pits; and that's before you take into account the bogs and marshes and stuff where they … where *we* … well … you know. It's a bloody death trap. Christ knows why they were even there in the first place, right? I mean, who would go there for *fun?*

Before the events of 1996, Scarclaw Fell was largely unknown. And today, most people have forgotten its name once more; despite that almost-famous photograph on the front of The Times; the hook-like peak curling through the clouds behind a spectral sheen of English drizzle. Most people have forgotten the name Tom Jeffries too.

Maybe that's about to change.

—Sometimes I wonder how things could have been different. If dad had called the contractor an hour before he did, they would have come out and knocked the place down – repaired all the fences and the signs, got in some proper security to keep people away and none of this would have happened. An hour and dad could have said, 'Sorry, it doesn't matter how long ago you booked it, things change.' That would have been that. I wouldn't be talking to you now.

Just one hour – and a boy is dead.

Face down in the marsh. Someone's son; someone's grandson.

He was only fifteen, wasn't he?

Christ.

Welcome to Six Stories. *I'm Scott King.*

In the next six weeks, we will be looking back at the Scarclaw Fell tragedy of 1996. We'll be doing so from six different perspectives; seeing the events that unfolded through six pairs of eyes.

Then, as always, it's up to you. As you know by now, I'm not here to make judgements. I'm here to allow you to do that.

For my newer listeners, I must make this clear: I am not a policeman, a forensic scientist or an FBI profiler. This isn't an investigation or a place I'm going to reveal new evidence. My podcast is more like a discussion group at an old crime scene.

In this opening episode we'll review the events of that day; introducing you briefly to the people present. We'll be hearing, not just from Harry, but also from one of the others who was directly involved; who was there; who knew Tom Jeffries personally; and for whom the shadow of what happened on that day in 1996 still remains, like some malevolent, unshakable stain on their life.

We will look back on what is, to some, a simple, open and closed case – a tragedy that could have, and should have, been avoided. To others, though, it is an enduring and enthralling mystery, to which there are no clear-cut answers.

At least not yet.

OK, now for a little bit of history. Buckle up, I'll be brief.

The fell itself rises from some of England's most beautiful countryside; Northumberland, north-east England. Scarclaw Wood was once an old glacial lake, filled with sand and gravel; the fell – a standstone escarpment – is now classified as an Area of Outstanding Natural Beauty. There are several Iron Age cairnfields on its higher ground and the remains of scattered farmsteads on its slopes. Evidence of standing stone rings and Neolithic burial sites only add more layers to the landscape. The summit of the fell curls in a hook shape; as if something has taken a colossal bite out of its base. This is presumably the reason why Scarclaw has its name. Like much of Northumberland, inscrutable 'cup and ring' artwork decorates the rocks on its lower slopes.

Beneath the fell's higher ground is a complex network of lead mines that date back to the fifteenth century. They're all abandoned now, shut down in the 1900s due to subsidence. There were attempts to reopen the mines in the 1940s, but these were unsuccessful. Most of the tunnels beneath the fell have collapsed; and the resulting hollows and the weakened surface have

*created strange hybrid marshes and traps: half man-made; half claimed
by nature. To attempt a walk across the marshland of Scarclaw Fell is
to dance a jig with death himself. Without warning, the ground could
simply swallow you up. Yet it is not only the marshland that is a danger
to the unwitting; the majority of the mine's ventilation shafts have long
been obscured by nature, so they are now great fissures lipped with moss
and heather. The only signs of what they were are the remnants of the
decrepit fences erected long ago. Visitors to the woods and the fell are
advised to stay on the paths. Large sections were fenced off long ago, but
there is still danger underfoot on Scarclaw Fell.*

*Amongst this no-man's land of reeds and marsh grass stand the remains
of an engine house: a pale, crumbling tower encrusted with moss, and a
wall with a single window; the only remnants of a remote hamlet.*

—I don't know what happened to that boy … I really have no
idea. None of us do. How the police never found his body is just
bloody … *ludicrous* though, isn't it? A bloody *year*.

*Harry and I record the interview in his car, in the driveway of Lord
Ramsay's Mayberry Estate. He assures me that is father is away and tells
me that it's probably futile trying to get even a statement from him.*

—We don't talk about it, Dad and I; not anymore. Best to leave
these things buried … Oh gosh, I'm sorry … poor choice of words,
but you know what I mean, yeah? Dad still blames himself for what
happened up there, but what could he have done? There were signs
already, they knew what was up there, didn't they? They'd stayed
there hundreds of times before. Hell, it was that lot who had insu-
lated the place. They did it one summer; climbed underneath in
those white decorators' overalls and nailed a load of polystyrene to
the underside of the floor. Mad, isn't it? I mean, it was nothing more
than a glorified barn.

It wasn't just them that used the place. We hired it out to Scouts,
Girl Guides, climbers, canoe-ers … canoe-ists? … speelenkers …

spelunkers? Those guys that go climbing down holes … As I say, I'm
not an outdoorsy type. They all knew what the dangers were.

*Harry's talking about the Scarclaw Fell Woodlands Centre; a self-
catering, single-storey accommodation centre that was far more advanced
than the 'glorified barn' he calls it. When it still stood, it had five dormitories with about thirty beds, gas central heating, a fully equipped
kitchen, toilets, showers, the lot.*

*Situated at the very base of the fell, about five miles through the forest
tracks off the A road, the centre was an L-shaped building with a car
park and a telephone line. The centre was hugely popular. It was quite
a distance from the danger of the mines and had plenty of picturesque
walks and a river nearby. If you didn't want to hire out the building, you
could camp in its grounds. According to the one remaining logbook, it
was fully booked all year round. Climbers, walkers, canoeists, spelunkers,
even Scouts and Guides all used the Woodlands Centre regularly. And
there are no records of any serious accidents occurring on the land around
Scarclaw Fell in the last thirty years. Presumably the danger signs did
their job.*

*Lord Ramsay acquired the land around Scarclaw Fell after what hap-
pened in 1996. The purchase was an ongoing battle that raged for several
years between with Lord Ramsay, the local authority, the National Trust
and the co-operative of groups that had used the centre. This battle is
irrelevant to our story; but suffice to say, money conquered all, Scarclaw
Fell became part of the Ramsay estate, the centre was levelled and most of
the fell was fenced off. But we're straying from the point. Back to Harry.*

—The environmentalists threatened to jump all over Dad's
case if he changed things at Scarclaw. Don't get me wrong, he was
going to make it nice! But he said he'd have to drain a lot of it …
the marshes … to make the holiday lets; and that was a problem
– habitats and stuff. Newts, frogs and other slimy things no one
cares about till they're suddenly 'endangered'. Those old mineshafts
were the main problem, though; they had some rare bats nesting in

them, didn't they? Bats are alright I guess … but they're a bloody legal nightmare, so I think he eventually just thought 'sod it' and left it all alone.

—*Did your father ever visit, go to the Woodlands Centre itself, have a look around? Before what happened, I mean.*

—He may have, I don't know. It wouldn't have made much difference to be honest. Dad's like a bloody Rottweiler with a bone once he sets his mind to something, you know?

Harry and I talk for a while about the legal wrangling to purchase the land. I ask him a few times why Lord Ramsay wanted Scarclaw so much, but I don't get a straight answer. Maybe he wanted some new hunting land, for grouse shooting, deer stalking, something like that? Parts of the land were, in fact, created as hunting parks around four hundred years ago. The ancient woodlands are a lingering testament to this. What I do know is that Lord Ramsay seemed to have underestimated the appeal of the land. Even after the tragedy; the fight for Scarclaw Fell went on for a long while.

Maybe, because Harry's aware that this podcast will be listened to by millions, he is simply saving face – for his father, his family, I don't know. Eventually, though, I have to broach the subject we've both been avoiding; circling each other like a pair of tigers.

—*It was you, Harry, who found him, wasn't it? You found Tom Jeffries' body?*

—Yeah … yeah … I found him…

OK, so I could have phrased it better, but there's something about talking to people with Harry's wealth and clout that makes me a little flustered: it's that unshakeable confidence they exude, I just kind of blurt things out. For a few moments he looks at me and I think he is going to ask me to leave. Thankfully, he goes on with an unflappable air that I have to admire. Stiff upper lip and all that.

—Legally, I can talk about it now. Now that the case is officially
… 'cold' is it called? Resolved? That's not to say I want to, you
understand. But I will, because … I don't know, maybe it's cathartic
or something, yeah? And you're not a journalist…

Harry's very aware of what will happen when Six Stories *airs, he's
not a podcast fan himself but he knows just how popular these things
are. He tells me he's heard of* Serial *and he's aware of the potential thousands, possibly millions that will hear* Six Stories *worldwide. He asks me
about whether I think the media will turn to him, or even his father, for
answers. Lord Ramsay is an old man, he says; he doesn't need that. I tell
him I don't know what will happen when* Six Stories *airs, that I can't
make any promises. It seems he appreciates my honesty. He says he'll tell
me what he told the police before he has to go.*

—So, yeah. OK. So me and a few of my mates are out there,
yeah? Having a little recce of the place, a bit of a mission, if you
know what I mean?

*Harry's talking about the lower regions of the fell itself, the woods a
mile or so from the relative civilisation that is the Woodlands Centre.
This seems at total odds with Harry's often flustered assertions that he's a
'city gent'. I make no comment.*

—And it's the middle of the night; I dunno, maybe one or two
a.m.; we're having a jolly, you know? A walk around the woods.
We've got the dogs with us and suddenly they start going fucking
mad – barking and yapping like they've caught a scent.

*Sitting looking at Harry, with his good skin, coiffed hair and a fore-
head permanently scarred with worry lines, I'm not sure I can picture
him and his friends, who I can only assume were 'country types', walking
round a wood in the middle of the night with dogs. The police report
states they were also carrying lights – great, powerful lamps – which*

lends further credence to the idea that the Ramsays were using the land for hunting. There are several species of deer in Scarclaw woods, not to mention foxes, badgers and other assorted wildlife that the upper class like to kill for pleasure. 'Lamping' they call it: catch a deer in a light, makes them freeze.

—Now, like I say, I don't know what's going on and I've had a few drinks, so I just go along with it, you know? I've got no idea where we are and we're going deeper and deeper into the trees, and the undergrowth is really deep, like right up to our waists – brambles and bracken.

As I've said, the Woodlands Centre is surrounded by forest; go just a couple of miles towards the base of the fells and you're in dense, untamed woodland. Harry's dogs stop two and a half miles north-west of the centre. This marshy area was fenced off and very dangerous; why Harry and his friends were traversing it in the middle of the night seems more stupid than gutsy.

—It's really fucking muddy round there, yeah? You can feel your feet getting wet, and before you know it you're up to your knees in sludge. The dogs are still going mad and there's this smell … it's like … well … it's hard to describe – kind of sweet; meaty; it gets inside you, you know? A stink like that, gets right into your brain, deep; takes a while to let go. I'd like to think we had sort of an idea about what it was. Like, where in the fucking woods do you smell something like that? So we turn the lights on and that's when we saw it … half buried in the mud. I swear down, I will never forget it as long as I live…

The dogs all shot off into the marsh and began digging, uncovering their find, heaving at it with their teeth, easing bones from sockets, tearing at soft, decomposing flesh and depositing their finds at the feet of their masters. Harry and his friends turned on their lamps, and instead of dazzling deer, they shone down upon the decapitated and half-rotted corpse of a child. A child whose body had been missing for a year. Fifteen-year-old Tom Jeffries.

—Like I say, I'll never forget that sight. We honestly thought it was a prank, at first – like one of the guys was messing with us and someone was going to start laughing, and a camcorder was going to appear. But we all just fucking *stood there* staring. I sometimes see it in my sleep; half buried in the mud, hands bunched into claws like it … like *he* was a fucking *zombie* or something, desperate to rise from the grave.

The local police were duly summoned and the crime scene investigators erected their tents. Rather than a national scandal, it was more like relief that the body that had eluded police, investigators, scientists, and even psychics, for the best part of a year, had finally been found.

Tom Jeffries had gone missing on a trip to Scarclaw Fell Woodlands Centre with a group of other teenagers and two supervising adults. Unlike today, when such disappearances run riot on social media, Tom Jeffries' disappearance was largely ignored by the national press. Of course it was reported, as was the discovery of his body; but the moral outrage that dominates society today was simply absent back in 1996. Maybe it was just the times; there was no such thing as social media in the nineties, and the internet was not the crazed animal it is now.

Or perhaps it was something to do with Jeffries himself. Was it something to do with his personality, his reputation, that simply didn't warrant a national outpouring of grief? Was it because, at fifteen, Jeffries wasn't enough of a 'child'? Was it because he was male, white, and from a stable, middle-class background; an average school student, who blended in, had no real enemies and enjoyed a large group of friends?

Would Tom Jeffries have been remembered more if he had been a little white girl from a privileged background? This is just one of the questions that Six Stories will seek to answer…

In this series, we'll look at the case of Tom Jeffries from six different angles. Six people will tell their stories; six people who knew Tom Jeffries in six different ways. When the stories are told, you'll be able to decide what conclusions, if any, can be drawn from a death shrouded in uncertainty.

Welcome to Six Stories. *This is story number one:*

We've never had anything like it in Rangers. It was terrible … just a terrible, terrible thing. It drove us apart in the end. No one knew how to cope with what happened up on Scarclaw Fell … and a lot of them just *didn't*; didn't cope, I mean.

It all fell apart. Everything we'd done. It'd been such a huge part of our lives. Such a shame.

This is the voice of Derek Bickers, sixty-two. Derek, along with his friend Sally, were the last adults to use the Scarclaw Fell Woodlands Centre. They had booked it for a loose group of teenagers – their own children and their friends – a group that referred to itself affectionately as 'Rangers'. That day in August 1996, the group consisted of five teenagers and two adults. One of those teenagers was Tom Jeffries.

—'Rangers' – *to an outsider, it sounds rather like it was some sort of organisation … which it really wasn't, was it?*

—No, Rangers was never a proper organisation. There were just a few of us at first, just like-minded parents and friends, that sort of thing. We just wanted something for our kids to do; that's it really. It was never anything more than that. The name came much later; a Lord of the Rings reference I think. And I don't want to say I was the chief, or the boss, it wasn't like that really.

What's that? Oh, when it started? Oh, way back; a few of us were planning a camping trip when the kids were little – three, four years old. We'd set the tents up in the garden and Eva and Charlie were charging round them, in and out, like kids do…

Eva is Derek's daughter. Eva Bickers was fifteen years old at the time of the trip to Scarclaw in 1996. She was a friend of Tom Jeffries. Charlie is Charlie Armstrong, the son of a friend of the Bickers and of Tom Jeffries. He was also fifteen years old in 1996. He was at Scarclaw too.

—They were grubbing up great handfuls of leaves from the lawn, chucking them at each other; they were covered in mud, twigs in their hair. We were all saying how much they were going to love it – the camping trip, I mean, how they just seemed so at ease in the leaves, the mud, all that. Not like kids today, all phones and iPads. And at least we were *trying* to get them to connect with the outside…

It probably sounds a bit silly now, all a bit middle-class: a bunch of us old hippy types off in the woods, going back to nature, all that. But it wasn't; it really wasn't like that at all. We just had fun. That's all it was about in the end, just having fun.

I conduct this interview with Derek Bickers on the phone. He's never heard of me or Six Stories. Sometimes this is just as well. Derek was crucified in the press at the time of the tragedy. He had reporters outside his house, and photographs of him at university – hair over his eyes, acoustic guitar in one hand, the other smoking a joint – were leaked by someone close to him. That betrayal wounded him deeply, more that the headlines that accused him at best of negligence and at worst of pretty much murdering Tom Jeffries himself. It was something that Derek never really recovered from; and, as far as I know, he never found out who had done it.

Again, it all makes you speculate: should a tragedy like the one that befell Tom Jeffries in 1996 happen now, what might be the impact on someone like Derek of the trial by media and the press condemnation that would surely ensue?

Derek Bickers was questioned extensively about Tom Jeffries' death, but was never charged with his murder. He has spent the years since he was released by the police, keeping his head down, trying to get on with his life. I can only imagine how the weight of such an experience could

*wear you down, even if you were a formidable outdoorsman like Derek.
It is clear, when he speaks about the past, that he has fond memories of
his time in the wilderness with the group. Derek is a former mountain-
climber, canoeist, and fell-runner; six foot something with a head so bald
it shines, and a neat, grey beard. I ask him whether he continued his
relationship with the outdoors after Scarclaw.*

—I ran. I've always run; but I ran a lot after Scarclaw. Great long
routes, cross countries, miles and miles, head down. If something
like that ever happens to you, running is the best thing. I'd recom-
mend it to anyone. I used to run until my legs had gone, my knees,
my ankles; till I was dead on my bloody feet. It was the only thing
that helped … it just kind of ordered it all in my head.

*There was speculation that Derek would at least be charged with
negligence. Tom and the other teenagers were in his care. Tom Jeffries'
family, however, were adamant they did not want to press charges
against Derek, and eventually the lack of evidence and the perseverance
of Derek's friends and family prevailed. The coroner's report was incon-
clusive on the issue of foul play and Tom Jeffries' death was described
as 'accidental' or 'by misadventure'. Yet this did not stop the rest of the
country, or indeed, the world seeing Derek Bickers as the face of what
happened. At least for a while.*

—*So, in 1996, Rangers were still going strong?*
—Yeah. Even though the kids were older. We'd kept it going – the
camping trips, the walks, all that.
—*There were more members though, right?*
—Yeah; well, there were more people who knew about it by then.
Our kids had invited their friends from school; the other parents
had heard about it and liked the idea. There were a good, maybe,
twenty members of Rangers. It was still informal; it was still more or
less just walks in the woods, rock-climbing trips, all that, but now
we had a name.

—What were the age ranges of the group?

—Well I guess you could say from zero to adult. There were babies, toddlers, pregnant women, teenagers…

—But they didn't all go on the trips did they?

—Not all of them, no. By then, we'd started a loose weekly meeting in the church hall. It was just a social thing really; people brought cakes, coffee; the younger kids charged about and played and the older ones helped plan the excursions.

—And you say there was no underlying, ideological theme running through the group – not like the Scouts or something?

—That's correct. It was more about friendship, about acceptance. Just a network of parents and kids; friends of friends; something to do, all that.

—Can you tell me more about the kids who were involved in the trip to Scarclaw?

—There weren't many of them. That summer in '96 there was one of those bugs going round the schools; the kids were dropping like flies – vomiting, temperature. It would have been a bloody nightmare out on the fell, we nearly cancelled the whole thing.

By then Rangers was, a bit more organised, I suppose. We had to be: dietary needs, consent forms that sort of thing. These were other people's kids we were responsible for; we couldn't muck about. We had a meeting; me and the other adults…

Anyone who helped out with the trips to the countryside did so off their own backs. People gave up their own time to help out with the weekly meetings and the trips. Derek was not by himself on the trip to Scarclaw in 1996; there was another adult present. He maintains that there was no real hierarchy to the group, that the 'leaders' were just responsible adults – people who helped out of the goodness of their hearts.

—It was the kids themselves that were determined to go to Scarclaw that summer. I mean really determined. Even if it was only going to be a few of them. They would have been gutted if we'd cancelled. We'd been booking the Woodlands Centre at Scarclaw for years. The kids loved it, knew the place like the backs of their hands. That summer as well, it was beautiful…

Sorry, I'm going on, aren't I … So, the kids, the people who were there: there were only five kids in the end. Eva, my daughter, was one of them. She was … fifteen. They all were about that age. And then there was me, obviously. And Sally.

Sally Mullen's son, Keith, was ill at the time of the Scarclaw trip in 1996. Sally, like Derek Bickers, was one of the original members of Rangers and she had agonised for a while about whether she would come and help out on that particular trip. Her husband, however, had taken some leave from work, anticipating that Keith would attend the trip, so he was able to stay at home while Sally went to Scarclaw with Derek and the other kids. This is another 'what if' moment. If Sally had decided to stay at home, would the trip to Scarclaw have gone ahead? I don't want to speculate on this with Derek, though, there's no point.

Unlike Derek, Sally Mullen seemed to somehow slip under the press radar. There are several reasons I can think of why that happened. First, she is female. As abhorrent as sexism is, a man is far more likely to be a killer. That's just how it is. Also, Sally suffers from an intense form of sleep apnoea, meaning that she needs specialist equipment, assisting her breathing while she sleeps. This made her highly unlikely as a suspect. In order to kill Tom Jeffries she would have had to get up in the early hours of the morning, dismantle her sleeping equipment on her own and then re-apply it after she had finished.

—Sally *came out of it all smelling pretty clean, didn't she?*
—As she should. She's as innocent as the rest of us. Look; I took the brunt of it, I know that. I did it to protect not only Sally but the kids as well. They were *children*, for god's sake.

Derek was vociferous in his defence of the others and took particular offence at how the teenagers were treated by the police, accusing them of being heavy-handed in their questioning. I believe it was this anti-establishment tone that turned the press against Derek, whereas they left the quiet, compliant Sally Mullen alone.

—*Can you tell me a bit about Eva? Your daughter.*

—Eva's a good lass; she was a good baby as well, if that makes sense? Didn't do much in the way of crying; slept all night. She was just normal; a normal lass. She did well at school – wanted to be a vet.

—*Would you say that Eva and her friends were rebels? At the time, I mean.*

—Eva's never been the rebellious type. Well, I say that, but all kids rebel, don't they? That's just normal. Sus and I, we always tried to be understanding, easy. 'Chilled out' – that's how Eva's friends used to describe us. I don't think we were any more liberal than anyone else, but screaming and shouting never did anyone any good, did it? There wasn't a lot of conflict in our house. We talked. I think that's important when you're raising a girl. You know what kids are like when they get older.

—*That's a good way to raise a child, Derek. No wonder Eva was happy.*

—We're tolerant people; if Eva wanted to dye her hair, wear strange clothes, that sort of thing, we always let her express herself. My thought was always that, if you start telling kids they're not allowed to do things, the more they're going to want to do it. Of course we had rules; Eva was fifteen, still a kid. She was a kid when what happened on Scarclaw happened. She was a child.

—*You knew the other kids too, didn't you? You and Sally knew their parents, right?*

—That's right. Most of them had been in Rangers since it began. Charlie Armstrong – he was Eva's best friend, since they were kids.

Charlie Armstrong is the boy that Derek has already mentioned. The one who had thrown leaves with Eva in the Bickers' garden. Charlie's mum was involved with Rangers, but she and Charlie's father had

booked a weekend away when Charlie was due to go to Scarclaw. Both
of them declined to talk to me.

—*Tell me about Charlie.*

—Charlie and Eva went to different schools; I think that's how
they kept their friendship going; they saw each other at Rangers
and at weekends, without the nonsense you get about *boyfriends and*
girlfriends, and all that stuff in the playground.

I've known Charlie's mum and dad for years; they're good people;
they've got a similar attitude to me and Sus: chilled out, go with the
flow, that sort of thing.

Charlie was a little more ... I dunno ... a bit more *outgoing*, if
that's the right word, than Eva was back then.

In the inquest into Tom Jeffries' death, this was the debate that nearly
saw Derek Bickers and Sally Mullen charged with negligence. As I men-
tioned previously, it was the parents of Tom Jeffries who were the most
vocal in protecting Derek and Sally. As we will discover in further epi-
sodes of this podcast, all the teenagers at Scarclaw that night had been
drinking alcohol and smoking cannabis. Charlie Armstrong was appar-
ently one of the main instigators or ringleaders in all of that. We'll get to
it in due course.

—*You say that Charlie Armstrong was 'outgoing'.*

—I don't know if outgoing is the right word, though; he was a
strong character – that's probably a better phrase. Charlie was definitely the alpha of the group, the leader of the pack. He smoked
cigarettes; and his mum and dad knew he did. He was into his music
... death metal or something like that ... not that that has anything
to do with anything. He had the long coat, the long hair, T-shirt with
bloody devils on it, or some such; all that. I think he was excluded
from his school a few times.

This is another point of interest and something that was raised at the inquest. *Charlie Armstrong was thought of as the leader of the older teenagers. His appearance and music preferences were raised more than once in the press, to the derision of the parents, as well as Charlie's peers. Remember, this was before Columbine and the 'trench-coat mafia' hype in the US. Marilyn Manson was still relatively unheard of in the UK.*

It is true, however, that Charlie Armstrong was excluded from his school a number of times. I managed to track down ex-deputy headmaster Jon Lomax to get his take on it. Mr Lomax is an old man now, but his mind is still sharp and he reminisces about his school life with an unbound delight, his answers to my questions punctuated with laughter. Our phone conversation is brief.

—*Mr Lomax, you remember an ex-pupil of yours called Charlie Armstrong?*

—It's funny you should ask, actually, because, even with the attention he got after what happened up at Scarclaw, I would still have remembered him.

—*What do you remember?*

—He was a true rebel. Or a pain in the arse, whatever you like! He was forever stood outside my office.

—*Really, what for?*

—Oh, just little acts of defiance; nothing that important in the grand scheme of things. He wouldn't tie up his tie properly – had it knotted halfway down his front or not on at all; holes in his blazer; smoking; that sort of thing.

—*You must have overseen hundreds of thousands of children in your time; it's funny how Charlie stuck with you.*

—I suppose so, but you do remember the ones like Charlie, more than you do the ones who behaved… What I remember most about Charlie, was just how smart he was. He was a lazy underachiever; it used to drive his teachers potty! You know the sort, forever getting 'could be very good if he applied himself' on his report. Underneath it all, though, there was no harm to him. He wasn't a nasty child, and, believe me, I have encountered perfectly nasty children – nine times out of ten with perfectly nasty parents!

—*He was excluded wasn't he?*

—Yes. Maybe more than once, I don't recall. But the first time does stick in my memory; mostly because of how his mother behaved about it.

It was a lot of silliness really, but the point is, schools need to have standards. It's different these days, I know, but Charlie *and his mother* both knew fine well what we allowed and what we didn't.

—*What did he do?*

—It was his hair. I mean, we tolerated him having it long. Ten … even five years before and he wouldn't have been allowed to have it that long: but 'collar-length hair for boys' was omitted from the policy in 1990, I believe. But he stuck out like a sore thumb, a thumb that had been hit with a hammer! Bright pink, it was. I mean, he did it just for the attention, you know; just to break the rules. But his mother wasn't having any of it. *'How's the colour of his hair affecting his learning?'* she said in the meeting. That wasn't the point, of course. You couldn't just turn up to school with bright-pink hair, could you? What would other people think of us as a school?

—*So what happened?*

—It was funny, you know, because we'd been tipped off. Kids don't think teachers can hear them most of the time, but someone had overheard one of Charlie's friends talking about how he was going to do it at the weekend – dye his hair. When Monday morning came around, we sent him home with a letter, saying he wasn't welcome back until his hair was a 'natural' colour. Quite right too!

—*You say his mum kicked up a fuss about it?*

—She did; said she'd go to the press, that sort of thing, but it never happened. Charlie came in a few days later with it all dyed black. And his forehead too!

This interlude provides an insight into the sort of person Charlie Armstrong was back in 1996. He was impulsive; an individual; an innovator who didn't care what anyone thought of him. I have no doubt he was heralded as a hero when he came back to school after the pink-hair debacle. Maybe that was the point: he just wanted to show everyone he could do it.

I continue talking to Derek about the other young people up at Scarclaw.

—Err ... there was Anyu Kekkonen, Eva's friend from school. She was quite new to Rangers; she joined when she was twelve, I think.

Anyu's mum is Inuit; her side of the family came from Labrador. Her dad was an old friend of ours, but he'd died a while back. Anyu was a quiet girl back then; sweet, dark, serious, almost swarthy. Most people didn't know a lot about her, to be honest with you: she was quiet in front of groups of youngsters; polite but ... inscrutable ... in front of adults. She seemed at ease; and she had a real practicality to her – she was *sensible*; the voice of reason. As she and Eva grew up, Anyu would be the level-headed one, whereas Eva would sometimes be a bit irrational. When they were in middle school, Anyu used to call for Eva in the morning, and it would make me and Sus laugh, Anyu's little voice: *'Now, you know we've got PE today; have you got your kit?'* And then Eva would come flying back into the kitchen with her shoelaces half done and toothpaste on her face. She was twelve going on eighty-five, was Anyu.

Besides Eva Bickers, Anyu Kekkonen was the only other female teen in the group who went out to Scarclaw that day. I have heard that Anyu and her mother relocated back to Labrador, northern Canada in the wake of Scarclaw, but no one seems to know. Derek tells me he isn't sure but I am not convinced.

—I was friends with her dad, when he was alive. Jari was a fisher-man; a Finn. I'd studied a bit of Finnish at uni, and when I worked on the docks we got chatting. He'd just moved here with his wife. Eska is nice and everything, but reserved – like Anyu really.

—Do you think Eska might have wanted to return home after her husband's death?

—I couldn't say, to be honest with you. I have no idea, she never mentioned it...

—Was Eska part of Rangers?

—That's a hard one, to be fair ... I don't think *she* felt she was ever part of it, if you know what I mean? After Jari died, we welcomed her with open arms; of course we did. But she was distant, almost aloof. But that was just how she was. I don't think she was being purposefully rude or anything. I think she just felt a bit of an outsider. It was Jari who'd brought her to England, taken her from what was a pretty grim place up there, poverty, all that. I think Eska always felt she was 'below' us in some way ... which was a real shame.

—What about Anyu? She was sort of in-between worlds wasn't she?

—Anyu didn't start coming to Rangers till she was older. Maybe Eska didn't like being too far from her – you know, after what happened to Jari.

—Do you think there is a possibility they returned to Canada?

—There is, I suppose, but I really don't know.

—Anyu spoke Inuktitut?

—Did she? Oh ... well ... maybe then. I don't know.

I don't want to press Derek too hard about Anyu – or any of the others to be honest. Their stories will come. But the research I have conducted about the ex-members of the Rangers throws up very little when it comes to Anyu. It seems that being quiet, in the background of things, was her defining characteristic.

Derek and I talk instead about the dynamics of the group; specifically about the dynamics among the kids, the ones who were there on that trip in 1996.

—Kids are like packs of wild animals. And the pack has certain characters. There are leaders, voices of reason, the brains, the brawn, the wild card, the outsider ... the victim. I've worked with kids my whole life, and you see it again and again. It's maybe an evolutionary thing, I don't know; maybe some sort of survival mechanism?

—*Did the Rangers have defined roles like that?*

—Yes, I suppose they did. Charlie, he was the leader; the alpha. My Eva, she was sort of second in command, I suppose. Anyu was the strategist; the brains behind the operation.

—*You wouldn't think, would you, that something like what happened was possible?*

—Look. The way Sally and I saw it was that these were sensible kids; responsible kids. We'd known them all their lives, most of them. We understood them; respected them. And what was most important, we felt that they respected us.

—*Do you think it was possible that the other two perhaps threw out the balance of the group?*

—You mean…

—*Tom Jeffries and…*

—Brian Mings.

—*Yeah … Brian Mings.*

—Yes. Yes, you could say that…

We've reached the halfway stage in this week's podcast and I think it is important to take a little break from the interviews and summarise what we know so far about what happened at Scarclaw Fell in 1996. It is important to mention that foul play was ruled out by the inquest into Tom Jeffries' death. Derek Bickers and Sally Mullen were cleared of any wrongdoing or culpability for what happened, as were the remaining members of Rangers: Eva Bickers, Charlie Armstrong, Anyu Kekkonen and Brian Mings; all of whom were fifteen years old at the time. Tom Jeffries was also fifteen.

The police report states that Tom Jeffries was reported missing from Scarclaw Fell Woodlands Centre by Derek Bickers at 6.36 a.m. on August the 24th, 1996. Police attended the centre at 7.30 a.m. and a preliminary search was conducted of the surrounding woodland. The young people involved, as well as Derek Bickers and Sally Mullen, were questioned together and separately. I have been able to obtain some of these recordings, extracts of which we will hear in the following episodes of Six Stories.

After the questioning, the search parties were alerted to the idea that Jeffries may have walked off into the woods and passed out under the influence of alcohol and cannabis. All of the young people involved admitted that they were all under the influence of said substances at the time. None of them reported seeing Jeffries leave the centre, and none of the others had left the grounds of the centre that night. They all maintained that they were asleep when Tom Jeffries disappeared.

After the initial examination of the surrounding woodlands, the perimeters of the search were extended to include the lowlands of the fell, where there were disused mineshafts and marshland.

After twelve hours, Tom Jeffries' body had still not been found.

After twenty-four hours, the search perimeters were widened further. A task force of combined police forces and mountain rescue were drafted in. The young people as well as the two responsible adults were questioned further. No arrests were made.

[Audio extract from taped interview with Derek Bickers, 24/08/96]

—Look, we knew they smoked, we knew they drank – teenagers are the least subtle people in the world. But what were we going to do? If we lost our rags, kicked off with them, they would have still done it, but further away. They would have done it where we didn't know where they were, wouldn't they?

—*Are you saying, Mr Bickers, that you were aware that these young people under your care were drinking and taking drugs?*

—Yes … yes … there's no denying it. But I want you to know that I take full responsibility for all that. It's on me, not them, not Sally … me.

—Who bought the alcohol for them, Mr Bickers?
—I have no idea. Is that really what's important here?
—Did you buy the alcohol for them, Mr Bickers?
—No. No, I didn't.
—Do you realise how serious this is?
—Do you think I'm fucking stupid, officer?
—That's not what I said.
—What do you think is better, officer? A load of kids, who *are* going to be drinking and taking drugs – whatever you do to try and stop them – doing it where we know they're safe and we can intervene if they get into problems, or doing it in the middle of a fucking *forest*?
—A child is missing, Mr Bickers; a child under your care.
—I know that … Christ, I know that…

Derek Bickers has never changed his stance on what happened with the drugs and alcohol, nor his views. Whilst he had his detractors – and there were many – he also had his supporters. There were interesting columns in some of the left-leaning national newspapers that supported Bickers' view, the most famous one making the point that Bickers was acting truly in loco parentis and should be admired for it. The words of this same article were used by the tabloids in order to make the point that Bickers was some sort of monster. Indeed, with his grey beard, perpetual shorts and love of the outdoors, Derek Bickers was an easy caricature: a 'loony' left-wing parent who let his kids do what they liked. Derek Bickers' high standards of morality and the empowerment that he allowed his daughters have been overlooked, which is a shame.

I talk to Derek about this for a time, but even today, his view has not changed. I admire that, and we could dedicate much of this episode to a debate about the subject. However, I don't feel that this should be the focus of the podcast. However, in my opinion Derek Bickers and Sally Mullen were acting in the best interests of the young people in their care. Of that I am in no doubt.

Listeners to Six Stories *will come to many different conclusions and have differing views; of that there is no doubt either. I, however, want to concentrate on the events that led to the disappearance of Tom Jeffries and the discovery of his body a year later. I steer the conversation with Derek Bickers back to the group dynamics we were discussing earlier.*

—There were two more young people in the group that day, weren't there? Aside from Eva and Anyu.

—That's correct; Brian and Tom. Like I say, there were only five of them.

—Can we talk about Tom first?

—Yeah…

—Is that ok?

—Yeah. Sure. It's just…

—You don't want to speak ill of the dead?

—That's correct. I wouldn't. I mean, I have no reason to speak ill of Tom. But … it's not like he was a horrible person or anything. It's just…

—Would it perhaps be an idea to briefly mention Brian first … to provide context?

—Yeah … yeah. That makes sense. If that's ok, I mean…

—It's fine. Whatever's easiest. I think if you tell us a little bit about Brian, it might help us understand your view of Tom.

—Yeah, you're right. OK, Brian … what can I say? Brian was a good lad too; they all were, but Brian was … I'm not sure how to put it. He wasn't like the others; he didn't have the same confidence. He was…

—Weak? A victim?

—I wouldn't use those words, but in a way, yes. I suppose you could say that. I would say Brian was a 'follower'; he was a 'lame'…

—What do you mean, a 'lame'? Was that what the others called him?

—Sorry, no. I'm talking sociolinguistics here. There was a study done by a guy called Labov in New York in the sixties – about speech patterns in social networks. I won't bore you with the details, but he distinguished a pattern within these groups. There were the group 'leaders' who socially 'controlled' the use of language in the group. I've worked with kids for a long time and I've seen it; there's the leaders—

—In terms of Rangers, were the leaders Charlie Armstrong and possibly Eva?

—Possibly. Although, if we're using Labov's terms, I'd say Eva and Anyu were 'secondary' members, in that they *belonged* to the group, but had little control of the group norms. Then there were the peripheral members, or as Labov named them, the '*lames*': these were the members of the group who were in some ways 'detached', be that ideologically or geographically. Labov's study was about language. He found that the 'lames' used less vernacular than the group and were, therefore, less likely to invoke any sort of linguistic change.

—So, you said Brian Mings was a 'lame'?

—Only in that he seemed like an 'outsider'. He never seemed to become part of the group – the total opposite of Tom Jeffries.

—Let's stay with Brian for now.

—OK. Look, Brian was no different to the others. Not really. He just … OK, so Brian Mings joined Rangers not long after Anyu Kekkonen. He was from the private school over the way and didn't know any of us. His mum knew Sally, I think, something like that – they worked together, maybe? Anyway, Brian was getting bullied in school. It was bad; his mum was going spare. He didn't have any friends; his dad was long gone – alcohol, mental health, something like that. And I guess she thought that Rangers might be good for him.

—He was bullied?

—Yeah, I think so. I didn't really know. It didn't matter. I just remember thinking that the outdoors, and Eva and the rest of them would be good for him. The kids, they're good people; kind. They would accept him. Which they did … until…

—Until Tom Jeffries joined?

—Yeah. Until Tom came along.

Brian Mings' mother never turned up to a Rangers meeting; she dropped Brian off at the church hall near the Bickers' house the very first time and left him to make his own way after that. Brian, unlike the others, was awkward and a little insular. He had, as Derek says, been the victim of bullying – not just in secondary school, but all through primary. It was fortunate that Sally Mullen knew his mother, and I do not doubt Derek's assumption that hanging about with other kids his age – Eva, Charlie and Anyu – was good for him. During his first few years with the group, Brian's confidence grew and grew – to the point where he went from more or less mute to actively, and sometimes rather raucously, helping plan the excursions and trips with the others.

—For Brian, I think the meet ups were a bit of a release. I think he felt he could be himself with the rest of them. Sure, he was a little immature and actually a bit of a pain at times; Brian could be very vocal, very *insistent* with his views. But we all understood that. He'd been kept silent for so long, Rangers was the place where he could be 'heard' and all that.

Brian came with us on every trip to Scarclaw Fell. He did rock climbing, canoeing, orienteering; loved it. It was great to see him, actually. You could see the happiness in his face. Like I said, he was on the periphery, yet he was still part of the group. It made me sad sometimes; I sometimes wanted to tell him to stop it, you know? Stop being so desperate to fit in. He even started dressing like them a bit; you know, wearing big boots like Charlie, growing his hair, that sort of thing, bless him.

—*Then Tom Jeffries came along?*

—Yeah. Then Tom joined us and the dynamic was … different, let's say.

—*In what way different?*

—This is hard. Tom Jeffries wasn't really *like* the others. That's not to say he wasn't welcome or anything. We were inclusive, we didn't discriminate. We're not that sort of group! We *weren't* that sort of group.

—Can you explain what you mean by Jeffries not being 'like' the others?

—I'll try. Look, I don't know the ins and outs of teenagers – the labels they like to hang off themselves: hippies, punks, all that nonsense; whatever they like to call themselves – I still don't!

—Are you saying Tom Jeffries was not your typical sort of kid?

—Yeah; that's a good way of putting it. So, Eva, Charlie, Anyu – even Brian – they were all, let's say, 'individual' in terms of their dress sense, what music they listened to, all that. When Eva was younger, she used to get a fair bit of stick in school; nothing too serious, and she could handle it, she wasn't overly bothered. You know about Charlie don't you? Well, he was forever getting in trouble at his school for his hair or his uniform. There was talk that he had a tattoo, that he'd done it himself or something. I don't know; I never saw it.

As far as we were concerned, none of that mattered. As I said, at the heart of it all, these were smart, sensible, mature kids.

Sorry. I know I'm going on again. It's been, what, eighteen, nineteen years since it happened; but that doesn't make it easier, it really doesn't…

—Just take your time.

—So …Tom. I mean, it wasn't like he just came to us off the street. His mum was a friend of … someone's, like I said, the group was bigger then – it had a wider network, and we knew her, Pat Jeffries. I think she was looking for something positive for Tom, something that would distract him, take him away from all that other nonsense he had got caught up in…

This 'nonsense', as Derek calls it, was a little bit more that it sounds. A lot more, in fact. Perhaps Derek wasn't told about the extent of it; perhaps he didn't believe it to be significant. However, he's right to say that Pat Jeffries was trying to guide her son in a different direction from the path he seemed to have chosen.

As Derek states, Tom Jeffries wasn't like the others in terms of appearance or behaviour. In school (Tom attended the same private school as

Brian Mings but moved in very different circles to Brian), he was more of a follower than a leader.

If we're sticking with Derek's sociolinguistic analogy, Tom would have been a 'secondary' member in the groups at his school. He hung around with the kids in the years above him: the nearly bad kids; not the outright thugs and bullies, but the weed smokers, the shoplifters, the dealers; the ones whose cousins would turn up after school in their cars, Cypress Hill throbbing from the windows.

In 1993, when Tom Jeffries was nearly thirteen, he was involved with a minor disturbance in which three boys threw coins at a homeless man. The other boys – aged seventeen and nineteen – were charged with assault. Tom Jeffries, who was alleged to have been the third boy, denied any wrongdoing and was never charged. There were other things too, floating like slow-moving predators in the murky waters of Tom Jeffries' past: rumours, things that could never be proved, things that ultimately, in my belief, tainted the national outpouring of grief that would have occurred if, say, Eva Bickers or Anyu Kekkonen had died up on Scarclaw Fell. I ask Derek about them.

—What did you know about Tom when he started coming to the meetings?

—Look, I take kids as they come. There's no nonsense with me. If they want to start dicking about, that's when we might have a word. But I don't believe in treating anyone any different because of some supposed reputation, alright?

—Did you know about the incident in 1993 with the homeless man?

—I did. It came out at the inquest, but, yeah, we knew about it before. That *was* three whole years before Tom joined us, though, to be fair.

—Did you know about the other things Derek? The fires?

—Look, when kids like that come to us, we don't screen them. Pat Jeffries was very open about Tom, about the sort of stuff he'd been getting up to. Coming to knock about with us was a clean slate for him – that's how we saw it, anyway. It's not like he killed anyone or anything. He was just a bit of a wayward lad. That's all.

Tom Jeffries, to be fair, did not have that much of a reputation in the area. First of all, Tom came from a well-to-do background, as did Eva, Anyu, Charlie and the others. The incident with the homeless man, to my knowledge, was not repeated. Yet Tom was well known, amongst his peers at least, for being a little bit into fire. He'd come close to being excluded from school for setting fire to a pile of exercise books on the school field one lunchtime, and using a can of deodorant as a flame thrower. Also, his attitude to girls could be thought of as 'unhealthy'; although you could also argue that it was simple teenage preening. Tom often boasted about his vast experience with girls and women, who were always older than him.

There are some people, who we will hopefully talk to in later episodes, who maintain that there were other reasons that Tom Jeffries joined the group. These reasons will become clearer when those others tell their stories. Derek Bickers certainly did not know about any of this.

—As far as I knew, Tom Jeffries was an average lad; just another teenager. He was fifteen years old, for Christ's sake. What's a fifteen year old going to do?

—*Where was Tom in terms of your Labov analogy? What was his status in the group?*

—Now, that's interesting. As I've said: when new members join, our kids are very welcoming, very accepting; and they were with Tom.

—*Brian knew him from school, right?*

—Yeah, so there was a bit of familiarity, there. I think Charlie knew him a little bit too – friends of friends, something like that. It was interesting, because Tom just seemed to slip in, and gain 'leader' status, without any effort at all? He liked Charlie, and like the others, was a bit in awe of him. And then Tom swiftly became Charlie's right-hand man.

—*Why do you think that was?*

—I honestly don't know. We didn't listen to their conversations; we didn't know what had gone on. It was probably something to do with cigarettes. You know what teenagers are like. Tom and Charlie both smoked regularly by then. Something to do with that, I imagine.

—And *drugs, and drink too?*

—Very possibly. I don't know.

—*Tom Jeffries attended one other trip to Scarclaw; is that right?*

—Yeah. He went once before. It was a much larger contingent, then: about ten kids, and six or seven adults. It was a winter trip; there had been snow, loads of it, up on Scarclaw, so we thought it'd be fun. There's some good places for sledging up on the other side of the fell, near where we do rock climbing.

To reach the spot Derek is talking about, you have to drive. As the fell rises the woodland becomes dense and wild. There are signs showing where some of the mineshafts appear; but there are plenty of places where there are no signs at all; where the full extent of the danger is not indicated. The adult leaders didn't permit the kids to go past the very specific boundaries or fences. The rock climbing was overseen that weekend by independent instructors who were friends of one of the other adults.

—*What can you remember from that weekend in winter? Just in terms of Tom and the others?*

—Well, not a lot, to be fair. As far as I recall, their behaviour was impeccable. Like usual.

—*What about in the evening? At night?*

—What about it?

—*Well, we were talking about dynamics before; did you notice any difference, with Tom there?*

—Look, like I've said, we trusted them. We didn't get involved. Maybe we should have. If there had been a problem, *I know* they would have told one of us. I just *know…*

'Maybe'. 'Maybe we should have got involved'. It's the issue some say the inquest pivoted on. I think Derek Bickers' views on his leadership and care of the young people is clear by now. Like I say, he has been

acquitted of any charges and of any wrongdoing. However, by his own admission, there was a lot that Bickers didn't know about the dynamics of the group; possibly as a consequence of his hands-off approach. Possibly. But don't all teenagers – even impeccably behaved ones – hide some things from their parents? Remember, Eva is Derek's daughter. I don't blame him for wanting to give her her privacy during the Rangers trips. A bit like a teacher whose child goes to the same school – there's a certain distance it's wise to keep.

I fully expect Derek to slam the phone down and refuse to speak to me when I mention the next aspect of what happened at Scarclaw Fell. It's a touchy subject, but if we're going to discover what really happened up there, it's something we're going to have to breach.

—*Derek, we need to talk about Haris Novak...*

There is a long and terse silence after I say this. So long, in fact, that I think Derek has either hung up or is just lost for words. Finally, he speaks, and his voice finally reflects his age.

—Yeah. OK. There's no getting away from it, I suppose. I'll tell you what I know...
—*Wasn't it the kids who 'discovered' him ... as it were?*
—I don't know. Honestly, I don't know how they came across him, who 'discovered' him; what went on. I have no idea. All I know is that none of them told us about him; and they should have done. They bloody should have done...

As was widely reported in the media at the time, the prime suspect in the disappearance of Tom Jeffries, other than Derek himself, was a local man called Haris Novak.

Novak, at the time of Jeffries' death, lived nearby – in the village of Belkeld on the other side of the fell – and spend a lot of time in the woods. The newspapers, especially the tabloids, were quick to speculate about what he had to do with Jeffries' disappearance. Why, they asked, was a thirty-odd-year-old hanging about with teenagers? The photographs of him – looking much older, with his camouflage clothing, wild beard and thick glasses – made him look predatory. That, or a survivalist. Novak, however, was neither of these things, and proved nothing but helpful during the inquest. No charges were brought against him at any point. Not, as Derek well knows, that any of that mattered.

—All I know about Haris Novak was that he was a recluse, a loner, a bird enthusiast. He had hides and tents all over the fell. He knew where the mineshafts were, all that. Of course he was a suspect; he was a perfect fit.

—*Did you ever believe Novak had anything to do with it?*

—No. And he was proved innocent, wasn't he? He had an alibi that night, didn't he?

—*Did you, or Sally, or any of the others ever think he did it? At the time, I mean?*

—Look, we didn't even *know* about him until the police brought him down from the fell. We didn't even know he existed.

—*But the kids knew him, didn't they?*

—That's correct. The kids knew him. He was a secret that none of them should have kept from us. None of them.

—*Do you think that, if they had told you about Haris Novak, what happened to Tom may have worked out differently?*

—Possibly. I don't know. Maybe if plenty of things had been done differently, Tom Jeffries would still be alive. But that's something we'll never know, so there's no point speculating, is there?

Isn't there? Personally I think yes, it is worth speculating about the case of Tom Jeffries. As we'll see in next week's episode, there were certain things that, if Tom had disappeared today, would definitely have been done differently.

There are other things about Tom Jeffries' death that need contextualising in order that we can make sense of them. But the most pressing questions raised so far in our tentative review of the case are these:

Why did Tom wander away onto the fell by himself?

Why was Tom's body not discovered for nearly a year after he vanished?

We will attempt to answer these questions – along with several others – during this series.

Derek Bickers was consistently polite and helpful during his interview with me for this week's episode, and for that I would like to thank him. Derek and Sally were both deemed completely innocent in what happened that day in 1996; and while some might speculate that both of them should have done more, I certainly believe that they were both sensible and responsible adults who were looking out for the children in their care.

In the next episode, we will talk with the man that Derek and I alluded to at the end of this interview: Haris Novak. As we will find, it was not easy securing an interview with him, but he did, eventually, agree to talk to me.

Today, we have only touched upon the mystery of what happened to Tom Jeffries. But, trust me, it will deepen and branch out, like those ancient mine veins beneath Scarclaw Fell, and you will be able to begin making your own judgements about what happened.

This has been Six Stories.

This has been our first.

Until next time…

Scarclaw Fell 2017

I wasn't there the day they knocked down Scarclaw Fell Woodlands Centre. Dad was, though. He said he wanted to see it happen; see the first bite that the machines took from that place. I think he thought that, by knocking it down and building The Hunting Lodge, he could lay what happened to rest. Scatter the memories to the wind.

My boots are pinching at my ankles but I keep going. I can feel the base of Scarclaw Fell calling to me through the trees – its marshes, those rotted fence posts and trailing wires sticking out of them like the carrion-picked ribs of some long-dead beast.

Up there, that's where things get dangerous.

Up there, nature has obscured the danger signs, creeping brambles pulling down the posts; nettles displaying their own barbs to the wire. Up there, past the green-fingered spread of the trees and the constant stone tongue of the river.

But I'm not ready to go that way, not just yet. Here's a wooden sign, poking up from a patch of perpetual shade. Its lower half is green with moss and it points the way I am going. 'Belkeld'.

I put my head down and plough on.

Tomo had all the gear in the boot of his Jag but no one had suggested doing anything with it, not even Tomo. We were all waiting for someone else to take charge.

What in god's name Tomo was doing with all that stuff – the lights, the guns – was a mystery. On reflection, I think he was perhaps trying to impress us. Jus's father used to ride in the Heythrop Hunt; my father had just bought Scarclaw Fell. Tomo lived in Pimlico, his father was the director of some online search engine.

New money. His real name was 'Jazz', his surname something-Russian. Hardly see the guy these days. Save for when I did the interview, and he came as ... well, I suppose you'd call it 'backup'...

I was glad, if I'm honest, that no one really wanted to do it: the idea of killing deer by shining lights at them just seemed ... well ... like cheating, I suppose. 'Lamping', Tomo called it. That just sounded like something you said when you were going to have a fight. I don't think Tomo even knew what he was supposed to be doing. He'd brought these two lurchers and we'd locked them in one of the dormitories. Great noisy things, they were; panting and whining and scratching at the doors. What a bloody mess.

What were we going to do with the body if we caught a deer, anyway? Feed it to the dogs? None of us knew the first thing about butchery. I don't think any of us had ever killed anything bigger than a fish. It would look like the Texas Chainsaw Massacre if we brought some creature back down from the fell. And what if someone came by? It was all Dad's land by then, but that doesn't stop people. Ramblers' rights or something. What if some journalist, or one of the parents came poking about, saw blood on the walls? Even back then my family's name would have been dragged through the mud.

Jus said he'd seen one kill and he never went again – not even to the hunt ball. Dad once laid out poison for a rat at the Mayberry Estate when I was little. I stayed up all night, tears wet on my cheeks.

So the whole deer-hunting thing was something we just went along with, I suppose; it was what people expected from us: city boys out in the country to kill things.

But whatever we tell ourselves, it wasn't deer that we were hunting that summer night in 1996.

I push on, along where the track widens; a carpet of leaves – autumn scales beneath my feet. The call of the marshlands becomes fainter the further I walk. The trees thin; that dead boy just a will-o-the-wisp. A dream. I can't start thinking of things like that. Not while I'm here on my own.

I've learned an awful lot on my visits to The Hunting Lodge. This isn't my comfort zone, the countryside. I don't think it ever will be. I spent the afternoon yesterday up a ladder, nailing a nesting box to one of the silver birches that you can see from the kitchen window. I'll get one of those cameras in there and link it to the television. Bill blooming Oddie eat your heart out. There's not many twitchers who can afford to stay at 'The Hunting Lodge', but some of the rich kids who do like to see their wildlife alive. It might broaden their horizons a bit, you never know.

Not far now and the woods end. Not far and I'll be on the other side of Scarclaw Fell. Where the woods stop, the fences begin. Pale wood and grey barbed wire, looking stark and self-conscious beside the swells of gorse and grey plains of scree beneath the fell's summit.

'What's all this chuff?'

Tomo was poking about through a big folder of all the Scouts' and Guides' stuff on one of the bookshelves. A few dead leaves fluttered out.

'Leave it,' I said.

I didn't like to look at it. The posters and pictures on the walls; the leaf-rubbings and animal pictures – looking at them folded a crease of guilt in my belly. I drank beer to block the feeling out.

'Come and play, Tomo, mate.'

'Fuck that, you always fucking get Mayfair. It's not fair.'

Tomo's face was red with booze. He opened up the folder and my heart sank as paper spilled onto the floor.

'Come on, mate, leave it.'

Tomo poked at the papers with the toe of his brogue. He'd cleaned the mud off his shoes with blue-roll as soon as we got inside the Woodlands Centre.

Mine and Justin's boat shoes still stood sopping on the windowsill.

Suddenly Tomo was on his knees, leafing through the drawings. Most of them had leaves glued to them, whirling green and brown crayon patterns.

Jus looked at me and I saw worry in his eyes.

'What's he doing?' Jus mouthed.

I shrugged.

The lurchers were making a hell of a racket, howling and scratching on the other side of the dormitory door. Jus's eyes flicked over in that direction then back to me.

I realised then that we were out of our depth; that these woods in the shadow of Scarclaw Fell had swallowed us without our noticing.

I'm out of breath when I reach it. All the gorse and trees have long since been uprooted, leaving this place like an old, open wound. The fences are now topped with coils of barbed wire – too much for me to climb over. I've managed to get as close as I can, though. I stare into the darkness from behind the fence, uncomprehending. A child behind the bars of a predator's enclosure.

An email has driven me here.

The email that drove me from home. From safety, where there's Wi-Fi, concrete and chrome, filled with faces, beating hearts, the pulse of cars and life 24–7.

Re: Scarclaw Fell blazed my trail back to The Hunting Lodge – the place I swore I'd never return to. But it wasn't the subject line that drew my eye. Believe me, after what we found out there that weekend, emails regarding Scarclaw Fell go straight to spam.

Not this one, though.

Twenty years since that night and requests for interviews are still not as rare as you might think. I've had them all: the tabloids, the broadsheets, radio show researchers; they all want me to talk.

But the only people I've talked to so far are the ones who matter: the police.

'Dear Mr Saint Clement-Ramsay. I am not a journalist, nor am I a researcher, an aide, an editor or an author.

'Nor am I a fan.'

Maybe it was that word that struck home: *fan*

It's what Dad and I call them: the ghouls and goblins that used to hammer my inbox with questions. I still get them out of the blue sometimes. They fill in the online booking forms for The Hunting Lodge with requests to hold séances and vigils there. Even reality TV shows ask to use it as a location.

'More fan emails,' I tell Dad, and his eyes twinkle, head sunk so far into the pillow, it looks like a great, white boa is devouring him.

'All I am interested in is your voice. Your story. Your point of view.'

There was another word in amongst this cloak-and-dagger proposal that hooked me in and sent me here to contemplate one of the biggest decisions of my life: *podcast*.

Call me a toff, a snob; make jokes about ivory backscratchers, but don't call me ignorant. I know what a podcast is. There was that one that everyone went crazy over a while back. *Serial*, it's called. About some bloke in the States that's in prison for allegedly killing his girlfriend.

Jus texted me a link at the time, but I didn't listen to it. I did after I got that email.

A scratchy phone line from inside a US jail.

People listened.

Millions of people heard a 'guilty' man's voice.

If he was guilty in the first place.

'All I am interested in is your voice.'

I let Scott King email me again. And again.

I let him keep trying for three months – to see if my voice was really what he wanted.

In those three months I listened to his podcasts in the car on my way through the London traffic. Scott King and *Six Stories*. I listened to them all until I felt I understood. About him, about his mask, about how he gives everyone a voice.

I talked to Dad.

Then I replied.

'Look at this guys…'

It was as if Tomo had finally found what he was looking for. He stood up, flushed face now shiny with a film of sweat, and held up one of the crayon pictures. More leaves floated down. I saw Jus wince.

'Stop it Tomo, mate. That's just old kids' stuff. Leave it alone.'

Jus's last word trailed off. The Woodlands Centre suddenly seemed very old and very empty – like we were a troop of those urban explorer types; or else Carter and Herbert standing in front of the tomb of King Tut.

The lurchers were still grizzling with hunger and the noise of them was like a swarm of angry bees inside my head. I stared at the picture Tomo held aloft in trembling victory.

Later on, when the approaching darkness left daylight whimpering at his feet, he would tell us a story he'd heard about Scarclaw Fell. In hushed tones, his tongue bloated with booze, he would tell us why he'd brought the dogs, the guns.

'Just in case, boys; just in case.'

Episode 2: The Beast

—It lives on the fell. Behind the fences. I've seen it.

And sometimes it goes in the woods. That was where I first saw the beast – in the woods. When I was just a young boy. I don't know how old I was – maybe seven, maybe twelve?

We were in the woods, Mum and me. She had her blue coat on and I was wearing new trainers: *Transformers* ones from the shoe shop in Belkeld. Sheena fitted them for me. We were walking in the woods and I turned around, looked behind me and I saw it.

And it saw me.

—Oh yeah, everyone knew him round 'ere; friendly as owt, that lad. A bit … you know … I dunno what you call it these days; but he were nice with it, no harm in him. Like I say, everyone knew him and yet none of them lot had the decency to come and ask any of us about him. They all thought he'd done it. But we knew. We knew…

The first voice you heard was that of Haris Novak. The second was the landlord of the Hare and Hounds pub in Belkeld.

Today, Haris is forty-seven years old. He was born and spent most of his life in the village of Belkeld, on the other side of Scarclaw Fell from the Woodlands Centre.

Haris and his mother relocated after the disappearance of fifteen-year-old Tom Jeffries in 1996, and the subsequent trial of Haris by the UK tabloid media. Haris, like the others present at Scarclaw Fell, was questioned extensively by the police. And, like the others, he was never charged with anything.

These days, Haris lives alone, in a location I have been asked not to divulge. There are some who will always see Haris as the guilty party in the case of Tom Jeffries.

Welcome to Six Stories. *I'm Scott King.*

In the next six weeks, we will be looking back at the Scarclaw Fell tragedy of 1996 from six different perspectives; seeing the events that unfolded through six pairs of eyes.

This is episode two, in which we will talk to someone many would say is still the prime suspect in the case of the death of Tom Jeffries. Many others also say that Haris Novak was an easy scapegoat.

—I was … thirty years old when I first met them. It was a Saturday, a bright and lovely day in May, and I was walking along the street to the pub for lunch. I used to go to the pub for lunch on a Saturday. The Hare and Hounds, it's called. I used to go there and read my book. My favourite lunch was gammon – gammon with gravy and turnips. I met them in the street. There was only four of them that day: two boys and two girls. They were nice people; I liked them.

Haris Novak, as you will have already noticed, has a distinctive way of talking. His voice is high; it has the innocent sincerity of a pre-pubescent, and coming from his rugged, bearded face, is a little disconcerting. He meets me in the back bar of a pub, accompanied by his cousin, who sits close enough to hear us, but does not intrude. Haris' cousin, who does not want to be named in Six Stories, *was the one who rallied to Haris' cause after his trial by media back in 1996. The cousin is the one who got in touch with me when I found Haris. Initially, she was very sceptical about what I wanted to do, but over time, we have built up a level of trust and we have both agreed on my line of questions. Haris' cousin has also told me that she will stop this interview at any time, without warning, should she feel that Haris is being exploited or misrepresented.*

I have agreed to this. I think it's only right after what happened to him back then.

—So, can you remember if you approached them first, or did they approach you? The very first time you met them.

—I approached them. I am a friendly person and I like making new friends. I hadn't seen them before in Belkeld. They were young as well. Most people who come here are old people; they come to Belkeld to do canoeing and things. Climbing and things. I don't like doing those things. I like watching the animals in the woods. I wondered if they knew about all the different species of animals in the woods.

As was reported to grotesquely sensationalised effect in the press, Haris Novak was a veteran of Scarclaw Fell. He knew the place like the back of his hand: the woods, the hillside and even what lay beyond some of the fences.

The Sun *printed a particularly unpleasant story, referring to Novak as a 'local oddball', alongside a gloomy photograph of the outside of his mother's house: a dilapidated cottage that perches wonkily on the side of the fell, a mile or so outside of Belkeld. It was easy for the papers to present him as unhinged, a loner, a Norman Bates or an Ed Gein. Back in 1996, there was far less understanding of someone like Haris.*

—They were outside the pub, the Hare and Hounds, four of them: two boys and two girls.

—Did you…?

—The boys were wearing similar clothes. The bigger one with the long hair, he was wearing big boots and a black coat – a long one, like one mum used to have; a raincoat. He had a hat on, a black one, a beanie one. The other boy, he was smaller; he had big boots, too, but not a hat. His hair was the same colour as yours. I thought they were brothers, because they looked a bit the same. Brothers sometimes look the same; they're called identical twins.

—*And the girls?*

—Oh, I didn't think they were sisters or anything. They were very different. There was a taller one; she was ... err ... she was ... she had dark eyes, chestnut-coloured hair, hair the colour of chestnuts, all in little ... what do you call them, plaits? Little coloured elastic bands on the ends of them. The other one, she was ... she had a really *round* face, a *circular* face, red lips and dark hair, too. They had big green army coats on, with the little German flag on the sleeves. Furry hoods.

Contrary to some beliefs, autism doesn't equate to some sort of photographic memory power. I don't pretend to be an expert, but what I do know about Haris Novak is that he has trouble with social boundaries – understanding where they are. The people in Belkeld knew him well and were used to his idiosyncratic ways. But to a stranger, Haris' mannerisms can be somewhat perturbing. Often, Haris is over-friendly or else completely withdrawn, there's no middle ground. He also struggles with understanding other people's emotions, with reading their body language and facial expressions. And he also has specific learning difficulties. All this traps him in an eternal child-like state.

I ask him about how the teenagers responded to him when he approached them the very first time. This was back in 1995; a year before Tom Jeffries vanished.

—I don't know why they were there. The boys were smoking cigarettes next to the pub. I asked them if they were there to go canoeing or go rock climbing, or to look at the animals in the woods. They were laughing, they kept laughing, so I was laughing, too.

They said they didn't know why they were there and that made me laugh. We were all laughing. It was nice, it was sunny and we were laughing. Like friends.

From what I can piece together, this was a weekend trip to Scarclaw in the spring of 1995. According to the logbook at the Woodlands Centre, there were fifteen kids staying, including Charlie Armstrong, Eva Bickers, Anyu Kekkonen and Brian Mings. Tom Jeffries was yet to join the group.

—I asked them, I asked them some questions. First, I asked them if they were OK, if they were lost. They said they were fine. And next I asked them what they were doing, and they said they didn't really know, which was strange, and I asked them if they were looking for the bus stop. Lastly, I asked them if they were new-age travellers, because they were dressed funny, like hippies – *peace man!* – They started asking me things.

—*What sort of things?*

—Well, first they asked me if I could buy them some beer. But you're not allowed glasses outside, except the beer garden, so I said I'd go and talk to Sam, the landlord. I know Sam very well. But they said not to; they said that it was OK, because they weren't thirsty anymore. That was funny and we laughed again.

Then they asked if I would go in the shop for them. They wanted cigarettes. But I told them about the dangers of smoking, because smoking can give you cancer.

Charlie, Eva, Anyu and Brian would all have been around fourteen years old at this point. According to Haris, it was Charlie and Brian who were smoking. He says he never saw either of the girls smoking, but it was Anyu who asked him to go to the shop for cigarettes. I can't help feeling sorry for Haris when he describes what happened next.

—I asked them where their mums and dads were, and the older boy, the one with the long hair, said that their parents were all dead, that they were orphans. I felt sorry for the poor little orphans, all alone like that, so I gave them some money that Mum had given me for my birthday.

—*How much money did you give them?*

—All of it. I thought they could get some food or some new clothes, because their clothes looked all ripped and dirty. I think it was about fifty pounds. I was going to buy some clothes for myself, but the little orphans needed it more than me.

Then the big one, the one with the long hair – Charlie, he was called – he told me I was cool. He said I was cool.

It would be easy to condemn right now; a bunch of privileged teenagers taking advantage of a vulnerable adult. I don't think, however, that this was necessarily the case. Remember, autism wasn't widely understood back then. Also, Haris isn't incapable, he's well aware of what to do if he feels someone isn't being kind to him. He had plenty of people in Belkeld who knew him and who he could have told about the teenagers if he felt they were abusing him. I honestly don't believe Charlie, Eva, Anyu or Brian had it in their natures to be malicious to Haris. Not at this point, anyway.

It may well have been the case that none of them had encountered someone like Haris before. According to Haris, one of the girls – he doesn't remember which one – tried to give him his money back. But he insisted. Once Charlie Armstrong told him he was cool, he decided that he would tell them his secret.

—I said, if they were orphans, that I knew a place where they could stay. I said they could come with me to the woods; but they had to be careful.

—*Why careful?*

—There's secret places in the woods, high up on the fell; dangerous places.

—*The old mines, right?*

—Yes, the old mines. They're very dangerous; there are fences and signs that tell you not to go inside. You can fall; there are drops of up to two hundred feet, and you could break your legs and no one could hear you and you could die down there quite easily.

—*So why did you want to take the orphans there? Why not take them to the safe parts of the woods?*

—Because there's nowhere for them to stay there. There's nowhere that they could sleep. It gets cold, it gets windy, their clothes were tatty and they would have got cold. I know where the dangerous bits are. I know the secret ways and how to stay safe.

As you've probably guessed, this was brought up at the inquest. What you probably don't know, and what wasn't widely publicised at the time, if at all, was that Haris Novak was questioned by police in the wake of Tom Jeffries' disappearance on his own. These days, you would imagine a vulnerable adult like Haris would be better protected. But we'll come to the questioning later; the trauma of that is still very fresh in Haris' mind, even after all these years. His cousin agreed to talk to me about that, alone.

Let's continue with Haris' story.

—So, you took the orphans up the side of the fell, to the mine?

—Yes. You have to walk for a while. You have to climb high, through the gorse bushes and through the heather. And that's where there's a secret place. It just looks like the fell-side, but I know it's there.

Haris' 'secret place' is now fenced off. What he's talking about is a concealed entrance to one of the mineshafts. I'm amazed that no one else knew about it apart from Haris, but that's the way it was. Traversing Scarclaw Fell from the Belkeld side, where the 'claw' overhangs, you emerge onto a steep, uncompromising slope covered in gorse and heather. The going is tough, so I suppose the reason why no one knew about the mine entrance was that there was no real reason for anyone to want to climb this way. Haris, however, spent most of his time on the fell, watching wildlife.

—One of the boys, the shorter one, he kept saying he didn't think it was a good idea, and said they should go back. The bigger boy was laughing at him and calling him a 'wuss'. The girls weren't really paying much attention, they were just following along.

We got to the secret place. It's a pile of rocks. You nearly can't see it because of the heather. You have to be really, really careful because it's muddy and you can slip. You have to hold on. I showed them how to climb down to where the mine is. It looks like a sort of mouth and you have to duck to get in.

—*Did they go in with you?*

—Yes, they did. The smaller boy, he had a bit of trouble climbing down. His face was all red and his eyes were like he was going to cry, do you know what I mean? They were all wet and I told him that it was OK, that he'd soon be safe. And the others were laughing, so I was laughing, and the bigger boy, he said I was 'too cool' and he sort of hit me on the shoulder; but he was laughing and I was laughing, so it didn't hurt.

—*Why did you take them to this particular place, Haris? Why there?*

—Well, I had some supplies there: a wind-up lamp and some food. I come here sometimes to see the bats. There's some Natterer's bats that roost here; they come every year and hibernate in the winter. They're a protected species and you're not allowed to disturb them. I don't disturb them, I just watch them.

—*Did you think the orphans would like to see the bats?*

—Yes. People like to see animals. The bats are really interesting, but I also thought that the orphans could sleep here in the winter, just like the bats do. It's dry down there and I could bring them food.

They would also be safe down here … from the beast.

—*The beast?*

—Yes. The Beast of Belkeld.

I have done a lot of research into Haris' claim that there is a 'beast' in the area, and I have come up with some strange results. I will go into them presently; but first, it's useful to know a bit of the place's history. I talk, briefly, to a lady called Maxine Usborne, one of the volunteers at the local tourist information centre. Maxine is seventy-eight and still enjoys hiking on the fells every weekend. I speak to Maxine in person as she doesn't like telephones.

The tourist information centre in Belkeld is a tiny room in a small parade of shops. It is impeccably tidy, with posters of wildlife neatly tacked onto the walls. There's a display of flyers about the nearby tourist attractions: castles, gardens, farms and conservation. On the desk where Maxine sits, there are piles of home-made leaflets that contain instructions for walking in the area.

—*So, do lots of people come here to hike?*

—Oh, yes; even in the winter time, there's a lot of groups that like to come here. There's lots to do round here, you know: rock climbing and walks.

—*Can you tell me about Scarclaw Fell?*

—It's not as popular, because of the mine. It's dangerous on there and most of it's been fenced off. The woods are nice, though. They've been left, not been meddled with, and there's some lovely walks. But the fell itself … it's not terribly popular.

—*Do you know much about the mine – when it was a mine, I mean?*

—Not much to tell really, I'm afraid. It used to be a galena mine when it was first dug in the 1400s. Galena's a lead ore, a source of silver. It was quite prosperous, I imagine. Then it became a proper lead mine. The engine house was built in the nineteenth century to pump out the water.

—*It was closed though, wasn't it – the engine house?*

—That's right; they closed it when the tunnels began to collapse. There were a few accidents I believe. They tried again in the 1940s – to re-open them, I mean. There's a lot of lead in the fell, but it was just too dangerous, so they just left it. What a shame; it would have done wonders for the area.

Maxine is right. Despite the order and friendliness of the tourist office, the area around Scarclaw Fell is by no means prosperous. And I'm surprised there is little in the way of farming on the fell.

—I've heard that there is something else about Scarclaw – a story that keeps cropping up.
—Oh, you mean the beast?
—That's right, the beast.

This is interesting. I've talked to a number of people from Belkeld and the surrounding area, yet no one else, barring Haris Novak, has mentioned the beast. When I ask them about it, they just look at me blankly, shrug, and claim they've never heard of such a thing. I press Maxine for more information.

—Oh it's a silly story; an unwelcome story, if you really want to know. People round here, they don't like it; think it scares the tourists away. But that's just rot – the Belkeld Beast is an old wives' tale, a rumour, a whisper in the breeze, nothing more.
—When did it start? When did you first hear about it?
—Oh, when I was a girl, my mother used to tell me not to go up onto the fell because there was a monster there. I think everyone else's mothers had the same idea. It was when they were trying to re-open the mine and there was talk that a few men had died. Silly really, because they were killed by the subsidence – the tunnels collapsing in.
—Why did people say it was a monster then? Why not just say the mine was dangerous?
—I don't know, really. Maybe it was one of those stories, you know; like the one about the tailor:
'The great tailor always comes to little boys who suck their thumbs…'
My mother used to tell that one to my little brother; he used to wake up screaming in the night, checking his thumbs were still there, that they hadn't been chopped off by scissors!
—So you think the beast was just a cautionary thing – invented by the local people to keep their kids away from the mine?
—Nothing more.

It's a legitimate theory. Delve deeper, however, and there are signs that the legend of the Beast of Belkeld was around long before Maxine's childhood. Witch Covens in Northern England, *published in the early 2000s by a now-defunct publishing house in Lancaster, tells a seventeenth-century tale of a Belkeld woman by the name of Anne Hope who joined a coven of witches. The coven would meet at midnight 'atop Clawubeorg' ('clawu' being the Old English word for 'hoof' or 'claw'. It is not clear why this name was used, unless to protect the identity of the woman in question, or Scarclaw Fell itself). According to the book – the coven would dance – sometimes in their own shape, sometimes becoming animals such as hares or dogs. Anne was asked to join in the dancing, which, along with reciting the Lord's Prayer backwards, was to please a 'long black man' who granted the witches' wishes. Anne Hope was eventually arrested and tried for witchcraft. She eventually admitted (I imagine, through torture of some form) that she had caused a sickness that blighted the village of Belkeld.*

I ask Maxine if she has ever heard of this 'sickness'.

—It was around the end of the plague in London, and across the country at that time. I imagine that there was a lot of fear that it might spread here. I don't know about any recorded 'sickness' at that particular time, but very little was known about disease then.

The book does not explain whether this sickness was spread between humans or animals – witches were often blamed for diseases in farm animals. It is also known that there are rings of standing stones atop Scarclaw Fell, as well as the rock art, any interpretation of which evades us, even today.

Anne Hope was duly executed not long after her conviction for witchcraft and was hung in Belkeld. According to the book, she stayed defiant until the end, apparently 'cursing' the land. Afterwards, people reported seeing a 'terrible black figure' stalking the fell 'in the dead of night'. This figure was reported to be 'much like a bear' and was eventually 'commanded to leave, in the name of the Father, Son and Holy Ghost' by a local priest. There are no more records – none that I can find anyway – of this creature.

I tell Maxine this story.

—I've never heard that one before! It certainly could be true, though. There were witches executed in Belkeld, but you find me a place back then where there weren't! When my mother told us about the fell, she never mentioned a 'curse' of any kind. The Beast of Belkeld was just a silly tale to keep us kids out of the mine. Nothing more.

I relate the story back to Haris. Just in case. This is when he tells me about his first experience of the beast – when he was walking through the woods with his mother, in his new Transformers *trainers.*

—*Can you tell me about that day?*

—Yes, I can. It wasn't a nice day; it was raining and we'd been shopping. Mum had bought me new trainers and I was so happy. But I was also a bit worried.

—*Why?*

—Well, my new trainers were hurting my toes. They didn't have them in the right size, you see, they only had the smaller size. But I liked them, I liked them so much that I told Mum that they were fine. I was also worried because I thought I might get them muddy and Mum would get cross. When it is raining, we walk home through the woods because the trees shelter us from the pouring rain. We walk along the track in the woods and it sometimes gets muddy but sometimes doesn't.

—*So you and your mum were walking through the woods and it was raining?*

—Yes, that's what I said. I was being slow because my feet hurt a little bit and I was looking out for a woodpecker. I had heard a woodpecker in this part if the woods; they drum on the trees to mark their territory, you know. I was looking for it because I've only seen a woodpecker a couple of times. It was raining and it was getting dark because of the clouds. Mum was saying, 'Come along Haris! Come along!' And so I was walking quickly and then I heard a sound behind us.

Sorry to break Haris' story, but I should mention here that his sighting of the monster in the woods doesn't ring with the same authenticity as do his meetings with the Rangers. While he's meticulous with his other animal sightings, he's unclear what age he was when he saw 'the beast', or even what time of year this happened. If I had access to his animal diaries, we could have perhaps used them to jog his memory, but, unfortunately, they've either been thrown away or lost. Haris' mother passed away in 1999 and his cousin lived in a different part of the country back then. As we will discuss, this story of Haris' could simply be a coping mechanism, a rationalisation to help him deal with what happened to him in 1996.

Or it could be true. We may never know.

—So I stopped and listened because I thought it might be the woodpecker, but it wasn't a sound like that; it was a different sound, a terrible stamping sound. It was coming from the forest, from the trees.

—*And you're sure it wasn't thunder, something like that?*

—Thunder comes from the sky. Thunder happens when there's a storm. It was raining, but there wasn't a storm. It was a stamping sound, like big feet.

—*Did your mum hear it, too?*

—I don't think she heard it, too. She was going fast, saying 'Come on Haris, come on!'

That's when I looked behind me, back the way we had come, along the path. And that's when I saw it. It poked its head out of the trees and it saw me.

—*What did it look like?*

—It was big, with big black claws and teeth, and it looked at me with big, terrifying eyes.

—And were you scared?

—I wasn't that scared because my mum was there and I thought that it was scared more than me, because it was only there for a second and then it was gone.

—Where did it go?

—Back into the trees.

Interestingly, Haris is not alone in claiming to see creatures of this kind in the UK. Cannock Chase in Staffordshire, a site of countless UFO phenomena, is supposedly home to a ghostly 'pale-eyed' ape creature, sightings of which date back to the early 1900s. Shropshire Union Canal has its very own 'man-monkey', and ABCs (Alien Big Cats – mostly pumas and panthers) have been sighted in the British countryside since the 1760s. What is slightly unnerving about Haris' 'beast' is that it links, albeit rather tenuously, back to the 'terrible black figure' and the 'long black man' sighted on Scarclaw Fell and described in Witch Covens in Northern England.

According to Haris, he told the 'orphans' about the beast when they had descended into the tunnel. Then he had to go home for his tea. He says he was going to leave them in the mineshaft and told them he would come back with some food.

—Did you come back, after your tea?

—No. No, I didn't, because one of the girls talked to me before I went home – the tall, skinny one. She talked to me and told me that they were fine, that they would be going on their way and that I shouldn't worry because they would see me again. They would come and see me when they came back again. I was a little bit sad that they didn't want to stay, because they were my friends.

According to Haris, he didn't see Charlie, Eva, Anyu or Brian until a few months later; in the summer of 1995. Haris didn't speak to them this time – he just saw them in a minibus passing through. He remembers waving and the teenagers waving back from the back of the bus. The

Woodlands Centre logbook states that all four of the teenagers did visit in early August of 1995, along with Derek and a couple of other adults. They were there to insulate the building. They stayed for one night and left early the following day.

However, that winter, December 1995, there was another excursion to the Woodlands Centre. Derek Bickers mentioned it in episode one. This time, there was a much bigger contingent: fifteen kids in all – the youngest being eight and the oldest fifteen – that was Charlie Armstrong. I imagine Derek and the rest of the leaders were more willing to take the kids there in the cold, snowy conditions because of the insulation that they had installed the previous August. The logbook has a few comments from some of the younger kids: 'We built an igloo! It was skill!' 'Sledging is MEGA!'

This winter trip was Tom Jeffries' first to Scarclaw with the Rangers.

—Yes, I saw them again, in the wintertime. They came back and they were in Belkeld again. There were five of them this time: the four from the time before and a new one, another boy.

—Did you just see them the once?

—Yes. Only once. When they came through Belkeld. I asked them if they were hungry and the tall girl with the dark hair, she said that they were OK, that they weren't orphans anymore, that they had people who looked after them.

—Can you remember what they were doing in Belkeld?

—Just … I don't know … just hanging around, I think. It was cold and it was snowing, but there was grit on the pavements; loads of grit, because otherwise you can slip and fall. I told them that they must be careful because of the snow. They all had warm coats on so they were warm.

—Were they smoking cigarettes this time?

—Yes, they were smoking cigarettes. The big boy with the long hair, he was; and the smaller boy, again; and the girl with the dark hair, she was; and the new one, the boy, he asked if I wanted to smoke with them. I said no, because it's bad for you, and he started laughing. But it wasn't the laughing like the first time; it was different laughing.

—*Different how?*

—I don't know. It was different because I wasn't laughing this time, and the new boy, he kept turning away and repeating what I'd said in a silly voice. The others were laughing, but not properly. The girls, they were saying, 'Stop it, come on let's go', but he wasn't listening to them; he kept saying, 'Wait there, wait there.'

—*Can you remember what this new boy looked like?*

—Yes. He was thinner than the others. He wore a cap on backwards. He had big black jeans on, that were baggy, and you could only see the tips of his shoes poking out.

The person that Haris is describing is unmistakably Tom Jeffries. Jeffries was a thin and gangly boy, who wore a 'Raiders' baseball cap, perpetually. The hat still adorned Jeffries' corpse, but his jacket was never found.

—I asked them what they were doing on this snowy day, and they said they were bored so they'd come for a walk and they needed some supplies from the shops.

It was not a strange occurrence for the teenagers to be in Belkeld. Both Derek Bickers and Sally Mullen maintain that, so long as they were together, the older kids were allowed to walk through the wood and across the fell to Belkeld. It was a good hour's walk and there were five of them. Derek admitted to me that most of his judgements concerning the kids, he stands by; save for this one. He often wonders whether he should have allowed them to go off on their own like that. It was the only time that the kids had ever kept something from him, something important: Haris Novak.

—Then the new boy, he said he had a present for me. That made me feel better, because I was starting to get confused about why he was laughing. So he said he had a present for me and he gave me a little bit of black rubber stuff and he said it was a sweet and I should eat it. It didn't look much like a sweet and I didn't want to eat it.

The next bit of Haris' story doesn't make for pleasant listening. Either the shame of it was too much, or, like some things, the complexity of Haris' conditions simply didn't render it important enough to recall when questioned by police at the time of Tom Jeffries' disappearance. We'll discuss that further at the end of the episode, when we speak to Haris' cousin. None of the teenagers mentioned it – neither when they were questioned, nor during the inquest. Perhaps it was too shameful, or perhaps, it being nearly a year before, they didn't consider it important.

—The new boy, he kept saying, 'Eat it, eat it, go on.' Then the other boy – the one with the long hair and the skeletons T-shirt – he started saying it, too. He said, 'I thought you were cool, like us.' So I ate it because he told me last time that I was cool. It was horrible, it tasted like plants; like a mushy leaf or soil or something, so I went to the shop to get a drink, and when I came out, they'd gone.

—What happened after that?

—I was fine. I thought the orphans must have gone on their way again, so I thought I'd go to the secret place to see the bats; to see if the bats were there because the bats hibernate in the mine and they're an endangered species, so I went to have a look at them. I walked up into the village, where there's the cenotaph and the churchyard, and it was sunny even though it was snowy. It was a nice day. I thought I'd go the long way, past the cemetery. The birds were tweeting and I thought they were probably hungry because of the snow, so I thought I would put out some seed when I got home. And then I felt something hit me on my back.

—What sort of thing?

—Well, it felt like a hand, like someone had hit me, but when I looked around there was no one there. So I kept going, and then I felt it again. I was scared in case it was a ghost. There was only the cemetery on the left and the road on my right, and I got a little bit scared in case there was a snowstorm. And I looked and there was snow on my back, so I started to run. Then something hit my head and I nearly fell over. I looked round and it was the boys.

—*The orphans?*

—Just some of them. It was the long-haired boy and the little boy, and the new boy, They were in the cemetery, behind the railings, and they were throwing snow and laughing. It was a snowball fight. I wanted to play snowball fights, so I picked up some snow, but they were too quick and they kept moving. My snowballs kept hitting the railings, or the boys would dodge behind the gravestones. It wasn't really fair and they kept doing it. They kept throwing snowballs and some of them had bits of soil in and it hurt. My hands were getting cold, so I said we should stop now, but they kept doing it.

—*All of them?*

—Yes. The three boys. The new boy and the long-haired boy; theirs hurt the most. The other boy – the smaller one – his snowballs always missed. So I ran away and I could hear them laughing and I ran and ran at top speed until I got to the woods. Then I started feeling funny.

—*Funny how?*

—Sort of sick, sort of floaty, sort of all tingly. I wondered if I had got too cold on my hands. I'd taken off my gloves, you see, to play snowball fights, and I couldn't find them, so I went back the way I had come, and it was hard because I was suddenly out of breath and the road felt all weird, like it was sinking. And my head was cold and I realised I'd lost my hat too. So I ran at top speed again and got back to the churchyard and there was a funny smell.

—*What sort of smell?*

—It was sort of like cigarettes and something else, something sweet. My heart was beating really hard and that tingly feeling was in my legs and I was really thirsty. The boys were in the cemetery and they were all smoking a big cigarette and it looked funny because it was big and it smelled funny so I started laughing.

—*Then what happened?*

—They were all laughing again, the boys, and they told me to *shh, shh,* and then they told me to come into the cemetery. So I went in and I was feeling really funny then, like all sort of wobbly and tingly, and the world was going really slow like one of those flick-books. The boys wanted to tell me a story. The one with the boots and the long hair, he told me a story, and his voice was all low, like a cat purring, like a dog when it's trying not to growl.

—*What was the story?*

—I don't … remember … but it was frightening. It was a nightmare and everything was breathing: the church and the snow and the blue sky were breathing in and out, and I had this great big scream inside me, blowing up like a balloon, and suddenly it all came out … I was screaming.

—*That sounds awful…*

—Then the new boy, he got angry and he ran to the railings and started saying, 'Get out of here. Go on, get out of here!' But I couldn't stop laughing, and I was thirsty but I was laughing, and the new boy he started saying, 'Shh, shh.' But I couldn't … I couldn't stop and then he said that something was coming, and that's when I thought of the beast.

—*He said the beast was coming?*

—He did … or I did …I don't know; it was a bit like a dream. I think I had got too cold because my heart was thudding and I was thirsty and everything was soft and funny. And then the new boy said, 'Come here.' So I went over and he poked his head through the railings and told me that the beast was coming, that I had better run.

—*Did you?*

—I did run. I ran back into the woods and kept going because I could hear it behind me, and it was making a screaming, laughing noise, and I ran as fast as I could and I didn't look back and I didn't stop and I could hear its feet behind me and my heart was thudding and when I was nearly home I stopped because I couldn't run anymore.

—*And the beast?*

—I think it had gone. I think I outran it, because everything was still again

—*What about your hat and gloves, did you ever find them?*

—Yes. I found them the next day.

—*Where?*

—In the churchyard. Someone had made a snowman and they had put my gloves and my hat on it, and they'd put a cigarette end in its mouth and given it a … a penis … and Father Brown, he was really cross with me and told my mum. I got in real trouble and she said I was acting 'out of character'.

Telling this story is clearly traumatic for Haris; his voice quickens and he becomes more child-like, avoiding my eyes and shaking his head. I break off our chat to give him a breather, and his cousin takes him aside to calm down.

From what we've heard so far, it is pretty obvious what happened that afternoon. What is particularly telling here is the attitude of the teenagers to Haris in the presence of Tom Jeffries. Haris mentions the 'girl with the dark hair', which I assume is Anyu Kekkonen, who often reassured him and tried to give him his money back the first time. I'm surprised Eva Bickers hasn't really featured in Haris' account. In fact, neither of the girls seem to have made much of an impression on Haris. But then, it's the emotionally impactful moments rather than the pleasant ones that stay with us. Certainly, the snowballs and the drugs were a terrifying combination for Haris, as you would expect.

Notice something else though: Haris does not refer to any of the teenagers by name; he knows them only as 'the orphans'. As we'll hear throughout, Haris finds it hard to deviate from a certain neural pathway. To Haris, the Rangers were 'the orphans', and that was that. Haris doesn't recall meeting any of the others, or the adults. That makes sense; there would be no reason for any of the leaders or the younger kids to be hanging around Belkeld. Neither Derek Bickers, nor any of the other adults had heard of Haris until the inquest.

What surprises me most about this whole thing is that Haris never mentioned the incident with the snowballs to anyone – even his mum. Listen to this extract from the police interview with Haris from a few days after Tom Jeffries disappeared; it might give us an understanding of why.

[Audio extract from taped interview with Haris Novak, 26/08/96]

—*What are you saying to me Haris? Are you saying that on the 12th of December last year, you did or you didn't speak to and interact with these people? For the record, I am indicating the photographs of Tom Jeffries, Charlie Armstrong, Anyu Kekkonen, Eva Bickers and Brian Mings.*

—No … I mean … yes, I suppose so … sort of.

—*What does that mean, 'sort of'? You either did or you didn't speak to them.*

—I did. Sort of.

—*Haris. This isn't a question of 'sort of'. There is a missing child here; a missing child; and you're stopping us finding him by saying 'sort of'.*

—I met them … I met them, I met them, the orphans, I met them.

—*For the record, Mr Novak is pointing at the photographs in front of him. You can confirm you spoke to Tom Jeffries, Charlie Armstrong, Anyu Kekkonen, Eva Bickers and Brian Mings on the 12th of December 1995?*

—The orphans. I saw them.

—*Right, then. So whereabouts did you see them?*

—It was weird … everything was strange. Everything was topsy-turvy and funny and I was…

—*Will you just answer the question, please, Mr Novak?*

—It was like a dream. It might have been a dream. It felt like a dream. It *was* a dream.

Haris had an alibi for the night Tom Jeffries disappeared the follow-ing summer. He has no history of violence; nothing that linked him to the teenagers, save for these few fleeting meetings in Belkeld. I find it difficult to believe that Haris thought the teenagers were a dream. When he talks to me about them, he doesn't mention dreams. Despite Haris' disabilities, he does not hallucinate: he does not hear voices. When he goes to the toilet, I speak to his cousin about this discrepancy.

—*So, do you know why Haris told the police seeing the teenagers was a dream?*

—It's a coping mechanism. That's the best I can come up with. Ask Haris about certain things – he'll tell you they are dreams. His mum, for example: he doesn't talk about her much, not with me anyway. The night she died, when they took her to hospital, he was there the whole time; but if you ask him about it, he'll say it was a dream.

—*Does he believe them to be a dream now? The teenagers, I mean.*

—I'm … I dunno; it's hard to tell. Sometimes he talks about stuff and if you ask him whether it was a dream, some days he says yes and some days he says no. That whole thing, it was a fucking disgrace, the way the papers went after him. He didn't even have an appropriate adult in with him when they questioned him. Fucking disgusting. The whole thing traumatised him. There's great swathes of it he doesn't remember – or says he doesn't; or says it was a dream. Sometimes he wakes up screaming in the night about the beast. The fucking Beast of Belkeld.

—*What do you think about that? What's your opinion?*

—To me, I think the whole 'beast' business is another way he copes with what happened back then.

To be honest with you, I didn't have much to do with Haris' side of the family – not until the whole thing happened. His mum, she was just ... she was lost. So I visited more, to help them out. It was me who helped them with the move, got them out of Belkeld. Looking back, I think it's all mashed up, sort of, in Haris' head – what is real, what isn't. I'm not sure even he knows anymore.

—*He said he saw it as a child.*

—Yeah, he's told me that before but ... I don't know if that's just some sort of false memory – something he's created. He likes things to be logical, to be consistent. I have a feeling that the whole thing of seeing the beast when he was a kid might be just ... I dunno ... just a *safety net* sort of thing. Do you know what I mean?

—*It makes sense.*

—And I think something happened with Haris – something with Haris and those kids that he's not told anyone about. There are things – little things – that upset him, that could have traumatised him – things that probably didn't come out back then...

Haris' cousin has a point; in fact, she has several. First of all, Haris is classed as a vulnerable adult, and under the Police and Criminal Evidence Act (1984), police custody sergeants must secure an appropriate adult to safeguard the rights of vulnerable people detained by police. This was put in place to stop vulnerable people like Haris admitting to crimes they did not commit. An appropriate adult was never acquired for Haris when he was questioned. The police pushed Haris hard in the interviews, but, credit to them, did not attempt to make him confess.

The newspapers were far more vicious in the way they attempted to demonise Haris. The Daily Mail claimed that he had access to a 'network of tunnels' beneath Scarclaw Fell, when, in reality, the great majority of the mining veins have collapsed. There is no known way of getting from one side of the fell to the other using the mineshafts. That didn't matter though. A wild-looking, bearded loner who lived with his mother in a ramshackle cottage was good copy.

Haris did not spend his time in and out of the old mining tunnels either. He knew of one or two that had not been fenced off, where he would go to watch birds and other animals, and there was his 'secret place' – the entrance to the tunnel near his house where the bats roosted. Haris had dragged branches and old material over the entrances to these caves not, as the papers made out, to conceal what he was doing from people, but so as not to scare the animals he loved to watch so much.

When Haris comes back from the toilet, and both he and his cousin are happy with us continuing, I ask my last few questions.

—*Did you never tell Father Brown, your mum – anyone – about the orphans?*

—I didn't.

—*Why? Why keep them a secret?*

—I … I … I thought they were a dream.

I don't want to press Haris much further as I can see he is near the end of his tether, talking about that time. However, there is one other thing that came out in the inquest that I need to ask him about.

—*Do you think the orphans ever went to your secret place – the cave with the bats? Might they have gone there when you weren't with them that winter, perhaps?*

—Yes. Yes I think they did because they wanted to see the animals and people like animals.

—*Did you know that they went there?*

—Yes, I knew. I think they went there in the night when I was asleep, maybe to see the night animals you can see from there, like the owls. Sometimes you see deer, if you're still.

—*How did you know they had been there?*

—Well, I went there to see the bats in the morning, to see if they were OK, because they hibernate right up in the ceiling, all together. And I saw something on the ground; I saw lots of things on the ground and I thought the orphans were still there.

—*What things on the ground?*

—There were little orange cigarette ends and little white cigarette ends and a funny smell. There were empty bottles, too – plastic ones all chopped in half with plastic bags sellotaped onto them. I thought the orphans must have been there, but then they must have gone again.

—*Why?*

—Because of the beast. The beast must have scared them away.

—*Why do you think the beast scared them away?*

—I ... because I had a dream ... a bad dream, a terrible dream, a dream about the beast.

—*Would you mind telling me what happened in your dream?*

—No, I wouldn't mind telling you. It's OK because it was just a dream. In my dream I woke up early, went down to the secret place to check on the bats, to make sure they were OK. I went there when it was still dark and there was a smell, a funny smell, a bit like cigarettes, and it was the smell of the beast. I heard the beast in the mine tunnel then, at the back, where it's dark. I heard it coming out of there roaring and gnashing its teeth. It came out of the dark with its big eyes and I screamed and it was chasing me and I ran as fast as I could and I ran back home and got back into bed.

This all happened in the winter of 1995, during Tom Jeffries' first excursion with the Rangers. It is clear from what Haris says that there was definitely a significant change in the behaviour of the group with the arrival of Jeffries. While the snowballs incident leaves a sour taste in the mouth, it smacks of horse-play – behaviour that just went a bit too far. During the inquest, all the teenagers were vague about what happened with Haris, but all maintained that it was Tom Jeffries who instigated the incident with the snowballs and gave him the piece of cannabis to eat.

In August 1996, Haris Novak met the 'orphans' once more. A single time, on the 23rd.

—*Are you OK, Haris, to tell me about that day in the summer?*

—Yes. But I'm getting tired of telling you about them now.

— *I know. I'm sorry. It'll be brief, just what you can remember.*

What came out at the inquest was that the teenagers had walked into Belkeld in the late afternoon of the 23rd August 1996: Tom Jeffries, Charlie Armstrong, Anyu Kekkonen, Eva Bickers and Brian Mings. They had hung about for a bit, bought some food supplies and attempted to buy alcohol in the corner shop (they failed), before setting out across the fell, back to the Woodlands Centre. They encountered Haris Novak during this walk back.

—It was just nearly teatime and I was watching out for deer. There's a family of roe deer that live in the wood and I was watching out for them in my hide with my binoculars.

—Is that when you saw the orphans crossing the fell?

—Yes, and I went to say hello to them. I went to see if they were OK because it had been a long time and I thought the beast had scared them away. I had forgotten that they were real and not just a dream. I told them that I had found their things in the cave and I had kept them safe for them in my house. The new boy, he said, 'Well done, Haris; good thinking!' He told me that anytime they leave those things in the secret place for me, that I must keep them secret, that they would put them in a bag for me and I couldn't tell anyone. If I did, the beast, it would get me, it would get me if I told. I never told, I never did. I kept the orphans' bags in the coal scuttle. We don't have a coal fire anymore; we have British Gas. So I kept their heavy bag there when they were gone.

—You kept their bag? Why?

—Because they gave it to me. It was a kind thing to do.

—Then what did you do?

—He kept shouting, 'Quick, quick!' And so I started running, I was running back home to put those things in the coal scuttle and I was running and I could hear him shouting, 'Quick! Quick!' and that's when I fell.

To cut a long story short here: Haris Novak twisted his ankle running home from the fell. He managed to limp back to his mother's house and that's where he stayed for the rest of the evening and night. His mother testified to this at the time.

The place where Tom Jeffries' body was found was pretty much the opposite side of the fell – deep in the fenced-off, restricted area. Haris, despite his knowledge of the area, would have had a job getting there, even without his twisted ankle. While Haris has ventured beyond the fences to watch wildlife, he is anxious about breaking rules. Knowing him even for the short time I have, it is difficult to imagine him being in any way involved in the disappearance of Tom Jeffries.

Because no one has ever been charged with the murder of Tom Jeffries, the media were free to speculate on what happened. One of the theories is that Haris Novak held a deep-seated resentment of the teenagers after the incident in 1995 with the snowballs. He allowed this resentment to build over time and, using his 'network of tunnels' beneath the fell, somehow managed to lure Jeffries out on his own and kill him.

Oh yeah, and the twisted ankle was an elaborate lie that Haris constructed in order to create an alibi.

So what conclusions can we draw from my interview with Haris Novak? Haris was known by the teenagers – specifically those five and none of the others. I imagine that none of them let on about him because … well … what reason would they have to tell any of the leaders? Remember, during the encounters with Haris Novak, the teenagers were trying to buy alcohol or were smoking – both tobacco and cannabis. I don't doubt that the remaining Rangers are sorry for what happened with Haris. In fact, during the inquest, both Eva, Anyu and Brian made a point of extending their apologies to Haris and his family.

It is interesting that Haris' cousin maintains that there is something that happened between him and the five teenagers that has not come out. That same feeling struck me during my chat with Haris Novak.

I believe Haris' cousin when she says that Haris has almost created a 'buffer' in his mind – behind which the trauma of 1996 cannot touch him. And I don't want to try and push or pull him over it. Instead, in the following episodes of Six Stories, *I'm going to talk to the people who definitely will know what happened.*

The other teenagers who were there.

In the next episode, we will gain a clearer picture of what happened at Scarclaw Fell on that summer night in 1996.

This has been Six Stories, *with me, Scott King.*

This has been our second story.

Until next time…

Scarclaw Fell
2017

I don't stay long. There's nothing to see here anymore, no rustic elegy; just a silent, black blight on the side of the fell. An empty question. I sometimes wonder if the bats are still there, roosting beneath the rock; whether the removal of the vegetation and the erecting of the new fences has driven them away. Maybe they've flourished? If I had the courage to come out here at night, I might find out.

That's not going to happen.

I keep going – leaving the canopy of trees and crossing the more exposed part of the fell. This is the track to Belkeld, curved like a scar. It feels almost sacrilegious, following the Rangers' footsteps like this. Scarclaw bends its head over me and scowls.

No one comes out here anymore. I worry sometimes what would happen if I met someone. Would I tell them to get off my father's land; my land? Would I smile, nod, comment on the weather and cast my gaze down the side of the fell, following the fists of gorse and flecks of scree?

Above me, the pale wall of cloud betrays the rising sun. It is light now, yet it still cannot penetrate Scarclaw's shadow.

Not far now.

For a while I thought Haris Novak's 'secret place' might become a bit of a … what's the word? I don't want to say 'shrine'. A talking point? A place of interest? Something like that. I'd thought that I'd sometimes have to come up here and chase away ghouls. But there's just nothing, not even the rusty voices of the crows; just the perpetual fug of not-quite-rain, not-quite-mist. Cleared of all vegetation, this hole in the side of the fell is an ugly wound. It bleeds its darkness across this land.

My land.

I've asked Dad a few times about knocking the fences down, filling it in.

But if the bats are still here then we've no chance. Imagine the headlines if we touched anything up here. So all we do instead is raise the fences higher.

I move on, leaving the Secret Place behind. Even the name is a misnomer now.

I can't help the internal speculation, the questions pulling at me. What would have happened if all these fences, this purge of the land, had been done quicker? Imagine if those kids had never come to Scarclaw.

Shoulda woulda coulda, as they say. What's done is done.

But we didn't want to do that; we didn't want to come marching onto these lands and just *take* them from under everyone's noses like they all thought we would. I remember the meeting over in Belkeld, when Dad's purchase of the land was more or less complete. A grim afternoon, much like this one. A draughty church hall; bad tea and stale biscuits. Rural officials in suits and wellingtons. Muddy Range Rovers in the car park. There was a bloke there who said he represented the users of the Woodlands Centre. Scruffy beard and shorts; hairy cyclists' calves and midge bites on his ankles. He smelled of old sandwiches and BO. Nearly thirty years ago now and I still remember that.

'Hasn't Lord Ramsay got enough ivory backscratchers without buying up all the proles' land as well?' he said in that self-satisfied way that those working-class imposter types have. 'Scarclaw Fell is for everyone, not just the super-rich.'

'And what would you know about the proles?' I wanted to say. 'You've more in common with the rich, you smug prick.' But Dad gripped my arm, pretending the cold air that whirled around our ankles was making his hip ache.

That was Dad's way. Quiet. Dignified.

I reach my destination; a mile from Belkeld. It's possible to pass by and miss it these days. That's good.

I often wonder if we'll get some of those beards and shorts types popping up around here. Will they take selfies at the old Novak Place? Lament the loss of this land? I've never seen any so far. Anything that was worth looking at was taken for evidence; the doors and windows boarded up. There's not even any graffiti. Scarclaw Fell seems to be wanting the old Novak place back; slowly drawing the cottage back into the soil. Weeds and brambles clog the little back garden and you'd need a machete to find the empty shell of the coal scuttle. The grates on the doors and windows are steel.

Coming here is more sad than anything else. I picture what it must have been like, living out here on this lonely slope. I imagine myself behind those walls; the metallic reek of rain, stewed meat; maybe a grinding whistle from an old radio in the corner, the shipping forecast as night falls over the fell. I think of what that must have felt like for a boy growing up here: sleepless nights staring from the window at that endless blackness.

There are times I have wondered if it were possible to see the Woodlands Centre from here. I stand as close as it's possible to get without touching the crumbling bricks of the Novak house and stare back the way I have come. The woods and the curve of the fell obscure the horizon in daylight, but I wonder if, at night, the lights shining out from the windowless curtains might have caught an eye, planted a seed? We'll never know.

'Father's out back, dear, counting the sheep,

Hush now my love and go straight back to sleep.

Father's out back, dear, locking the barn,

Making sure that the animals come to no harm.'

Jus and I looked at each other and started to laugh. Tomo stopped, long breaths replacing the rhyme. He held up the crude painting before us: intertwining green-and-brown snakes behind a black stick-figure in the foreground. He shook it, as if he had just proved something.

'What in blazing hell are you going on about?' Jus said, his laugh loud.

Tomo didn't smile back. He just let the picture fall from his hands. Outside, the rain began a sustained assault against the windows. The Woodland Centre roof reverberated with its tattoo.

Darkness was coming.

'You two are a pair of cunts, you know that?' Tomo said, his cheeks reddening. The word hit me like a fist. But it only seemed to make Jus laugh harder.

'You're fucking priceless, Tomo, mate!'

A whisky bottle appeared in Tomo's fist. He took a nip, winced and stared down at the painting, which had fallen, face-up at his feet. I didn't like the look on his face; it had slackened, as if all the fight had left him. Yet something else was there; something hard I'd never seen before.

I strode over to the doorway and flicked on the light. The gloom in the Woodlands Centre was alleviated and I felt my spirits lift a little. But that lift swiftly became replaced with a knot of unease. There were no curtains, nor blinds on the windows of The Woodlands Centre and in this rain-lashed dark, I realised the lights made us suddenly very visible.

Tomo took another long swig of the whisky and held the bottle tight to his chest as Jus reached for it.

'Piss off.' Tomo's face was still red with irritation. 'You two think you know everything.' He was beginning to sound like a little kid.

Jus looked at me but I was intrigued.

'Come on mate,' I said. I hadn't laughed at him, not yet. 'What were you saying before?'

'Dun't matter.'

But it did. With the lights on, the room seemed bigger and we seemed smaller. It mattered here, with the stark walls, grimy windows and grubby lino floor.

It took a few more moments of gentle cajoling and a few good glugs of the whisky before Tomo would speak again.

'When I told my dad I was coming out here, to Scarclaw,' he said, rubbing the toe of his brogue with his thumb – despite the booze, he sounded horribly sober – 'he told me to watch out for the…' He stopped, puffing out a little gasp where a word should have been. 'He said there was something out here … on the fell.'

I gave Jus a look, stopped his laughter with my stare.

'What do you mean, "something"?' I asked. I felt out of breath, like my lungs had deflated.

The wind had picked up outside and the spindly thrashing of the trees behind the windows kept catching my eye.

'Don't fear the dark, dear, swift is the night,

For nothing will harm you, wrapped up here, tight.

That's just a shadow, dear, don't fear a sprite

Don't pay your mind to the tricks of the light.'

Tomo's voice seemed to echo. All I wanted was to be wrapped up in my sleeping bag in one of those bunk beds. It would feel safer in there; I would let the alcohol hang heavy on my eyes and my mind, let it pull me down into sleep. And in the morning, as soon as light came, we could get the fuck out of here and back to London.

'What's a sprite?' Jus asked.

Tomo ignored him and carried on.

'That's just the wind, dear, not a knock at the door,

Father's protecting us, he's out on the moor.

That's not the scraping and sneaking of feet,

That's just the rustling of sheep who can't sleep.'

'Stop it, Tomo,' Jus said; he was suddenly pale.

Tomo ignored him. He stared straight forward, his recitation firm and quick, exorcising the rhyme out into the room.

'Mother, is that father's form at the door?

It's taller and longer than ever before,

His face is all white, coat black like a loon,

His teeth glow like blades in the light of the moon.'

'Fucking shut up!' This time Jus punched Tomo in the arm, a swift, feral movement.

Tomo ignored that, too.

Silence again.

We all jumped as the dogs, who had been quiet for a time, all began to bark. My heart yammered and I could feel a swelling panic building inside me. I wanted my dad. I was twenty-one years old and I wanted my dad to come and make everything OK again.

'Tomo?' Jus said. 'Tomo, man, what the fuck is wrong with them?'

We all looked in the direction of the dormitories where the baying was coming from.

Tomo got to his feet, dazed, as if he'd stepped out of a dream.

'Come on,' he said and turned his back on us, walking toward the sound of the dogs.

Jus and I followed him. What else were we to do? That panic in my stomach felt huge – a pulsating, swollen thing. I could feel tears – tears of all things – pricking behind my eyes. Why in heaven's name had we come out here?

Tomo stopped at the door of the dormitory. He placed his hand on the door-knob. The dogs were going insane; we could hear their claws scraping on the floor. I pictured sharp teeth and pink gums, flecks of froth at their mouths.

'Tomo mate,' I said, 'are they...' I gestured to the door. 'Are they going to be OK, when you...'

But I saw in his eyes that Tomo knew as much as I about what was going on here. With a hopeless shrug he turned the handle.

'Hang on Tomo, mate, hang on!' Jus shouted.

I braced myself for a flurry of teeth and fur to come bursting from behind the door.

What we saw was worse.

The lurchers were at the back of the dormitory, throwing themselves at the single-paned window. Their barks were frantic, furious. .

With our eyes we followed the furore of the hounds. And then we all saw it. All at the same time. Beyond the window, framed by the flailing fingers of the trees and the slash-marks of rain.

That shape.

That black figure.

It stood, looking in.

We all saw it, we all did. We all saw it look up and see us.

We saw it vanish into the night.

I tell myself that, yes, I'll come here at night. That I'll get a few others, perhaps. We'll walk out here to the old Novak house and we'll not be scared. We'll prove once and for all to ourselves that there's no monster, sprite, troll, hob or whatever. They say, if you don't look at a monster, it grows. One minute there's a single eye staring at you, and before you know it, there are twenty-one.

Even in the daylight, there's darkness on Scarclaw.

I stand here in the daylight and look at the darkness.

Then I turn and walk on.

Not looking back.

Episode 3: Daddy's Girl

—First of all, no one called him TJ. No one except him. He used to write it everywhere, though, in that stupid little graffiti writing, you know; that sort of squiggly nonsense that you can't read? Well, yeah, that.

God, he was such a little *dickhead*.

Sorry. No, really, I am. I'm sorry that he's gone, that he died. I know that his parents are probably listening to this and probably hate me now but … yeah, what can you do? He was a horrible little dickhead and I hated him.

That's it really.

Welcome to Six Stories. *I'm Scott King.*

In the next six weeks, we will be looking back at the Scarclaw Fell tragedy in 1996, we'll be looking back from six different perspectives; seeing the events that unfolded through six pairs of eyes.

In this week's episode, we'll talk to Eva Bickers, the daughter of Derek, and one of the teenagers who was on the trip to Scarclaw Fell Woodlands Centre in 1996.

Eva Bickers spent a significant amount of time with Tom Jeffries and will be able to offer fresh insight into what went on the day he disappeared.

At first, as you'll hear, Eva is defensive and sketchy. She seems unwilling to say much about what went on that weekend. She has her reasons for this, as will become clear.

Today, Eva is thirty-four. She lives in a different part of the country from where she grew up, and it's about as far as you can get from Scarclaw

Fell. Who knows whether this is intentional or not? She does often travel to visit her father in her home town. We conduct our interview over Skype.

—You'll have to excuse me; I'm a little … er … overwhelmed. I'm actually a big fan of yours.

—*Oh really? Thanks, that's very kind.*

—Yeah. I used to listen to you religiously; every morning, when I was running.

—*Did you ever think that what happened to you might one day become one of my series?*

—You know, I almost … *fantasised* about it, if you know what I mean? Well, not *fantasised* as such, but I practised. I practised what I would say.

—*So you're prepared then?*

—It's funny, because now you're here … well, not *here* … but now I'm talking to you in the flesh – well, not even in the flesh, you've got your hood thing on – but now I'm *talking* to you, I'm not sure I know what to say.

—*I think sometimes it's best to start from the start.*

—Right. Where is that, though? I mean, where is the start of all this?

—*Why don't we talk about Rangers?*

—What about them? It wasn't their fault.

—*No. That's true.*

—It's been proved. Like, legally.

—*I know, I—*

—I know you've talked to my dad. It still haunts him, what happened. Sometimes he gets … I know it upsets him and I know he cries. Talking to you just re-opened the wound.

Maybe Eva is right. In fact, there's not much 'maybe' about it. Put yourself in Derek Bickers' shoes: no matter how understanding Tom Jeffries' parents were about what happened, Derek will always blame himself in some way. I don't doubt this is the same for Eva. She was close to Tom – closer than her father was – and I imagine she saw a different side to him than either Derek or Haris. So I proceed with tact; at any point, Eva could simply hang up, stop talking to me.

—*How about we start from the beginning, I mean the very beginning.*
—I don't know … I…
—*Your dad told me about what's obviously a very treasured memory of his: you and Charlie chucking leaves at each other in the garden.*
—Oh yeah. He always tells that one but I don't actually remember it. It's, like, my dad's favourite story. I don't know why. But yeah; that's how young I was when it started I guess.
—*You knew Charlie from that age?*
—Younger. I think we shared changing mats when we were babies; our parents were friends; best friends.
—*So what are your earliest memories of Rangers? Was Charlie there?*
—Of course! Charlie and I were the founding fathers! Look, I think I sort of know what's coming, and I'm going to say now: I don't think Charlie had anything to do with what happened to Tom. I just don't.
—*Maybe we're getting a little ahead of ourselves? I'm not here to make accusations.*
—I know. I'm sorry. It's just … it's so *hard*. When I listen to your podcasts, I'm sometimes, like, *screaming* at the people you talk to, to open up. But now I'm on the other side, it's just so…
—*Different?*
—No. Yeah … I dunno. I'm just saying, OK? Charlie was a lot of things to a lot of different people. But he wasn't a killer. That's all I wanted to say, first off, OK?
—*OK. Look, I'm not doing this to try and lead you to a place you don't want to go.*
—I know, I know. Like I say, I'm a fan, I know what you do and, like, I made up my mind about a few of the other cases you've looked at in your other series.

—Lots of people come to lots of different conclusions.

—Yeah, I get it. That's the point. I know all that. I'm just saying, though … about Charlie.

—I understand. He was your friend.

—Yeah.

I do understand Eva's caginess, and her devotion to her friend. The teenagers were too young to be named in the press at the time. However, by the time Tom Jeffries' body was found, Charlie had turned sixteen, and, now being the only one who could be identified, he had a hard ride from the press – that is, once Haris Novak was ruled out as a suspect. Charlie got nowhere near the condemnation that Haris Novak received, though. But many articles leaned heavily on Charlie's appearance and music tastes, as if that has something to do with what makes people kill.

Eva tells me that she stood up for Charlie then, just as she does today. She says, however, that she and Charlie, have not been in touch since.

—So you and Charlie grew up together?

—Yeah, we were always at theirs, or they came to us. We went on holiday a few times together, the families. Well, me and my mum and dad and Charlie and his mum. France, Italy; we went camping in the Black Forest in Germany when we were about eight – that's probably the earliest solid memory of the two of us I have. It was amazing, magical; like something out of a story. I remember the *smell* of it. It smelled *green*. Yeah, those were good days. That was when it was just my family and Charlie's. Before anyone else came along.

—What did it mean to you – that friendship; those excursions into the country, when you were that age?

—It was nice. Sorry, that's a terrible word … It was a really precious thing that we did. Precious memories. I loved the outdoors, the woods, that sort of thing. I still do; even after what happened at Scarclaw. I still love the hills and forests. I'm thankful to my dad, you know, for making that effort when we were little. You see so many mums and dads who just don't give a shit – just staring at their phones while the kids are charging around. It's really sad.

—*So you and Charlie, you said you were, what, the 'founding fathers'?*

—Yeah! That's what we used to call ourselves, when we got older; when more kids started joining in.

—*And growing older, sometimes it gets awkward with boys and girls who are friends, doesn't it?*

—Yeah, you're right, it does get awkward; especially in school and stuff. That's the thing, though: Charlie and I weren't at the same school, so there wasn't that, you know, that silliness, that 'Ooh, who's your boyfriend'. Neither of us would have given a shit anyway. I wasn't into all that cliquey stuff at school. I was … I dunno … I used to get called 'hippy' a lot.

—*Really? Why was that?*

—Oh, because of the way I dressed; because I didn't wear a Kappa tracksuit or have a gold chain around my neck. Honestly, I envy kids today with their clothes – lads in skinny jeans and that 'geek chic' stuff. Back in the nineties, you would have got battered for dressing like that!

—*Did that ever happen to you? Did you experience violence?*

—Nah. Me and Anyu used to get all that 'Did you get your clothes from Oxfam?' stuff, but we didn't care.

—*Anyu Kekkonen, she was a school friend of yours, wasn't she?*

—Yes. Me and Anyu became friends in, like, year eight or something. She'd just joined the school and didn't have anyone. I just started talking to her, you know? That was the other thing about being in Rangers; you were just so, like, *open* to other people; so non-judgemental. When there's a new kid in school, no one wants to talk to them; people are so scared of being seen as different, like some of that newness might rub off on them. Anyu was a little bit foreign – her mum's Inuit and she has that … that *look* about her, if you know what I mean: dark skin and sort of oriental eyes. Not a bad thing, she just … Anyway; so I didn't give a shit; I just went right on over and started talking to her, and that was that.

—*Anyu started coming to the Rangers meetings, didn't she?*

—Yeah, eventually.

—*Eventually?*

—Well, yeah. But that wasn't *her*, or her mum. People say that Eska was a bit funny, but she really wasn't. She was just … I think she often felt a bit out of place. I don't think she ever settled in England, if you know what I mean? She was very traditional. She had some crazy stories…

—*Stories?*

—Yeah, like, folk tales from up there, the Arctic.

I notice Eva does this when she speaks about her friends: she'll start, introduce them, and then suddenly clam up. I understand that she's protecting them. But it does make me wonder why she's doing it, when no one in the case of Tom Jeffries was ever charged and his death was deemed accidental.

Perhaps Eva is worried that, when the podcast airs, it might kick up the whole thing again and the four of them will be under scrutiny from the media. I don't know. I've learned it's best not to push too hard when people don't want to talk about certain things.

— *So was Anyu's mother OK with her going off with you lot?*

—I think she was, but only, like, halfway. Anyu was her only real link to this country – the language and everything. I think Eska found it hard when Anyu wasn't around; she didn't have people to talk to. She wasn't, like, overbearing or strict or anything. I went for tea at their house loads of times and Eska was lovely. It must have been so hard.

— *Your Dad says Anyu was quite reserved. Was that just with adults, or with you kids, too?*

—You know, I'd like to say that we drew her out of her shell, but Anyu didn't really have a shell; she was just … it was just that some people found her inscrutable. Most people actually. She had … there's a good term for it now, isn't there? 'Resting bitch-face' – when your natural look is a bit … grumpy. Anyu was more … I think people found her aloof. But she wasn't. It was just the way she came across. She was beautiful as well, in a really unique way. I think a lot of people thought that. Anyu used to get so annoyed that loads of the boys were too scared to talk to her.

—*Your dad told me that Anyu was the 'sensible one' in the group – the level head.*

—Ha! Yeah, that's totally right. She was dead smart, too. If we got lost and stuff, it was always Anyu who knew what to do. If one of us drank too much at a party and was sick, Anyu would be the one holding back our hair and giving us water.

—*So Anyu didn't join in with all that?*

—Oh yeah, Anyu did it, too. She was just … you know how some people are really just 'cool', like in control all the time: that was Anyu. She could put away more vodka than any of us, but she was never a mess with it, if you know what I mean? She was level-headed even then. I was so jealous of that!

—*Was there a lot of drinking and stuff going on during your outings?*

—See, this is what the media and all them tried to do at the time. They made out like Rangers was some hippy free-for-all, where kids were allowed to smoke crack and worship the devil. But it wasn't like that at all. You show me one group of teenagers – *normal* teenagers – who don't behave like that. The thing with us is, we were a bit more … sensible … I don't know if that's the right word. Let's just say we weren't troublemakers. We didn't go round breaking things and fighting. We just kept ourselves to ourselves.

—*Was Scarclaw Fell a place where you did it most?*

—Well, we did do that sort of thing there; but we did it at home, too. There were parties all the time; weekends and all that. Scarclaw Fell was a good place because we were with our best friends and – it sounds daft to say it now – but like, my dad was there too, so we all felt safe there. That's why, when Tom went missing, it was just so … It just *destroyed* us. It ruined it all.

—*Aside from you, Anyu and Charlie, there was another member of the group? Brian Mings.*

—Oh, Brian. Yeah, he was there, too. He was always there.

When Eva talks about Brian Mings, I notice a shift in her voice. It's very slight; probably unconscious. Her face changes, too – again, only slightly. Her smile seems more pronounced … almost forced.

—*Can you tell me a bit about Brian?*
—Well yeah, I suppose. There's not much to tell.
—*He joined Rangers about the same time as Anyu, right?*
—Correct. His mum was a friend of Sally's or something … I don't know.
—*You don't know?*
—Well, yes, I do; I do know. His mum was a friend of Sally Mullen and he just … he just *joined,* like the rest of us. That was all, really.

There is a bit of an awkward silence at this point, and I wonder if Eva wants a break. She's been happy to talk to me about her friends and the early days, but it feels like, as more of the group appear, the closer we get to Tom Jeffries, the more reluctant she is to open up. We sign out, and I call Eva again an hour or so later.

—*Are you OK?*
—Yeah, I'm fine. Sorry, it's just that it's been a long time since … since all this, and I don't want to get things wrong. I don't want to come across in a bad way and I don't want to misrepresent people, do you know what I mean?
—*I do, I honestly do. You've come across fine. You've heard my series before and you know that there are no conclusions drawn – not by me anyway – that it's all about honesty.*
—I know, I know. It's just, I've noticed a theme in a lot of your podcasts is, well, bullying. They're often about people who've been treated badly – like that lad from Devon who killed those people from his school; or that guy who was put away for that bomb at his work.
—*Bullying is a sensitive issue for you?*

—Yes. I mean, I wasn't really *bullied* as such, but I knew people who were.

—*Your friends were bullied?*

—Some were. I know Charlie used to get a lot of stick in his school for how he dressed; his hair, the music he liked. Anyu, too, a little bit, when we were younger: 'Are you Chinese?', 'Did you used to live in an igloo?' – that sort of crap.

—*We were talking about Brian Mings before we had a break.*

—Oh yeah, that's right.

—*Your dad described Brian as a 'follower', a bit of an outsider. Would you say that was accurate?*

—We were all outsiders. Not just him.

—*So, from what I understand about the group, Brian would have felt safe with you all; he would have been accepted?*

—Yes. Yes he was accepted. He *was* accepted … just like everyone else.

—*And were there any … problems?*

—Problems? Like what?

—*With Brian? Any problems with him and the others?*

—What do you mean by 'problems'?

—*Well … you tell me.*

—OK, OK, I know what you're getting at. Brian liked Anyu. He *really* liked her; it was obvious. To all of us. But, you know, no one mentioned it; no one shamed him about it. We all just, well, we kind of just accepted it. Even Anyu.

—*How did Anyu feel about it? You know, when it was just the two of you.*

— She was sort of flattered. But Brian, he was just … he wasn't her type. She just wasn't into him.

—*To me it sounds like you want to say something else, but you won't. For Brian's sake, I mean.*

— It's just, it was a funny situation because, no matter how much he liked her, it just wasn't going to happen, you know? It just wasn't. Anyu didn't go for people like Brian.

—*People like Brian?*

—Yeah … he was just too … what's the word? … He was just too *weak* for her or something. It's weird; when you're a teenage girl, the nice guys – the sweet guys – they just don't *cut it*. Maybe it's something to do with evolution or whatever, but when you're a teenager, you go for the arseholes, the dickheads, the alpha males. Then you grow up and wonder, *what was I even doing?*

—*So was there someone that Anyu liked? Presumably you two talked about these things?*

—Yeah, I think so. Yeah, I imagine there was.

—*OK…*

—Well … I don't remember. It was a long time ago, and, well, you know, it doesn't matter in the scheme of things, does it?

—*I suppose not.*

—I spent a lot of my time trying to keep Brian away from Anyu, if I'm honest.

—*Really? Was he really that persistent?*

—No … look, I think I'm making him out all wrong here. Brian liked Anyu and she didn't like him back. It was that simple. But Brian seemed unable to accept it. Maybe it's a boy thing; maybe he just thought if he was persistent, one day she'd finally crack or something. Let me make something clear, though: he never got *weird* about it. He never got all stalkerish with her, and they were still friends. I guess that was one of the nice things about it.

—*That must have been slightly odd – to have this unrequited desire hanging over them the whole time. Did stuff not get a bit … strained?*

—It just became sort of *accepted*. Brian liked Anyu. Anyu liked … well, that was all, really. It was never going to happen. They went through funny little stages; like, he would really try with her for, like, a week; and then the next few months he would just let it go. Then he would try again. But, you know, this whole Brian and Anyu thing, it didn't really have much to do with what happened to Tom.

—*I think I'm just trying to really get a good picture of the group*

*dynamic. These sorts of things can get overlooked, and it was never prop-
erly reported what exactly was going on.*

—There was nothing 'going on'. We were just kids.

*Eva, like the others, was fifteen at the time of Tom Jeffries' disap-
pearance, and therefore, there are complex legal issues surrounding her
interviews with the police. Long story short: I cannot play them; I don't
even have access to them.*

*However, I have been able to talk to Eva Bickers' old form teacher
from her high school. Dorothy Whetworth knew Eva from year seven, all
the way up to year eleven, and remembers her well. I speak to Dorothy
on the phone.*

—*So, Eva Bickers…*

—Yes, yes, oh yes. It was such a shame about what happened. She
was only young. She didn't come back in after … after what happened, which you can understand. I always thought there was a big
Eva-shaped hole at leavers' assembly. Such a shame.

—*I guess you knew her quite well…*

—You see them grow up … you do. They come to you in year
seven, all pigtails and smiles, and you watch them turn into adults
before your eyes. It's amazing really.

—*What sort of a person was Eva? What was the side of her that you
saw, anyway?*

—You know, Eva was … I almost don't want to say because it
sounds trite … but you could say Eva, for most of her school life, was
run of the mill. She never got in trouble, she rarely got detention.
She was polite and respectful all the time. We had a good relationship, she and I. We were never especially close, but we had a mutual
affection for each other, I think.

—*So nothing to write home about then?*

—Well, no, not really. I talked to her father quite a lot at parents'
evenings. He was a lovely man. You could see Eva was well brought up.
I think that's what made what happened with her all the more shocking.

—I guess you don't see it coming with girls like Eva?

—No, that's right. You see it with certain others: there are patterns of behaviour, and then years later, when you see they've been put in prison for stealing or mugging old ladies, you think, 'Yep, we all saw that coming.' It's horrid really, but it's the way it is sometimes. There was none of that with Eva. Well, perhaps one thing. There was … I mean, it was probably nothing…

—Go on…

—I mean, you don't tell your teacher things do you? But I had the feeling Eva wanted to tell me something a few times, but the opportunity was lost. You know how it is – classes, other kids, people coming in and out…

—What do you think it might have been?

—They're funny creatures, teenage girls – all tough on the outside, but really they're still traipsing round in Mam's high heels, wanting desperately to be grown-ups. They don't give much away, to be fair to them. But … I mean, I have two of my own, and you can tell when something's gone wrong.

—So you think something went wrong for Eva?

—I couldn't say for sure, but I'll tell you what I thought at the time. Throughout year ten, Eva had really started to find herself. She was experimenting with her own style – dyed hair, too much eye-liner, that sort of thing. I knew she was smoking as well. They always think you don't know, but she reeked of it. I wanted to say something, but that would have pushed her away. There's other things you pick up as a teacher as well. It's like the smoking thing: children think you can't hear them, but it's amazing what you *do* hear; you know all the gossip!

So … how do I say this with some decorum … Eva was becoming, um, *popular* with some of the boys. She wasn't sleeping with them, I hasten to add! At least I'm ninety-nine per cent sure she wasn't But she was … she was *developing physically,* and … well … you know what teenage boys are like.

—Was Eva aware of this, do you think?

—Oh, I think so. Some of the nastier ones would shout things at her. Remember, she was smoking as well, so often would spend time in the smokers' corners that they all think we don't know about. And of course that's where a lot of the rum 'uns would congregate.

—*But, from what I know about Eva, she wasn't a bad girl; she wasn't in trouble.*

—That's correct, she wasn't. She was a conundrum, our Eva.

—*So why then did this well-behaved, pleasant girl, with a secure background, start smoking in school? With the bad 'uns? It seems, from what you've said, out of character.*

—Yes and no. I had the feeling, with Eva, that there were things outside her school life that were starting to creep in.

—*Did you know about Rangers?*

—Not until what happened in '96. I had no idea. I think Eva kept it safe, you know. A precious little box that only she could look into as she pleased. I understand Anyu was part of that group, too. But I didn't know her; I didn't teach her.

—*Eva had a firm little core of friends in Rangers; friends outside school.*

—Yes and it makes more sense now I know about that.

—*What does?*

—Well, I don't want to sound like an old lady here – even though I am – but you can sometimes see when there's, you know, *boy trouble.*

—*Again, that seems a little out of character for Eva.*

—She pretty much had the pick of the boys, you know. I don't think she knew it herself; or if she did, she didn't care. It always seemed to me, though, that she was saving her heart for ... someone else...

—*What made you think that?*

—As I say, you hear things. You see them every day; you notice subtle changes. But there was a definite *moment* that I remember. One spring, when Eva was in year ten – I'll never forget it – she told me she had been away in the half-term for a couple of days...

This, if Dorothy is remembering correctly, was May 1995, when the group went to Scarclaw Fell and met Haris Novak for the first time. Tom Jeffries was not with them.

—And Eva was just *radiant*. It was as if she had swallowed a bit of sunshine and it was streaming out of her. I think I asked – I must have done – I said, 'Eva, you seem happy,' something like that; and she just smiled. I'll never forget it, that smile; it was utter bliss, contentment. 'I just had a really good time, miss,' she said. And that was it. But I knew – I don't know; a woman's intuition perhaps? – that there was a boy involved. I left it at that, but I was happy for her.

During my next Skype chat with Eva, I ask her to recall that trip to Scarclaw Fell in 1995.

—Oh, I don't know. We used to go there a lot.

—*That spring half-term was the first time you met Haris – you, Charlie, Anyu and Brian. What can you remember?*

—Not a lot, really. It was a long time ago and it was just a trip. Nothing special happened. Not really.

—*Are you sure?*

—Is this about Haris? Look, I still sometimes beat myself up about it. Of course I do. Haris Novak was ... I mean, we should have just left him alone. None of us knew; none of us understood about his ... his ... conditions. We just ... we were bored teenagers and he gave us all that money...

—*And he showed you that bit of the mine, didn't he?*

—Yes, he did. It was amazing, it really was; just this little pocket of darkness hidden in the fell. It became our 'place'. We just used to hang about in there, smoke. Charlie used to tell us stories.

—*So, you'd go there a lot?*

—Yeah, we did. We were fourteen; it was a cool place, a hole in the ground. No one could find us there. I mean, c'mon...

—*I get it. Was Haris there with you?*

—No, not much. He was at first, but only for a bit, in and out. He used to bring us all this stuff, like crusts of bread and cold beans in a little Tupperware. It was sweet really. But then he'd go away again. Looking back now it seems really weird, but then we were just ... we were teenagers!

—*Why did you never tell your dad, or Sally, or anyone about Haris?*

—I ... I just ... There was no reason to. I mean, there was no conscious decision to keep him hidden. It was just, why would we need to tell someone? It's not like he was a paedophile or a nutter or something. He was just like the local ... er ... He was just like a funny little man, you know?

God, my dad, he went spare after he found out; after Tom disappeared. He thought Haris was like ... well, I suppose you'd call it 'grooming' these days.

—*And was he?*

—NO! Of course not! He wasn't like that. We were like ... like little pets to him. I can see how *weird* it would have seemed to anyone looking in, but we just sort of got on with it.

—*Going back to that trip to Scarclaw in the spring. Was there anything else that happened? Anything significant?*

—What are you trying to say?

—*I'm not, I'm just ... it was the first time you met Haris; the first time you found that 'place'. It was a big time, was it not?*

—I wouldn't call it 'big'. We used to go up there quite a bit, during the day, I mean. It was just a thing to do, you know, to get away from the adults and the little ones. We didn't actually *do* anything in there, not back then. Not really. Just a few fags and stuff.

—*You said Charlie used to tell stories.*

—Yeah. He was always really good at that sort of thing. He would nick candles from the centre and we stuck them in the walls, and he would tell us ... god, it gives me the shivers just thinking about it now: he would tell us about Nanna Wrack.

—*Who's that?*

—I don't know if he made it up, or if it was a story from the area, a folk tale or something? He probably made it up, if I'm honest. Ugh, it was horrible…

—*Can you remember it?*

—Oh, I can't do it like Charlie did, but he used to make us go all quiet, and then speak in this really low voice, just above a whisper. He used to tell us how Nanna Wrack was the 'Marsh Hag', that she made the mines fall in, that, if you got lost on the fell, she would rise up out of the marshes – her teeth all black and her hair all stringy and filled with mud – and Charlie, he would be speaking so quietly, then he'd suddenly do this … this *scream*, and I swear to god I've never been so scared. I reckon I'll still have nightmares, thinking about it again.

—*That's pretty intense…*

—Yeah, but it became our 'thing'. We would always ask him to tell it, every time. And he would add stuff to it, like, he'd make the premise longer and longer – draw it out for ages until we were just *waiting* for this scream. It was brilliant! Nanna Wrack became this sort of *bogeyman* … a *bogeywoman* … that we'd created. If you heard the wind whistling, you'd say, 'That's Nanna Wrack.'

—*What do you know about the Beast of Belkeld?*

—The what? I've not heard of that. Maybe it's where Charlie got it from, all that Nanna Wrack stuff. He used to tell the little ones at Rangers not to go walking on the fell on their own because Nanna Wrack would reach up with her long fingers and pull you into the marsh. It was a pretty good deterrent, to be honest. I think my dad approved.

—*Was this story Charlie's 'thing' then? I mean, was he known for this story?*

—He only told it when it was just us lot – the four of us in that mineshaft. It was funny: Brian used to try and snuggle up to Anyu, put his arm round her in case she was scared. Bless him. I think he was more scared than her! He used to try and tell the story, if Charlie wasn't there. But it wasn't the same…

—*What about Tom Jeffries?*

—Oh, no. He wasn't there then. Not the first time Charlie started telling it.

I want to pause here to reiterate something. The marshlands of Scarclaw Fell are around the far side from Belkeld and the mine. If you're looking out from the Woodlands Centre, they're up on the left and quite a trek to get to. As far as I know, there was no reason for any of the teenagers to go there.

The marshlands are where the body of Tom Jeffries was found by Harry Saint Clement-Ramsay in 1997. I asked Harry about both the Nanna Wrack story and the Beast of Belkeld during our interview for episode one.

—I think I've heard something about it. I'm not sure. There's loads of that stuff: boggarts and witches. Something about stone circles. St Augustine built churches all over the old pagan sites in Northumberland. Got rid of all that crap...

—*Why were you and your friends out in the marshlands, anyway – the night you found Tom Jeffries' body, I mean?*

—As I say, it was just a recce; a jolly. We were just looking about.

—*In the middle of the night, with lamps?*

—As I've said, we'd had a few drinks...

More forthcoming than Harry is another teacher from Eva Bickers' school. I have been given his name by Dorothy Whetworth. He asked me not to identify him and his voice has been altered digitally. He tells me something that I've edited in after the interview with Eva, which corroborates the fascination that the teenagers had with Scarclaw Fell.

—*You taught both Eva Bickers and Anyu Kekkonen?*

—Yes, they were in the same group. GCSE art.

—*And you told Mrs Whetworth about something that bothered you in 1996; something about both of them?*

—You see, people often ascribe traits to students. For example, if a teenager writes a story in English class about a murderer, or in art draws people being decapitated, it suggests that they're disturbed, somehow; or that they'll actually go and kill someone. I don't buy it, though. What these people fail to point out is that ALL teenagers are morbid. All of them. Sex and death – that's at the forefront of their minds pretty much the whole time!

—*But there was something about Eva and Anyu's work that you noticed, right?*

—I wish I still had these pieces. They're really good, but they're … they deviate from the girls' usual work, their usual *style*.

—*Can you remember what these pieces were of?*

—Oh yes. I couldn't forget them. Partly because they were their final GCSE pieces before that summer in 1996, partly because they'd both done the same thing. They were these *monsters*, or witches or something, rising out of water – all claws and teeth. It was just so … so *off* for those girls to do something like that.

—*What did you think?*

—I honestly didn't know. Maybe it was like a private joke or something.

I mention these artworks to Eva, but she passes it off; says she doesn't really remember, that it was probably, like her art teacher says, a private joke. What I think is that both Anyu and Eva were paying tribute to a place and people – a person – that made them happy. Nanna Wrack was a figment of Charlie Armstrong's imagination. It is clear that both girls looked up to him. Maybe there was more. Eva has indicated that there was someone that Anyu liked; maybe that was Charlie. It's strange how these things work.

There is one more school-related incident that is important to mention at this point. Dorothy Whetworth tells me about another time she noticed something different about Eva.

—It was after Christmas: January 1996. Here's another thing about schools: that term – the one after Christmas – is always the worst. It's cold; Christmas Day is long gone, and there's really nothing for the kids to look forward to, so they're understandably a bit glum when they come back. But Eva … Eva was just … it was like someone had carved out her heart.

—*Wow. So the total opposite to the previous spring then?*

—Yes. That's what I thought at the time. In the spring, Eva came in just *glowing*; and now, after the Christmas break, she comes back, well, as if something had been sucked out of her. Like a little piece of her spirit had gone missing.

I can't find the words to ask Eva why, more than twenty years ago, she came back into school feeling happy, and another time came in sad. Maybe it was nothing. Like the paintings of Nanna Wrack, maybe it was just yet another layer to Eva's life. What does link these two events, however, is that in each school holiday, Eva visited Scarclaw Fell.

Crucially, Tom Jeffries was not there in May 1995; but he was in December.

My final interview with Eva is a few days later. I email her, explaining that I will be asking her questions about Tom Jeffries and to prepare herself.

When we speak, Eva seems stronger somehow; as if resigned to getting all of this out – exorcising some old ghost. I ask her about the time when Tom Jeffries joined Rangers. And that's when she calls him a dickhead and tells me how much she hated him – the clip I played at the beginning of this episode.

—*So, what was it about Tom that you didn't like?*

—Oh, everything. Just everything. He was gobby, you know? Like the kids in school who sit at the back, always shouting stuff out. He was always going on about weed the whole time, in front of the adults, too. I think my dad had a word with him at one point.

—*Was it always like that? I mean, even at first?*

—Yeah, he came in with that attitude. You know what the very first thing he said at Rangers was – after his mum dropped him off?

He looked at us all – Charlie, me, Anyu, Brian – and said, 'Hippies, eh? I like hippies cos they smoke *the herb.*' What a twat!

—*Yet he was accepted. He integrated himself into the group with a degree of ease.*

—That's right. *God*, if I could go back in time … I just … I don't know how or why, but he was suddenly Charlie's mate – his best bloody mate! They were suddenly off together and the rest of us didn't get a look in.

—*And Charlie had been your best friend since…*

—Since we were kids; babies even. Then this little … this lad came in, and, *poof,* off they went.

—*You still seem angry about this.*

—Ha. Yeah, I am a bit. I mean, me and Charlie, we've not been in touch since. I've not been in touch with any of them, if I'm honest. But Charlie … we went way back.

—*Why do you think it was? Why did Charlie suddenly just allow Tom in like that, instead of someone like Brian, who had been part of the group for much longer?*

—Oh, it was the drugs and drink and stuff. Tom had the gift of the gab; he had an edge to him. Charlie loved all that.

—*You said before that they used to 'go off' together. Do you mean that literally?*

—Yeah. And I mean it figuratively as well. Sometimes Charlie and Tom, they used to just disappear off together when we were on trips.

—*What do you think they were doing?*

—Smoking. There wasn't anything sinister about it. They just used to go off and smoke together.

—*But didn't you all smoke? You, Anyu, Brian?*

—Yeah, we all did. I don't know. I think Tom just wanted Charlie all to himself. We all looked up to Charlie, remember. He was like … an enigma or something.

Here we can see how the dynamic of the group shifted – as Eva's dad, Derek, alluded to in episode one. The arrival of Tom Jeffries plunged

*Eva – and, I'm guessing, the others – into uncertainty. Why was their
leader suddenly so taken with this new person? What is clear is that Tom's
removal of Charlie's attention really affected Eva. I ask her about the
others' reactions to having Tom Jeffries in the group.*

—Well Anyu, she was so chilled, she was virtually horizontal,
and she just went with it. I think Tom found her difficult. He never
really spoke to her. I actually can't remember those two ever having
a conversation.

—*And Brian?*

—That wasn't very nice, really. You know Tom and him were at
the same school, right? That private one. They didn't hang about
together or anything. But Tom … he was … he just wasn't very
nice…

—*You sound like you want to say more.*

—Yeah, I guess I do, but, it feels weird. Not weird – it feels *bad*,
because, I guess I wish I would have *done* something about it. But
I was so fucking *angry* that Tom had come along and just whipped
away my best friend like that, as if I didn't even matter. I was so
wrapped up in that, I just kind of ignored what he did to Brian.

—*What he 'did' to Brian?*

—Oh, it was just stupid stuff, you know. So whenever, like, my
dad or someone called out Brian's name when they were doing the
register at a meeting: 'Brian Mings,' Tom would shout, 'Does he?'
in front of everyone. Soon, all the younger ones were doing it and it
was just annoying, you know? Stuff like that.

—*So there was other stuff?*

—Well … we all knew that Brian liked Anyu. But he was nice
about it, like I said. He wasn't too heavy or stalker-y. He was just like
a little lost puppy sometimes, following her about. But Tom, *god*, he
used to make such a fucking *issue* about it: 'What you doing, Brian?
Why are you sitting there, you've not got a chance!' All that sort of
thing. Just to embarrass him in front of everyone. He just went on
like that all the time, just chipping away

—How did Brian take it?

—He didn't really do *anything*. I sometimes wanted to tell him to stand up for himself or something. But I was just too focussed on what was going on with Tom and Charlie to really notice.

—Do you think Brian hated Tom?

—No, I don't think so. I would have done. If I was Brian, I would have wanted nothing to do with him but, despite all the ribbing, Brian was always trying to impress him – just like he used to do with Charlie.

—That seems odd.

—It was more *sad*. Brian was that desperate for approval, I think he thought, if he could impress Tom, he'd finally be in with Charlie.

There was this one time, when we were away at Scarclaw. We were all smoking in the mineshaft, and Brian just … he just used to say things, *stupid things*, and we always wanted to tell him to shut up, but you didn't, you know, because that was Brian, that was just how he was. Anyway, we're there and he comes out with something like, 'Yeah, I smoke every day. My mum wishes I would stop.' Remember we were about fourteen or fifteen. Anyway, Tom just looks at him and says, 'You're not even inhaling properly.' Brian went all red and we looked – Tom was right, Brian was just taking the smoke in his mouth and puffing it out again. I mean, you just couldn't write this shit.

—Teenage posturing, right?

—Yeah, that's all it was. Just harmless stuff. But Tom couldn't just let it go. So him and Charlie showed Brian how to inhale properly – like right into his lungs – and, *god,* I thought Brian was going to throw up. He was coughing and his eyes were streaming. Tom and Charlie, they were in hysterics, just screaming with laughter. Brian didn't speak for the rest of that day. He just stayed quiet, walked behind us all the way back to the centre.

—To me that sounds like bullying.

—Yeah, looking back on it now, I suppose it…

There was one other time as well. And this was really bad … *Jesus.* It was when we used to have meetings in the church hall. Sometimes we'd get there before the adults and we'd have the place to ourselves. We usually just hung about or smoked cigarettes around the back. Anyway, one of these times, Brian came in with this new coat on – one of those 'bondage' ones with these detachable straps across the back. It was too big for him, but he was trying so hard to be *different* – like Charlie. Tom and Charlie, they were just … they just gave each other this *look*. It was horrible, just sort of mean and clever at the same time … wolf grins…

Brian just sort of stood there. Charlie and Tom go over to him, pretending to admire his coat. Asking him to turn around and all that. Well, Brian thought it was great at first, but then they started unhooking all the straps across the back, and you could see Brian getting all wide-eyed, his face going red. That's when Charlie grabbed him, held him down and they just tied him up with the straps off his coat. Tied him up and pulled his shoes off, chucked them out the window. It was horrible, you could see he was nearly crying. And Charlie and Tom they were just laughing, like it was the funniest thing they'd ever seen.

I waited till Brian had got himself free and had gone outside to try and find his shoes, and I asked Charlie why he'd done it. Said that he was being a dick. But just as he opened his mouth, Tom was like, 'Come on, mate, let's go for a spliff.' And off they went, just like I wasn't even there. It was like it wasn't Charlie anymore.

—*You think that was Tom's influence?*

—Right. It's hard to explain, but it was all about power with Tom. He had this this *way* of, like, getting into your head. He was sort of able to…

—*To exert power?*

—Sort of.

—*To seduce you, almost?*

—Yeah … that's a … that's an appropriate word…

—*Go on…*

—I … Look, I don't know why I'm telling you this. Everyone in the world will know it when it goes out, but … I don't know…

—*Maybe just say it. Let it come. Don't think too much…*

—Oh fuck it. You know what? It feels like getting this stuff out is a good thing; like, finally, I *can*. It's been hanging about inside me for so many years that it just needs … expelling. So, yeah, that winter, that time when it snowed and we went to Scarclaw…

Eva is talking about December 1995, the first time Tom Jeffries visited Scarclaw with the rest of the group.

—At first I was really dreading it, all because Tom and Charlie had been such … such dicks at the meetings in the weeks we were planning that trip.

—*How so?*

—Oh, it was stupid. Like they'd regressed, become twelve again. Kept giggling and whispering and nudging each other.

—*It sounds like they had some secret … something like that?*

—Yeah, well, maybe they did. I don't know. Maybe they had some plan.

—*Did you have any idea what it was? An inkling?*

Eva pauses for an inordinate amount of time. Then she takes a breath as if steeling herself.

—It's weird. It's like I knew *something* was going to happen. I knew it, but I still couldn't *do* anything.

—*What sort of thing do you mean?*

—That's just it, I don't know … but something. It started in the minibus.

—*On the way to Scarclaw?*

—Yeah. My dad used to pick everyone up. And when we picked up Tom, it was like I was ready – to stand up to him this time, to assert myself, I guess; to actually try and stop Tom and Charlie just *going off* without me again.

But when he got in the bus, it was like … well, I actually thought

Charlie had had a word, you know, because Tom was just, nice. He was … he wasn't like Tom!

—*You're shaking your head.*

—Yeah, I know. I just can't believe I was so *stupid*. So *naive*.

—*Go on…*

—So, Tom was talking to me loads – really talking, you know? Like a normal human being. I wish I could have trusted myself back then, because I knew, *I knew* what he was doing. He was just laying groundwork. But I guess, I was only, like, fourteen. How could I really be sure?

—*'Laying groundwork'. That doesn't sound good. It sounds ominous.*

—Yeah, well, as I say, I was young. I wasn't that *experienced* … with boys, I mean.

—*What about the others? Anyu, Brian, Charlie – had they noticed Tom's change in behaviour?*

—All Charlie seemed to care about was getting my dad to put his bloody cassette on the knackered old minibus stereo – that horrible screaming music he loved. Me and Tom, we were right at the back. Anyu and Brian, they were like musical bloody chairs. Brian would go and sit next to Anyu, so Anyu would go and try and sit next to Charlie, round and round, while me and Tom just sat at the back … talking.

—*Can you remember much of the conversation you had?*

— I think I did most of the talking, in fact. Just babbled on. That was probably how he managed it – just let me talk, pretended he was listening. It's funny, because now I sort of see where Brian was coming from.

—*How do you mean?*

—Well, that whole thing about trying to impress Tom – that's how I felt – like I had something to prove to him. How does someone just *have* that? It's so weird.

Anyway, I knew Tom'd brought some weed with him. Him and Charlie, they were smoking a lot of it, and I hadn't really tried it properly – just a couple of drags off a joint – but Tom would have been on about it, how it made you feel, all that. I remember he was showing me these things he and Charlie had been making – 'lungs' he called them. They were the top half of a plastic bottle with a plastic carrier bag taped to them. There was a little metal gauze thing on the spout bit, and you burned the weed in there, then pulled out the bag to suck in the smoke – like an actual lung, you see?

—*And Tom and Charlie, they'd made them specially: for that night at the centre?*

—Yeah, that's right.

—*Can you remember that night?*

—I've spent the rest of my life trying to forget it. So why I'm suddenly telling you about it here, now, is … I dunno … Like I say, it's cathartic or something. Therapeutic.

We all got wasted that first night.

—*On weed? Tom's weed?*

—Yeah … and booze. Me and Anyu, we'd brought booze. Charlie had, too – like, far too much vodka. We stashed it all outside. We had a dorm to ourselves in the centre, us older ones. There was this window – a dead old one; all flaky paint – and it opened onto this sort of old porch thing round the back of the centre. So you could just sort of hop out if you wanted to and you were in the woods. We just hopped out that window and shoved our stash in this huge black rucksack thing that was Brian's. We used to push that rucksack right under the building. You could crawl underneath it. We'd done that the summer before, when we were nailing in insulation. Anyway, we kept our stuff outside and that window closed just in case, like, my dad or Sally or someone came in.

—*Would they have searched you, do you think?*

—Oh yeah, they would have. After it all happened, people thought my dad was just this old hippy who didn't give a shit, but it wasn't like that at all. In fact, I think we were more worried about, like, abusing his trust. Everyone, including me, we had a lot of respect for my dad.

—*And Sally?*

—Her, too. Yeah. We were respectful kids. We would have been mortified if they'd caught us. The booze thing ... they knew what we were doing; they weren't daft. But they were hands-off about it. But my dad, he would have taken us home, all of us, if he'd found out we were smoking weed. He would have lost his biscuits with me – I know that! If anything had happened, he would have taken the rap for it. We all knew that. I guess that was the thing that upset me most – Charlie just didn't seem to give a shit anymore; even about my dad.

—*So I think I know what happened that night ... with you and Tom...*

—Yeah. It was just ... he was so fucking *sneaky* about it. That's what made it so, just, *ugh*. He was even being nice to Brian...

—*Did that raise your suspicions at all?*

—See, in any other context it would have. But not at Rangers, not at Scarclaw. We just weren't those sorts of people. That's how he managed it. The little fucker.

I notice at this point that Eva is not looking at me, she's staring down into her lap. She's clearly embarrassed about what she's about to say. I also wonder if she realises she's contradicted herself: earlier she said she knew that Tom Jeffries was 'laying the groundwork'. My view is that Eva knew all along what was going to happen – right from the bus journey, probably – and a part of her wanted it, a part of herself she'll never admit existed and that she'll always regret. Retrospectively, I sympathise; when you're that age, sometimes you know what you want, but the reality of going through with it feels just too much. But you end up doing it anyway, even though you know it's probably a bad idea. It's like that craze for 'tombstoning' – taking a running jump off a cliff and into the sea in the summer: kids Eva's age just take the plunge.

As we grow up, we get fearful and we don't take as many plunges. Eventually the plunges stop altogether.

—*Go on. Just take your time.*

—So, after tea on that first night, us older ones, we did the washing-up and then went to our dorm; it was right at the far end of the centre, so we didn't disturb the youngsters. I remember all of us just sort of slinking away while my dad and Sally were giving out the hot chocolate to the little ones, and a part of me just wanted to stay, just wanted to sit in the big common room with all the others, in a circle, and have my dad crack his silly jokes and hold a plastic mug full of that lumpy hot chocolate.

But instead we went to the dorm, started drinking. Tom gave me a 'blow-back' off one of those 'lungs' – he took in the smoke and then blew it into my mouth. I was pissed already and, well … I knew what I was doing; it wasn't like I was unconscious or anything. But everything was just so weird, like I wasn't really there. I remember bits and bobs, but it's fuzzy, all just … fuzzy.

—*You don't need to go into detail.*

—No. OK. I don't really remember anyway. But when it was over, he just sort of slunk off. We were on the top bunk. Those bunk beds were made in the seventies or something, and the top ones were sort of like wardrobes on their back – a wardrobe with no doors, just these wooden sides. I remember, while it was happening, I was just sort of *staring* at the sides, reading all the graffiti, just sort of *absent* … like I wasn't there.

When he'd finished, Tom just said he was going for a cigarette and, *poof*, off he went, down the ladder and away.

—*So, it was consensual?*

—Yes … yes it was. What I'd give for it to have not been him, though. Tom fucking Jeffries…

The others were either asleep or outside. I kept hearing them coming in and out of that window, their feet in the snow. I stayed awake for most of the night after that – just lay there … the room just buzzing and pulsing and zooming in and out all around me. I lay there and a part of me just wanted my dad, you know … I just wanted my dad…

Recalling what happened with Tom Jeffries that night is clearly difficult for Eva. The fact that she and Tom slept together back in 1995 did not come out at the inquest. Both Eva and Anyu were asked if they had any romantic connection to Tom and both answered truthfully: no.

Eva, though aware she was taken advantage of, has never wanted justice for what happened that night with Tom. A part of her, she supposes, must have wanted it to happen, otherwise why else would she have done it? It's a tough one. Clearly Tom Jeffries knew what he was doing. We make these mistakes – these poor judgement calls – when we're teenagers. One could argue, it's a part of growing up. Certainly, that's the way Eva sees what happened that first night in December 1995.

I move on to the day afterward – the meeting with Haris Novak.

—It was just awful that day, just *awful*. I felt like shit. I know you don't get hangovers when you're that age, but I think it was like, just a mix of everything and I was so scared as well.

—*Scared? Of Tom?*

—Not *of* him, but scared that he'd tell everyone; scared that everyone knew what had happened and thought I was … I don't know … thought I was *easy*. I remember Brian tried to talk to me a few times when we were walking to Belkeld across the fell. He was gentle, you know, like, asking if I was OK. And I just was, like, 'Yeah, great, why wouldn't I be?' Just being overly chirpy until he gave up.

—*How were things between you and Tom that day?*

—Awkward. He didn't say anything but he kept giving me these *looks* – really sleazy, horrible, sort of winking, sneery looks that I couldn't tell whether they were supposed to be derogatory or seductive or what. It was … *ugh* … I remember really regretting it all then. Really feeling sick whenever I looked at him.

—*You all went to Belkeld.*

—Yeah, we went off over the fell. The younger ones and my dad, they were building an igloo in the snow. My dad, he's like, Mr Practical and was loving it – totally immersed. He was like, 'Yeah, fine. Off you go; be back by five,' sort of thing.

On the way there, Tom and Charlie, they were doing their little 'brothers' thing – giggling and plotting. And I was just so paranoid. Maybe I still had weed in my system, but I was sure they were talking about me, like, *comparing notes*, or something.

—*And Brian and Anyu?*

—Brian was carrying her bag, I think. I think he thought it made him look manly or something, but he just looked ridiculous. He was wearing these boots as well, like, the *exact* same boots as Charlie. I was walking with them but I was quiet. I wasn't really *there*, if you know what I mean?

—*I do. Eva, can you remember the incident with Haris Novak at the churchyard?*

—Oh god, yeah. Tom and Charlie, they wanted to go in the churchyard in Belkeld and smoke a joint, just because they could; because it was such a tiny village and they were arrogant, you know? Plus, there was literally no one about and well … we were fourteen.

—*Did the rest of you smoke with them?*

—I didn't, but Brian did, and Anyu probably. We were all smoking cigarettes, I remember that. We were round the back of the church, sitting on this sort of tomb, this mausoleum thing, and just … hanging about…

—*Is that when Haris Novak came along?*

—Yeah, I think so. I think we were about to leave and he just *appeared*, like he did.

—*This was the first time Tom had ever encountered Haris, wasn't it?*

—Yeah, and he reacted just like you would expect him to – like a total dick; started taking the piss. Charlie was laughing away, so was Brian, but you could tell he didn't really find it funny.

—*What about you and Anyu?*

—Anyu just sort of … She's so quiet, so *removed*, she just sort of ignored them. And I … well … I was so scared of doing anything *against* Tom at that point, I was so scared that he'd say something about me – like I wasn't very good, or my body was horrible, or something, because of how he'd just … left. So I stayed quiet.

It still comes back sometimes, that afternoon – more than what happened with Tom, even. It comes back when I can't sleep and just plays over and over again in my head, like some film.

—*What did happen?*

—Well, we just got ... the boys ... they just got carried away. Tom gives Haris this bit of weed and tells him to eat it. And Brian — bloody Brian — he chooses that exact moment to do the thing that's going to actually impress Tom and Charlie. That bloody moment he has a *good idea*.

—*Really?*

—I say *good*, but it was just awful. He has this fucking bright idea of getting Charlie to tell Haris the Nanna Wrack story. I remember thinking *no, that's the worst fucking idea ever*, but Brian's got this look on his face — this desperate, pleading look — and Tom and Charlie, they do that wolf grin at each other and start laughing.

—*Brian, I'm guessing, is over the moon at that.*

—I know, right? So Charlie, he's really stoned at this point, but I swear to god, in that graveyard, in the shadow of the church with all the snow and the crumbling gravestones, and that quiet in the air, he tells that story like he's never told it before. I swear to god, it freaked *us* out, and we'd heard it, like, a million times before. He starts going into this description of how she shambles along the fell with her hair like seaweed — like bladderwrack, which is where she gets her name from. And her skin is all pale and shrivelled, her teeth all black. He says how she reaches up from her lair in the marsh and grabs you and pulls you in. It was fucking horrible. I could see the weed was starting to hit Haris, and his bottom jaw, it just starts trembling. Tom is snorting away and so is Brian. He keeps looking at Charlie and Tom like they're fucking gods or something. It was just ... *sick*. I wish I didn't have to remember that. But maybe it's my comeuppance — my punishment for letting it happen.

Eva says she will always regret not speaking up, for not doing something about what happened next. Terrified and stoned, Haris Novak runs away from the churchyard in a volley of snowballs, leaving his hat and gloves behind. According to Eva, Brian, Tom and Charlie use them to make an obscene snowman.

Haris' version of this story is different: he goes to look at the bats or to the shop and the snowball fight begins on his return. I think that the reality of what happened that afternoon is lost in a haze of teenage stupidity and narcotic drugs. The important part is that no one made an attempt to stop the terrorising of Haris. That's what will live on here.

Before me, Haris didn't tell the police, or his mother or anyone else, that Charlie told his Nanna Wrack story that day. It makes sense. Like Haris' cousin says, things that traumatise him, he protects himself from. And this idea – that there was some 'creature' on the fell – along with the tenuous legend of the Belkeld Beast kind of fits together. Is it this trauma that provoked in him that false memory of seeing something when he was a boy?

Back to Eva Bickers; we move on to the last part of the interview. The summer of 1996: the trip when Tom Jeffries disappeared.

—It's hard because it feels like I got it all out then. I went through it all, over and over. To the police, my dad, everyone. So now, all these years later, it's like it's hard to recall it. Like it all got used up back then and there's nothing left.

—*Well, let's start like we did before, with the ride to Scarclaw in the minibus.*

—OK. Well, that was just a normal Rangers bus ride: my dad driving, singing that Ilkley Moor song; Charlie badgering him to put his stupid tape on; Brian trying to sit with Anyu. Nothing of note.

—*What about Tom?*

—Like I said, nothing to write home about. He was sat up with Charlie, on about weed most probably.

—*So Tom wasn't putting on the false charm this time?*

—No. Now, of course, I know it's because he'd got what he wanted from me. Anyway, you know the worst thing about that trip – the fucking worst thing about it? It was one of the most *normal* trips we ever had; one of the least memorable … well, up until what happened to Tom, happened.

—*I know you've been through it again and again, what happened that day, the sequence of events, but let's just get a few things clear.*

—OK.

—*There were just the five of you teenagers – you, Charlie, Anyu, Brian and Tom – plus your dad and Sally Mullen?*

—That's right. Everyone else was ill. We nearly didn't go, but … well, all of us, we just loved it there.

—*Now, that first night you were there, what was it like, compared to, say, December the previous year? Within the group, I mean.*

—Not a whole lot different. Charlie and Tom were still close. There were small things, though. Charlie had been getting into more trouble at school; he'd been suspended a few times and he was smoking a *lot* of weed.

—*Were you and Charlie still close?*

—Yes and no, sort of. We were when Tom wasn't around; but when he was, I just didn't want to be around the two of them.

—*Did Tom make any more passes at you, any attempts to err…*

—To get with me again? No … well, he might have done, but I just stayed clear, you know? That wasn't going to happen again. No way.

—*That first night at the centre…*

—That was a bit different from usual, I suppose. It was hot, really hot, that summer, and we just sat around with my dad and Sally rather than going to the dorm and getting wasted. It was nice. Peaceful.

—*So you didn't drink or do drugs that first night?*

—I didn't. Anyu and Brian, neither. In fact, even Brian was being less puppy-like; we were actually having quite a nice chat. I think Charlie and Tom were smoking, though. They went for one of their walks in the wood. Usually Brian would have tagged along, tried to follow them, but I think he'd given up by then.

—*Was Tom still picking on him?*

—No, not really; not anything big that I remember. Brian had a big spot on his chin – it was huge, with a big yellow head – and

I think Tom made a big deal of it, pointing it out so everyone was conscious of it, you know, put Brian in his place. I think Charlie was sick of Brian copying him all the time as well. I think they were just sick of him.

I remember me and Anyu, we went to sleep early. The boys may have stayed up, but it can't have been for long. In fact, all of us were just *tired*.

—*And the next day, you met Haris Novak again, right?*

—Oh god, I was actually really scared. Scared that we'd, like, *damaged* him the last time. I'd totally forgotten until then about Tom giving him the weed and the snowballs and stuff. Me and Anyu, we were ahead of the others – quite a bit ahead. We were cooking dinner that night and wanted to get back. The boys were just messing about – dawdling, smoking, so I don't know what Haris said to them. But it was like he had forgotten, too. We didn't see him for long – just said hello and stuff. He went away again sharpish, though.

—*Did Tom talk to him?*

—I don't know. It's hard to remember. Probably. They had this stupid thing going on with Brian's bag …that massive rucksack. Poor Haris kept carting it back to his house, full of Tom's 'lungs' and stuff. I was always terrified that Haris would tell his mother, and then she'd tell the police and we'd get in trouble. But that never happened.

—*And that night?*

—After dinner we went to the dorm. We had a bit of a drink, a smoke. But there were only five of us, plus the two adults, so it wasn't like we could get wasted or anything. We were pretty paranoid about it, to be fair, so it was all pretty low key.

—*So, you had a drink, a smoke; then what? Did you go to the mine-shaft again?*

—No. That's it. Then we went to bed. And in the morning … well … Tom just wasn't there. He'd gone.

—*And had he said anything about going? Did he seem out of it, not in control?*

—That was the weird thing. Tom was *never* out of control; he was never wasted. He left that to everyone else. Like fucking Charles Manson or some shit. No, Tom was just … Tom; just his usual dickhead self.

—*What do you think happened to Tom, Eva? What's your opinion, your theory?*

—I honestly have no idea.

—*You remember so much about the trip in December, but this night – the night Tom vanished – there just seems … I don't know … nothing. I mean, what did you guys talk about?*

—Just normal, teenage stuff, I imagine.

—*What about Charlie or Anyu – did they do anything out of the ordinary?*

—I don't know.

—*Do you think Brian Mings had anything to do with what happened to Tom?*

—It makes sense, doesn't it? It all points that way: poor, bullied Brian finally gets his revenge on the guy who picked on him. All that rage building up. Yeah, it makes sense. But it's impossible…

—*Really?*

—Yes. The night that Tom disappeared … well … Brian was with me.

Not long after this, Eva says she's had enough. She's been through these final hours over and over, she says; in her head as well as to the police. I understand. What is interesting, though, is, for all Eva has been open and honest with me about what happened at Scarclaw Fell in December, she is elusive and brief about the summer of 1996.

What we do understand, in terms of Eva Bickers, is perhaps the reason why her form teacher at school noticed a change in her after the Christmas holidays back in 1995. That's understandable, too.

So what conclusions, if any, can we draw from this episode?

Clearly, Charlie Armstrong had an effect both on Eva Bickers and, to some extent, on Anyu Kekkonen, whether that effect was his imagination or just his personality. We've also seen another side to Tom Jeffries:

a controlling, manipulative side that definitely did not come out in the press at the time.

There are some things that I still want to know more about, though. One of which is, if something terrible happened to Eva Bickers in the winter of 1995 (her experience in the bunk bed with Tom Jeffries), what explains her elation the previous spring? She's vague about that, too. Despite my prompting, she claims she doesn't remember anything 'significant'. But I'm not so sure.

There's also the question of Brian Mings' bag and the 'deal' with Haris Novak.

I feel that trying to prise any more information out of Eva Bickers is going to be futile and I don't want to end our interview on a bad note, so I agree not to contact her regarding this matter again.

Fair enough.

Next time, on Six Stories, we will find out more about the day that Tom Jeffries disappeared and a very different picture of the group dynamic will emerge from my interview with another member of the Rangers.

This has been Six Stories with me, Scott King.

This has been our third story.

Until next time…

Belkeld
2017

Fixed with cable ties to the old sign that reads 'Welcome to Belkeld' is a smaller sign, which says *'Bloomin' Britain Runner Up 2013'*. The announcement is flanked by two wooden barrels stuffed with drooping pansies, as if to hammer home the point.

I like to think of the *Bloomin' Britain* judges arriving in this tiny place, which isn't near anywhere, petunias tumbling from the hanging baskets on every lamppost, Sweet William standing taut at the roadside behind the trimmed grass; all of those colours screaming, pleading to forget 1996.

To forget Tom Jeffries.

Right now, the hanging baskets look a little half-hearted; the verges at the sides of the roads are untrimmed and dandelions peer out furtively between the swathes of long grass.

Guilt fills me and I pull my bobble hat down, pass the sign like a sinner.

The streets of Belkeld are empty, but I feel the prickle of a hundred thousand glaring eyes from behind net curtains. But they won't recognise me. And, anyway, what if they do? What happened at Scarclaw Fell in 1996 is no more my fault than it is theirs.

Perhaps what I'm worried about is that they'll tell me I should have left it all alone. That I've enabled Scott King and *Six Stories* to bring it all up again. The third episode had record listeners, apparently. There have been new articles in the broadsheets. There's even word King will do interviews. I doubt it.

I feel like I've helped construct a bomb.

A couple of cars pass and I stare at my feet; mud-stained boots, one in front of the other on the pavement. The church, St Sophia's, comes lumbering around the hill, and I can already see the graveyard gate is locked with a blue bike chain.

I can't stop here.

There's going to be a service later on this week, to commemorate what happened here. Belkelders will trim the verges and clean the net curtains; polish the brass horses on their windowsills. Some will share their experiences with the *Guardian* weekend supplement. Some will rue the Rangers, the police and most probably my father through the yell of the tabloids.

St Sophia's has already been tainted by what happened in her quiet graveyard. The benches have been removed and a home-printed sign is gaffa-taped to the gate, asking people to respect the dead.

I pass without another glance and reach the small parade of shops; the war memorial where a stone soldier stands, head bowed, tattered poppies at his feet. This is where I stop and compose myself, keeping my face turned to the plinth, as if reading the names carved long ago.

Haris Novak won't be here for the service; nor will any of those that were directly involved. The papers that painted Novak as a monster will lament the tragedy, still keeping their knives sharp. The people of Belkeld will suffer the flashes of the cameras, the mini media frenzy.

I can't stay here long. Morning has come and there are a few people about now, back and forth up the little parade of shops; cagoules and worn faces. Belkeld still has a proper butcher. I pass the closed Tourist Information Centre, next door to a Pet Supplies store and a key-cutters. I'm baffled how these places prosper.

I read there's been a surge in tourism here since the first couple of episodes of *Six Stories*. Amateur sleuths and bloody ghouls, I imagine. The same kind of weirdos who enquire about renting The Hunting Lodge.

The story of the Beast of Belkeld has been an unwelcome highlight of the series so far. There'll be T-shirts soon, mark my words. The Tourist Information Centre already has a few books in the window; a hastily cobbled together display: *Myths and Legends*, *England's Haunted Castles*, that sort of rot. Scarclaw Fell makes a couple of the covers. A pixellated Google image, or else it's been Photoshopped into the background. I bristle and wonder if they need my permission.

I walk past and keep going. There's only empty countryside in the distance; a bench that sits askew beside the pebbledash wall of the Nepalese takeaway that lies on the very edge of the village. I'll buy a coffee and sit on that bench before I leave. Give something back to a place I have taken from. A place that will never be the same.

I've looked into the story of Anne Hope, the 'witch' who 'cursed' Belkeld, and have only come up against the same dead ends as Scott King. Witches and curses are beyond my understanding of the world, but a line from episode two stayed with me. The 'long, black man' whom this witch coven was supposed to be appeasing. I've woken a few times in the night with the memory of what we saw that night on Scarclaw. Do I believe in the devil? I'm not sure. I certainly don't believe what we saw was the devil – what we pursued through the rain and the mud that night.

We had a crisis meeting.

It took seconds. We shut the dormitory door to muffle the sound of Tomo's lurchers and stood in the short corridor that turned its L-shape to the room further on: the famous dormitory.

'We all saw that, didn't we?' Tomo said. 'Outside?'

He had that little-boy look in his eyes again; round and begging. I didn't want to look at his hands; didn't want to see them shaking. A funny little part of me wanted to say no, wanted to ask him what on earth he was going on about, wanted him to have been the only one who saw that black shape outside. Who saw it stare at us and run.

'What the fuck?' Jus said. He looked furious.

I couldn't say a word, a bubble replaced my tongue. Jus was glaring at us both, but his lower lip was trembling. If he began to cry, I don't know what I would have done.

'If this is a fucking gag, boys…' he said, one fist clenched.

But no one answered. Jus knew himself this was no joke.

If this had happened today, we all would have had our phones out. Help would be on its way.

'Where's the fucking gun, Tomo?' I said, with a mouth that was not my own.

Tomo inclined his head to the door of the dormitory. The lurchers' skittering was subsiding. The shape that had looked in on us had passed. If it had been there at all.

'So you're saying we all saw it, right?' Tomo pleaded. 'Right?'

I couldn't look at him, or at Jus.

'Come on,' ordered Tomo.

I followed him into the dorm, bent-kneed, playing soldiers. My heart was thudding but my head was oddly straight. Adrenaline had long chased away any effects of alcohol. Jus slunk behind us. I didn't want to look at him in case his face betrayed the fear that thrummed through me. We had to keep it together.

The rest of Tomo's lamping gear was in the boot of his Jag, but the shotgun lay sheathed in a waterproof carry-case on the top bunk beside his sleeping bag. He drew it out as one might draw a broadsword.

'Is it loaded?' I asked.

Tomo looked down at the gun, alien in his hands, and nodded, a tiny movement.

It didn't matter. Just the sight of it would scare whatever – whoever – was out there.

'We've got the dogs, too,' Tomo said, as if thinking exactly the same thing. 'No one'll fuck with them.'

The two lurchers were circling around our feet. I saw Tomo flinch when one of their noses brushed his hand.

There was a noise, and we both turned to see Jus crawling onto one of the bottom bunks. He turned his back to us and began to curl into a foetal position. The soles of his feet were wet with spilled booze, twin screams soaking through his socks.

'Justin, for fuck's…' I began, but stopped.

The lurchers had begun growling again. Through the rain came the sound of branches against the walls; damp slaps, as if something moved past.

'What was that, before?' I said, trying to control the tremble in my voice.

'What?' Tomo swung the gun and picked up the dogs' leads. I felt my arsehole clench.

'That rhyme thing you were saying before?'

This suddenly felt like we were part of an elaborate prank. I stared into the corners of the dormitory, looking for cameras. Only spider webs and dust looked back.

'C'mere!' growled Tomo. The dogs were whining now, too excited to stay still. Tomo's hands were shaking.

'Let me.' I bent down, glad to have something to do. The lurchers began sniffing my face; I could smell their meaty breath. I didn't want to look at Tomo holding that gun. I clipped the leads onto the animals' collars and rose.

'It's something my dad told me,' Tomo said, fiddling with the gun. Was he trying to cock it, perhaps? Both dogs were pulling at the lead now. 'Some folk song or other. I don't know.'

'About Scarclaw?'

Tomo shook his head. 'No. At least, I don't think so. He used to say it when I was a kid. Proper shit me up, it did.'

Some other accent was creeping into Tomo's voice. Midlands perhaps?

'Mother, is that father's form at the door?

It's taller and longer than ever before.'

At that, Justin uncoiled from the bottom bunk and got to his feet. The dogs barked as he stamped toward Tomo and met him, chest to chest, eyes wet and face red.

'Just stop it,' Jus said through clenched teeth. His mouth was an inch away from Tomo's nose. 'Just fucking shut up, do you hear me?'

Tomo's hands rose in submission. 'I'm sorry Jus, mate, I...'

'There's nothing out there. No ghosts, no fucking ... whatever, OK?' He turned his fury to me.

I nodded, quick.

Satisfied, Jus continued. 'But this is your land, Harry.' He pointed to the window. 'And some cunt's out there trying to shit us up...' He turned back to me and I could see a new steeliness in his eyes. 'Are you guys going to fucking stand for that?'

Tomo and I looked at each other and shook our heads.

'There's lights in the boot,' Tomo said, nodding toward the window.

'The fuck are we waiting for then?' Jus said.

The dogs, sensing our sudden resolve, began straining at the leads even harder.

'Pass me the fucking whisky,' I said.

'Good lad.' Jus thumped my back and shoved the bottle into my hand.

The liquid was lukewarm and it burned hard. I felt an urge to throw it back up, but I didn't.

This was my fucking land.
'Give it,' Tomo said, and followed my example.

There is evil in the world. There is definitely evil in this world of ours. We carve monuments to our fallen, engrave them with the names of those whose lives were snuffed out when trying to stop evil.

We don't forget.

Episode 4: Nanna Wrack

—It's a dark, freezing night on Scarclaw Fell. The wind wails mournfully through the trees of the old forest and little bundles of sheep huddle together like balls of damp cotton wool. Frost freezes on the edges of the leaves, the trees glisten in the moonlight, and their branches caress the frozen earth like the withered fingers of some long-dead corpse.

The night rides on, endlessly, soundlessly. The last few lights in the village are winking out. But as a cloud passes over the moon ... yes ... there – something is moving.

Breath – little puffs of fog – and the crackle of breaking leaves and twigs. It's a traveller– not a man, not a hiker in boots and pack, but a boy, a little boy, and he's running; every step is agony as the frozen ground bites at his bare feet.

On and on he goes, higher and higher, the darkness surrounding him, spinning his bearings this way and that. Has he been this way before? Yes ... no ... maybe? The trees all look the same – hard and sneering. He stops. Rests. Takes a breath.

All he can hear is his own heartbeat ... shhhhh ... and the wind ... shhhhh ... through the trees...

One ... more ... step...

CRACK!

His foot plunges through thin ice, and he's up to his ankles in freezing water. Oh no, it's the marshlands – the place they told him not to go. The one place they told him that, if he went, he would certainly die.

But the dark, the cold, the panic in his belly, it's too much for him and he stumbles.

CRACK! CRACK!

He's waist deep in it now. It is so cold it chills his very bones and the mud sucks at his toes. He cries out, but only the night hears him.

He's got to get out of here. He's heard the stories about what dwells down here, in the dark place below the earth. The moon appears from behind a cloud, and, in the fleeting light, he sees a rock, an island, sanctuary in the sea of swampy earth.

The boy pushes his legs as hard as he can … forward, onward through this terrible frozen marsh. He's made it … up onto the rock, feet out of that freezing mud.

Thank god … thank god…

He stares around in the silence of the night. All around him is the swampy ground, the trees in the distance. All is quiet … shhhhh … so quiet….

EEEEAAAAGGGHHHHH!!!

There she is! Bursting from beneath the ice not two feet from him, with her hair a wild tangle of seaweed, her skin shrivelled and pale like the belly of a fish, and her eyes like black, whirling madness.

Nanna Wrack – the marsh-hag: she's found him. She's found him and she reaches for him, those terrible fingers with the bent, blackened, broken nails like claws … *snick snick.* And her terrible mouth opens and he can smell foetid death.

EEEAAAAAGHHHHH!!!

And as her clammy hands close around him, as those peg-like teeth tear into his flesh, as those terrible fingers heave him from that rock and pull him, down, down, down into that stagnant water, the last thing he remembers is the warm firelight of home…

Yeah … it went something like that, I think.

Welcome to Six Stories. *I'm Scott King.*

Over six weeks, we are looking back at the Scarclaw Fell tragedy of 1996; seeing the events that unfolded through six pairs of eyes.

In the last few episodes, I've talked to three people who were present at Scarclaw Fell in August 1996, when fifteen-year-old Tom Jeffries went missing and whose corpse was subsequently found a year later in nearby marshland.

I interviewed Derek Bickers, leader of the loose group of teenagers Tom Jeffries was a part of, who went on an excursion to Scarclaw Fell. I've spoken to Harry Saint Clement-Ramsay, the son of the landowner who found Jeffries' body; I've spoken with Haris Novak, a man from the nearby village of Belkeld, who encountered Tom Jeffries and his friends a number of times. And in the last episode, I spoke to Derek Bickers' daughter, Eva, who knew Tom Jeffries intimately.

From these people, I have been able to build up a picture of Tom Jeffries; how he was seen by his peers, and by adults. I've begun piecing together a sense of the dynamic in that group of teenagers. Maybe this will help shed new light on details that were overlooked or deemed irrelevant back then. Maybe not.

—So, yeah, that was the Nanna Wrack story. That's how I used to tell it. *Christ*, I haven't told that story in years. I haven't even really *thought* about it. It's amazing how these things just stay with you, isn't it?

The voice you're hearing is the same voice that told the tale of the boy lost on Scarclaw Fell; the tale of Nanna Wrack, the marsh-hag. This voice belongs to Charlie Armstrong, now thirty-five years old.

Charlie was seen, not only by the other teenagers, but also by the accompanying adults, as the 'alpha' of the group. Perhaps even more than that: he was revered by the others; looked up to and followed.

Charlie meant a lot to those who knew him.

—Oh, I don't know about that. I didn't really notice.
—*They certainly seemed to think very highly of you. You must have been aware of that.*

That's just ... ha! That's so *strange* ... because ... I ... I mean

I was just a mess back then, just a stupid mess. Full of anger and misery and doom. How *strange*. I can't get over that – that they looked up to me. I just can't.

I find Charlie in a big city (he's asked me not to name it). He's the manager of a chain bar – a job that seems totally at odds with what I know about him as a fifteen-year-old. Unlike Eva, he hasn't heard of me or the podcast, but he seems to like the idea of it, which, I guess, is a compliment. We conduct the interviews over the phone, usually late at night, after he's got in from work. A lot of the time he's tired and on more than one occasion he says there are some details that he just can't muster the strength to go back into.

—*From what I've heard about you, Charlie, I would have expected you to be doing something more … creative, perhaps?*

—Ha! Like what?

—*I don't know. A writer?*

—Ha! I haven't written anything since like, GCSE English, mate. But there you go. People change, things change, blah, blah, blah.

—*You've changed since Scarclaw Fell?*

—Since 1996? Of course, mate, yeah; of course I have. Who doesn't? I'm not that angry kid with long hair anymore, am I? That shit's for teenagers, isn't it? All that rebellion stuff – you have to … you have to change or else … well, you're stuck there aren't you; stuck in the past.

—*Have you been in contact with any of the others since?*

—Not at all. I think a few of them added me on Facebook. God, my memory's so *bad*. I think Brian did, Brian Mings. And I nearly sent him a message. You know, 'Alright mate, how's things, what you doing?' – all that shit. But I was just busy and then it became too late. He's not on there anymore I don't think. He seemed to disappear a while back, or he blocked me, I dunno. I wouldn't blame him.

—*What about Eva Bickers or Anyu Kekkonen, have you heard from them?*

—Nah. As I say, mate, I've grown up, moved on. They've probably got kids and stuff now, right?

—*I heard Anyu and her mum went back to Canada, to Labrador.*

—Oh. Right. Maybe they did. That's a shame.

—*What is?*

—I dunno – that they went without saying goodbye.

—*Maybe they moved on, too?*

—Maybe.

—*So, Charlie, I want to go back to 1995.*

—Aw, Jesus mate, I don't even know what fuckin' year it is now. *1995*, that's…

—*The year before what happened with Tom…*

—Yeah, OK. Look, mate, my memory's fucked. I'm so bad at remembering stuff. Honestly, it's like someone just came in and stole my memories, or, like, jumbled them around or something. I'll do my best for you, though.

—*That's cool.*

—Hey … err …mate … I know this sounds weird, right, but have we … have we met before?

—*What makes you think that?*

— I dunno. Something … something in your voice just then. Ha! See what I mean? We probably have met; we probably met the other day and I can't remember! See what I mean? Jesus Christ.

Charlie's charisma is immediate. He has something about him – an attractiveness that somehow makes you want to please him. I don't think it's engineered; it seems natural.

Charlie often describes himself back then and now as a 'mess'. He has huge problems remembering swathes of detail. He'll remember the brand of a stereo, but not the name of his favourite album; he'll recall the taste of a certain make of sweet, but where he went to primary school is fuzzy. He blames a lot of his memory problems on the amount of weed he used to smoke when he was growing up. He says it wasn't just because of Tom; school had its part to play as well.

—I fucking *hated* school, mate, fucking *despised* it. The Head, we used to call him fucking Mumm-Ra – the ever living. He was always on your case, the wrinkly old fuckbag – well, *my* case. Cos of my hair, my boots, my uniform, earring, nag, nag, nag. He didn't like the fact that I just fucking *wouldn't* tow the line.

I actually quite liked school – well some of it, like, English and stuff. But the Bitch-a-Tron just fucking *ruined* it for me. I can't even remember what she was actually called! Probably why I work for [name removed] now, eh? Ha!

Talking to Charlie is a very different experience from talking to the others. The way he talks is either tiredness or, as I begin to suspect as our interviews go by, the effects of alcohol. Charlie manages a bar and he's home late, so you can't really blame him. He jumps around a lot as well – from subject to subject, leaving a memory dead in the water just as he seems to be recalling it. There are some things he just seems to give a cursory nod; others he will really go to town on. The events at Scarclaw in 1996, he seems resigned about, as if they've simply been resolved and are therefore not really worth thinking about.

This makes many of our interviews difficult, as we have to wind around many paths before we find the right one.

—They used to think I had ADD – or, what's it called now: ADHD? – at school and stuff, cos I just couldn't concentrate. But my memory's like a sort of time-lapse coral reef; things just kind of blossom up out of nowhere, then fade away again.

—*We were talking about school. Back in '95, you would have been what, year nine, ten?*

—Something like that, yeah. I was smart; I wasn't thick. I was good at subjects, but I had all this energy, this *rage* inside me. I used to get into fights and stuff, with the … we used to call them 'charvers' back then. They call them *chav*s now don't they? You know the ones I mean though, don't you? Big lads who would call you 'hippy' and rob your dinner money off you.

I used to kick off, just go for them; and pretty soon they stopped. In fact, weirdly, we kind of found this sort of mutual respect for each other, and I used to smoke weed with them quite a lot; do buckets round the back of the art room at lunch times, that sort of thing.

—*Oh wow. So you weren't ever scared of them or anything?*

—Nah, no way. They were just kids. You see, back then, I used to knock about with much older lads, like, *outside* school. The olders, they were into their drugs, their music and all that sort of stuff. I wasn't scared of them, so I wasn't going to be scared of a couple of charvers from my year was I?

This is interesting. Neither Derek nor Eva Bickers have said anything about Charlie's 'older' friends, the ones outside school. Trying to track any of them down is like hitting a brick wall. Charlie seems reluctant to help me identify them. He tells me it 'doesn't matter' who they were. It may be, as I suspect as our interview progresses, that he either doesn't remember them, or some falling out or similar incident may have driven them apart.

—*So how did you start hanging about with these 'olders'?*

—It was weird; I just sort of met them down the park. They were up on the climbing frame, smoking and listening to music, and I would … I would just say to my mum and dad that I was going to play football or something, and I just started, like, knocking about with them…

—*Did the others in Rangers know about them?*

—I dunno. I doubt it. I might have said something … maybe. But, it's just, like, they weren't a big deal. They were just some lads who knocked about down the park and I was just this … this sort of little follower. Ha! They taught me how to smoke and everything. It was good, because when I was at school, all the fucking charvers who used to pick on me, they thought I was hard because I could smoke … and I could handle my weed.

—*You would have been, what, fourteen, fifteen at the time?*

—Yeah. But I started smoking in the park when I was about twelve. It's funny, cos, when I got chatting to a lot of the charvers at school, it was like, I could relate to them more than I could the kids in Rangers. The Rangers kids – don't get me wrong, they were my best mates – but I always felt like a bit of a mess next to them.

—*But you didn't fit in at school with the … the charvers either?*

—Nah, not properly. I felt more like *myself* at Rangers, but I never fitted in there completely. I always had something to prove. I was this long-haired fucking, like, *death metal* kid who hung about with the charvers at school, but then hung out with these, like, totally different kids outside school. And I fitted in with neither. It was such a mess.

—*It surprises me that you say you didn't fit in with the other Rangers.*

—I dunno. Fitting in's not the right word. It was, like, they all had nice lives and everything, and I didn't so I felt, like, the odd one out.

—*'Nice lives' – are we talking class here?*

—No. Yeah. Sort of. They were nice people. They were properly nice people. I mean Eva Bickers, she was just … she was my best friend. Without Eva, I would have … I don't know … probably just done something stupid. Anyu Kekkonen as well – *man,* she was just … Hey, did you say you knew where she was now?

—*I was hoping you might be able to tell me.*

—Nah. I wish I could, but I just … I just got away as quickly as possible from them after what happened to Tom, just because I knew they would probably think it was me who did it. And I just didn't want that … for *them.*

This is interesting. Charlie talks about the other teenagers in Rangers having 'nice lives'; in a way that seems to imply he didn't. As far as I'm aware, Charlie Armstrong's home life was no different from the others'. The Bickers and the Armstrongs holidayed together often, and it would have been nigh-on impossible for the Bickers not to notice any deep-seated problem with their close friends, right?

It makes Charlie choosing to hang out with these elusive 'olders' at the park in his spare time even more interesting.

—*Can we just go back to when you said the others had 'nice lives'? What do you mean?*

—Well it's just that they were all really *adjusted* and I just wasn't…

—*Why do you think that was?*

—It's like … we'd go on holiday – me and Eva and her mum and dad and my mum – and I'd sometimes look at them and just get this rage, this fury, this jealousy, at how *happy* they all were.

—*And you weren't?*

—Never. *Never.* All my life, I felt I was sort of *searching* for something, like *waiting* for something … it's hard to explain. And when this … when what happened to Tom up at Scarclaw happened, for a while, I thought that was it. I thought that was what I had been waiting for…

—*For someone to die?*

—No. Yeah … sort of … I dunno. It's hard to explain.

Charlie and I finish our first interview here. He's tired, drunk and gets increasingly incoherent, flitting between subjects. There's little to no point playing much more of it. What I can glean though is that, back then, Charlie was full of confusion and angst, a not uncommon trait for a fifteen-year-old boy.

Maybe there was nothing behind it; maybe Charlie was just a teenager. His family have not responded to any of my requests to speak to them – read into that what you like. Not everyone wants old graves raked over; and it's also possible that they just want to be left alone.

I listen back to my conversation with Derek Bickers for something, anything, to do with Charlie that may give me some more insight into him. The only other thing I can find is an anecdote that I edited out of episode one.

—It was one of those odd times when the older lot hadn't showed up at a Rangers meeting in the church hall – only Charlie.

—*Why hadn't the rest of them come?*

—I don't know: homework, can't-be-arsed, other things to do.

Anyhow, Charlie seemed pretty fed up because it was just him and a load of the little ones and us adults. I said to him he could go home if he wanted, that it was OK; but he stayed. He stayed for the whole thing, and you know what? He was just … he was *amazing* with those kids. By the end, he had them climbing all over his back, hanging off him. They were delighted and us … all us grown-ups, we were watching this sort of surly, long-haired lad, wearing a T-shirt with *Cannibal Corpse* written on it, just … it was like he was being a kid again himself.

—*Was that out of character for Charlie?*

—I don't want to say yes, because that makes him sound … you know … but certainly, if any of the others had been there, he wouldn't have done anything of the sort.

Just before the meeting was over and we were packing up; he slipped out for a cigarette and I went to speak to him to say thanks, to just tell him how great we thought he was and all that.

I went out the side door and saw him; he was just sat on the edge of a dustbin, headphones in, just staring out into the night, and … I don't know if he was crying or something, I can't remember for sure, but a part of me just wanted to give him a massive hug, just hold him. He looked just so *sad* … so … *lost*. I didn't, though. I wish I had.

So what can we make of that? The thought that comes to my mind is that Charlie was aching for a lost childhood – a playful innocence that perhaps he never had. But that idea seems contrary to everything we know about Charlie's home life.

The next time Charlie and I talk, I want to mention this incident, but feel like I can't, as if it would be somehow intrusive to do so. If he can't remember it, that's not fair either. Instead, I ask him about what home was like back in the nineties.

—Just normal mate; just normal. I don't know what you want. Like, you want me to say that my mum and dad beat me, or abused me or something, and that's why I killed Tom? Yeah? Something like that?

—*Whoa, hang fire. I haven't blamed you for what happened.*

—I know, I know. Look, it's just … I was just *waiting* to be blamed back then; that's what I remember. I was just waiting for someone to say, 'Oh, it was probably Charlie, all the evidence points to it.'

—*Why do you think they would have blamed you? Weren't you and Tom friends?*

—I don't know. Sort of, I suppose. I mean, I know he was a bell-end; I thought so then as well. We just smoked weed and stuff together is all. I smoked weed with a lot of people.

Sorry mate, you were saying something about…

—*I was just wondering why you thought they would have blamed you for what happened to Tom, that's all.*

—Cos I was the typical rebellious teen maybe? Like, I was the fucked-up one who did drugs, had long hair, listened to metal – all the death and black stuff. So I was just waiting for them to pin it all on me!

—*And did they?*

—It's hard to remember; that night was all a blur. I remember the police talking to me about it. I remember they had my tapes – Morbid Angel, Darkthrone – they were looking at them like they were a fucking contract addressed directly to Satan and written in my own blood. I remember one of them trying to be funny, trying to wind me up: 'You look like you belong in a fucking graveyard, you, lad.' Trying to get me to bite.

And they started asking me about some sort of animal sacrifice, or bollocks like that. Did I attack sheep or whatever? It was pathetic really.

I want to pause here for a moment. In last week's episode, Haris Novak said something about the Beast of Belkeld 'eating the sheep'. It is only by chance that I remember this passage. During the editing, I had to replay it to clear up a burst of background noise – that's why it sticks in my mind. However, on impulse, after Charlie mentioned animal sacrifice, I delved back into some police reports from the area and found that a group of rock climbers had found a dead sheep on Scarclaw Fell in February of 1996 and had reported it to the Belkeld police. The report itself states that the animal had been 'mutilated', yet I can't find anything more about it. If it was a natural occurrence, though, why did the police ask Charlie Armstrong about it – about something that had happened earlier in the year when he was nowhere near Scarclaw? I ask Charlie.

—Christ only knows. Loads of people thought I was into Satan because of the music I listened to – pathetic really, isn't it? Does anyone assume that all fans of country music are potentially suicidal? Course not. I thought they were trying to wind me up, to make me angry so they had a suspect. I *was* defensive, but I was more worried to be honest, I was worried about what had happened to Tom, and I had this horrible *heavy* feeling, like guilt; as if I *had* done something, as if it *was* my fault in some way that I didn't know about!

Anyway, they pinned all that sheep stuff on Haris in the end, didn't they?

—*Really? I've not heard that.*

—Oh. Maybe not, then. Maybe they didn't even know about it.

—*Know about what?*

—Oh, it was something Haris told us – when we met him that first time. He said he used to drag all the dead animals off the fell and bury them in his garden or something.

According to Charlie, Haris Novak would regularly find dead animals on Scarclaw Fell: sheep that had broken their legs; rabbits; birds. He would apparently take the corpses back to his mother's cottage and bury them. Whilst this feels potentially significant, what exactly does it prove? That Haris was a little strange? It's odd to me that this detail was never picked up on. Surely the farmers would have noticed their flock vanishing? And I imagine the tabloid press would have had a field day. I am frustrated that I didn't know this before I talked to Haris himself. But, again, I must question what part, if any, this detail had in the case of Tom Jeffries. Let's suppose that Haris Novak found Tom Jeffries' body. Haris isn't stupid – he would have reported such a thing. But let's just say he didn't, and he took the corpse back to his mother's cottage – why then did he replace it in the marsh a year later? It seems altogether rather far-fetched.

I want to concentrate on the night that Tom Jeffries vanished. According to Charlie, that night in 1996, they had all been drinking and smoking weed – Tom, Charlie, Eva, Anyu and Brian. Charlie says that he doesn't remember a lot about it, that it's blurry. He remembers being angry at one point and storming off. It was a warm, summer night, but the teenagers had spent the majority of their time in the centre, in their dormitory, using the window to get in and out. They were messing about in the woodland close by, smoking. Indeed, this was confirmed by investigators: footprints and cigarette ends showed that none of them strayed far from the place … except for Tom.

Interestingly, however, forensics were unable to confirm with total certainty that this was indeed the case. It was possible, they said, that someone else could have walked off onto the fell with Tom, if they were careful. The woods are thick and tracking Tom's route to the place where his body was found was impossible a year later. All the forensics confirm is that all the teenagers' tracks were found around the centre.

—*So you stormed off?*
—Yeah … probably…
—*Why?*
—Oh, just some teenage shit. Some fucking stupid thing, I don't know. A girl or something.

Charlie becomes infuriatingly elusive about this particular aspect of

*that night. He claims he has no recollection of why he stormed off, where,
and for how long. Eva Bickers did not mention it, either, claiming that
she went to bed early.*

*'Teenage shit' over 'a girl or something' usually means one of two
things: that a girl you wanted to get with didn't get with you, or else said
girl got with someone else. Eva and Charlie seemed to have a lot going on
between them. And, remember, Eva said she was 'with' Brian Mings the
night Tom disappeared. Maybe it was this that angered Charlie. Again,
that part of me that sees Charlie how the others see him doesn't want to
ask. What am I afraid of?*

*I can tell Charlie is getting frustrated with my questions. He keeps
asking me 'what the point' of all this is and repeating that he thinks he
knows me from somewhere.*

*I give him a break, and when we reconvene he seems considerably
calmer. I am more tentative this time and ask him about the trips to
Scarclaw leading up to summer 1996.*

—Help me out here…

—*OK, so the time you went to Scarclaw with Rangers; spring…*

—We went to Scarclaw a lot. I'm really sorry, mate, they all kind
of blend into one.

—*The first time you encountered Haris Novak.*

—OK, yeah, I'll try.

—*Haris tried to give you some money.*

—Oh yeah, *yeah!* I remember that … we were just … we didn't
know what the hell he was on about. Some mental problem. Sorry I
don't know the word…

—*He's got some complex problems, has Haris. But let's stay with that
time, just so you can remember. Haris showed you all a place.*

—Yeah! It was one of the entrances to the old mineshafts, like sort
of *under* the hill. God … yeah, I remember that place…

—*You sound almost wistful, Charlie.*

—Yeah, well, man, that was the place that me and Eva, we …
you know?

—*Did you?*

—Yeah, that first time, it was there, like, in the middle of the afternoon. We just went off for a wander and we had a smoke and … Wow, yeah, I'll never forget that … had I forgotten that?

OK, so now we know why Eva Bickers came into school so elated after that particular holiday. It makes sense. From my interview with Eva, it seems she really had a thing for Charlie, maybe she always had. I ask Charlie about how he felt about her.

—Ah, *maaaan.* Look, I don't really know. I was just a fucked-up person back then. I just … I thought, why would she want to be with me? Why? This angry kid.

—*Did it ever happen again?*

—No … no. But it was just so awkward. You know what it's like when you're that age? It was just, like, I didn't know what she wanted me to say – she probably wanted me to say something – and it just … it just got all fucked up.

—*That must have been hard to have to deal with, along with every-thing else.*

—Yeah. Maybe. The thing with Eva, it was, like, she was my *friend* … almost like a sister, sort of thing. I just didn't have that … that *attraction* with her. Not like I did with other girls.

—*You all went back to Scarclaw the following summer. To insulate the centre.*

—Yeah. I have a vague sort of memory of that. I remember wearing that stupid white-paper suit thing and crawling under that building. There were all these fucked-up spiders – massive ones – and everyone was freaking out.

—*Was there that awkwardness with Eva, still?*

—Not that I remember; I don't think so anyway. I think we sort of, you know, got over ourselves a bit, just never talked about it and just *got on.* When you're young, you just do that, you know?

—*Would you have been upset if Eva had … got with someone else, like if she'd kissed one of the others? Was that, perhaps, what made you angry, caused you to storm off?*

—Eva was my mate, a good mate. Like I said before, she was like a sort of sister to me. I looked out for her. But we just … I mean I wasn't focussed on that sort of thing back then. I was more interested in getting stoned. How sad is that?

—*Let's refocus here. I'm getting a bit lost. Let's go back to spring 1995, the first time you all encountered Haris Novak and he showed you the mineshaft.*

—Yeah.

—*That became a bit of a hang-out place – a 'den' for want of a better word.*

—A den is a good term for it – we were still just little kids at heart. We used to steal the emergency candles from the centre and burn the ends, melt them into the walls and just hang there. It can't have been for long because the leaders would have kicked off if they couldn't find us. So I reckon we just smoked a bit in there, drank and stuff. It was just something to do.

—*Haris found your paraphernalia, didn't he?*

—Oh god, yeah, *yeah!* But that was later, much later. I remember, cos we were going to give him this black bag of Brian's with all the stuff in. But I don't think we did. We weren't *that* stupid. It was just a dumb idea … probably Tom's!

—*Haris told me he kept things for you.*

—What, really? Wow … I always just thought that was, like I say, a stupid idea.

—*Haris also told me about the time you told a story. A story about a witch…*

—The marsh-hag. Nanna Wrack. Now that I do remember. How could I forget it? Wow … Christ. I haven't thought of that in ages.

—*Maybe you could tell it to me?*

Charlie tells me the story of Nanna Wrack. It's the passage you heard at the start of this episode; a sort of folk tale. He says he's not sure where he heard it first. As with most things, his memory is blurry. Charlie does acknowledge, though, that it holds extra weight when you think about what happened to Tom Jeffries and where he was found.

—Cos, like, everyone there knew it. All the little kids at Rangers, the leaders, the older ones – we all knew about this story. But ... I don't know ... it's just a story, that's all.

We are both quiet for a while, neither of us wanting to prod at the fact that Tom Jeffries' body was found face down in the marshland that Nanna Wrack is supposed to haunt.
Life imitating art.
Charlie is first to speak.

—We thought we saw her once, you know.
—*Go on.*
—Well that mineshaft thing, that place, after Tom joined Rangers, me and him, we used to go there quite a bit, just us together, without the others.
—*Why was that?*
—Just sometimes the others did my head in. Tom was like ... well, he was like the charvers at school. He had a darkness to him. He was his own person as well.
—*I don't follow.*
—Well, it's, like, the girls were girls. And Brian, he was just ... all he wanted to do was be like me; his clothes, his hair. He even started drinking those cans of, what did you call it, Tab Clear? ... He used to drink that all the time, just because I did. I used to hear him sometimes, telling the younger ones things that *I'd* said; things that had happened to *me*. He fucking did my head in. I could have said I liked to bum dead bodies and he would have fucking agreed with me! Sometimes I just wanted away with all that you know? I just couldn't deal with it.
—*The girls, too?*

—Well … ahh, that's a funny one. Sometimes I just wanted to talk to Anyu. But Eva was always *there*, going on and on and never letting anyone *speak*. I guess Tom … I dunno … I guess there just wasn't any of that *bullshit* with him. All he wanted to do was smoke weed and talk.

Sorry, what was I saying? Oh yeah, *yeah!* So me and Tom, we were at that place, it must have been that winter because it was really snowy. We were just chilling, having a smoke, and we were looking over the fell and … *man*, it gives me fucking *chills* just thinking about it … but we saw it … this *thing*. We … *man,* at the time we said we saw *her*.

—*Who?*

—Nanna Wrack. We saw Nanna Wrack – this fucking horrible *thing*. This figure, all bent and hunched, just scrambling over the fell in the distance.

—*Really? What made you think it was Nanna Wrack? Why not just a hiker, a walker, or Haris?*

—Maybe we were wasted or something, but it wasn't like it was human, just … *ugh* … just the way it moved – you know like when a spider scuttles along the floor and it gives you this fucking cold-blooded feeling? It was like that. Like all its limbs were too long for it. And it had this fucking … *Christ* … it had this fucking *hair*, like, I dunno, like a … like, I don't know what it was…

—*But Nanna Wrack is a story; a story you made up.*

—Yeah … I dunno…

—*I don't follow.*

—I just … I don't know if I made it up.

—*So what are you saying?*

—Just that, like, I was telling a story that was … that was already *there*, that was already in existence or something, like it was already … *there*…

—*The Beast of Belkeld perhaps?*

—Ha! That's a good name for it mate; it's got a ring to it.

—*No, I mean, had you ever heard of it … back then?*

—Is it a thing? Jesus Christ, are you serious? The Beast of Belkeld? That's just ... that's just *fucked up*.

—*That's why I wonder if you'd heard something before.*

—NO, no, not at all. Not that I can ... *Man*, maybe I had. Maybe it was a subconscious thing. But I just ... I don't remember ... *damn!*

It's frustrating. Charlie is frustrating. But I can't make him recall things and I'm no hypnotist. The story of Nanna Wrack does not sound original; it smacks of some folkloric tale. But even after a week or so, during our final interview, Charlie cannot or will not remember where he got the story from. 'Maybe I just made it up,' he says again and again. Maybe he did, but I think that's unlikely.

I have found talking to Charlie Armstrong to be the most exasperating story so far. It's a little like he is editing himself, only allowing me in to a point. Maybe that's a defence mechanism. But there is so much I need to know from him, and there are so many more questions my interviews with him raise.

Charlie's home life is particularly interesting. Teenagers rebel, there's no doubt about that, but with Charlie it seems much more than that: the boys in the park; the constant exclusions from school; hanging about with the 'charvers', never fitting in. He's certainly a complex character, and even after all this time, despite his allusions to just being an honest working Joe, I still feel that there's something he's holding back. It would be great to sit with Charlie and pick apart what is clearly a complex story, but we have limited time, so in our last meeting, I try and cover some of the key events from 1996.

Charlie seems calmer this time, but resigned. Work and these memories are catching up with him, and when I tell him this is probably the last time we'll talk, he seems glad.

—*So, I know it's hard, but I want to go over a few key events. Just tell me anything you can remember, is that OK?*

—Yeah. Honestly mate, I'll do my best for you. I've got nothing to hide. I just ... it's hard.

—*So, back in December '95, you and Tom saw Nanna Wrack.*

—Yeah, you know, I've been thinking about that, and I'm not sure…

—*About what?*

—That we saw her … that we saw it. I mean, me and Tom, we were just bollocksed – stoned off our heads – and maybe it was, like, a collective hallucination, because I'd told that story so much, you know, down in that cave thing.

— *What else do you remember from that weekend – the one with the snow?*

—I remember Derek and the young ones, they built this fucking *igloo* with the snow. It must have been fucking *deep* to be able to do that; I have no idea how they managed it.

—*But you and the others, you were elsewhere?*

—Yeah, mate. We were fifteen. We just wanted to go off on our own and stuff. We thought we were more or less adults.

—*I'm interested in the* dynamic *between the five of you – it was something that didn't really get spoken about at the inquest.*

—No, that's right. The police didn't really ask us anything about that, either. They were just all, 'Did any of you want to kill him? Did you know anyone who'd want to kill Tom?' That sort of thing. He had a bit of a past; he was a bit of a troublemaker, but that was all. There wasn't really anything else.

—*So none of you hated him?*

—Not as far as I know. Tom Jeffries was an acquired taste; he was a bit of a dickhead, we all knew that.

—*Yet you accepted him.*

—Yeah. Yeah, we did. We were nice kids. We weren't fucking knobs; we would have been nice to anyone.

—*What was Tom* like *during that winter trip to Scarclaw? I know there was an incident with Haris Novak.*

—Yeah. Yeah there was.

—*Do you want to…?*

—It wasn't anything really – just kids mucking about.

—*He was vulnerable. A vulnerable man.*

—I fucking *know* that now. It's not as if we *abused* him or shit. It was just a few snowballs. We were *kids*, for fuck's sake.

—*I'm not accusing you, Charlie; I'm just stating facts.*

—Sorry, yeah, I know.

—*It sounds to me like you regret what happened, like you're angry at yourself.*

—Yeah … actually that's a good way of putting it, mate. I am angry that we did that … that no one *stopped* us; no one said anything.

—*Do you think someone would have, say, if Tom hadn't been there?*

—I don't think it would have gone that far if Tom hadn't been there, if I'm honest. Tom and me, we just sort of wound each other up, you know; like the naughty boys who sit at the back of the class at school?

—*Who would have stopped you? Eva, Anyu, Brian?*

—Eva most probably.

—*And she didn't.*

—No, she didn't.

—*Why do you think that was?*

—Like I say, we all thought Tom was a dickhead. But he could get us weed – that was why we let him stick around, I suppose. And Eva she … she just … it went too far…

—*Eva slept with Tom on that trip.*

—Yeah and it was … I was just … so *pissed off* about it because … it wasn't like I *liked* Eva in that way. But it was like … I dunno … like she'd *betrayed* me or some shit. It just pissed me off.

I think, in some ways I understand. Before Tom Jeffries arrived, Charlie was the alpha male of the group – the undisputed pack leader. In nature, the alpha males have exclusive rights to the females in a pack and will destroy any young that is not their genetic material. The fact that Eva had slept with Charlie, despite his claim that he didn't like her 'in that way', and that he was then annoyed with her for sleeping with

Tom makes sense. In a sort of feral way. However, does this have any-thing to do with Tom's death? For me it's not enough.

Charlie tells me about how his alpha status was threatened even more by how the others reacted to Tom.

—Brian, he just, like, took *anything* from Tom. Tom could have called him worse than shit and Brian would have still tried to impress him.

—*Like he did with you?*

—Yeah. I suppose.

—*From what I understand, you preferred to spend time with Tom than Brian, even though you didn't particularly like Tom.*

—I guess I did. But it was because … well, he just had this sort of *way* about him, like you didn't like him but you sort of did, you know? Brian was just … annoying.

—*Brian and Tom went to the same school, right?*

—Yeah, but they were at polar opposites in the hierarchy. I don't think they even spoke to each other. Not even when they were both in Rangers.

—*Did Tom mention Brian much?*

—Not really; he just thought he was a joke, an idiot, like an annoying little insect.

—*Did Tom pick on him at Rangers?*

—Not really. Just sort of mucking about like the rest of us did; just daftness.

—*Like when you tied him up in his coat and threw his shoes out of the window?*

There is a profound silence. I hear Charlie breathing.

—Oh … yeah, wow. I'd forgotten about that. Yeah, that probably wasn't very nice.

—*Was there anything else?*

—Nothing *big*, just, like, Tom used to rip him off; sell him tiny crumbs of weed for a fiver, a tenner. But Brian, man, he was such a fucking *victim*.

—*And that annoyed you?*

—Yeah, because … because it so could have been me! Brian was really into Anyu and he was just so *shit* about it … like, he had no idea what he was doing, he just followed her about like a little lost puppy. You could never have a proper chat with her cos he'd just sort of *turn up* and butt in, or just fucking sit there *nodding* like he agreed with you. It so *annoying*.

—*But none of you said anything.*

—Well, *we* didn't. But Tom, he didn't give a shit – he would always say stuff. I remember once, at Scarclaw, we were drinking, and … well, I don't know how true this is, because I didn't see it, but Tom reckoned he saw Brian sort of 'topping up' Anyu's bottle. Like, he was pouring *more* vodka into it when she wasn't looking.

—*Really?*

—That's what Tom said, and he said it out loud, in front of everyone. Brian, he went *bright red* and started denying it. It was so awkward, it was horrible.

—*What did Anyu think?*

—Ha! She could have drank any of us under the table – maybe it was something to do with her heritage or something, I don't know … is that racist? I don't mean to be. It's just, like, she picked up her bottle and drank, as if nothing had happened. Like she didn't care.

—*What do you think? Did Brian do it?*

—I don't know. Maybe. He did like her.

—*When was this – that December trip?*

—No, it can't have been, cos I remember we were all stood outside, just a few feet from the dorm window, under the trees. There was no snow and it was warm, so it must have been the night … yeah … it must have been *that* night.

—*The night Tom disappeared.*

—Right.

—*What can you remember of that night?*

—Oh … that's tough. I've sort of erased it from my mind after all the … all the stuff with the inquest, so…

Just before we hear Charlie's account I want to draw your attention to something: Brian 'topping up' Anyu's drink and Tom pointing it out. This small event, if it indeed happened, shows a different side to Brian Mings – a craftier, sneakier side than we know about. It also shows a slightly different side to Tom – was he protecting Anyu? However, if this story is not true, the roles are reversed; putting Tom Jeffries in an even worse light.

—That day we all went to Belkeld, the five of us, to get some bits and bobs. We saw Haris Novak on the way back, but he didn't stop. Man, I spent most of that weekend just out of my tree, so my memories, they'll probably be a bit shit.

—*That night, though? When Tom disappeared.*

—Like I told the police, his family, everyone – it was just a sort of blur…

—*Just do what you can.*

—The thing was it was just, sort of, a nothingy night. None of us were more or less wasted than usual. I remember being tired, though, really tired, and looking at the clock and seeing that it was only early. Maybe we just did too much too quick, you know?

—*But there was the thing with Brian and Anyu's drink.*

—The more I think about it, it was probably just Tom being a prick, trying to embarrass Brian. Anyu didn't seem more wasted than us lot. Anyway, if I remember right, we didn't actually stay up that late. And then, in the morning, we woke up and Tom was … he was just gone…

—*Can you remember who noticed first?*

—I dunno. We were all awake, a bit bleary, and it was like a collective thing. Someone just noticed his bed was empty. And it was weird, cos it was really early, like sixish. Then we got the police and stuff, and the rest is … well, I'm guessing you know the rest.

One thing stands out here – to me anyway. These were five fifteen-year-olds who'd been drinking and smoking weed. Teenagers sleep like the dead, excuse the pun, and tend to lie in. Why were all the teenagers awake at six a.m.? I put this to Charlie.

—That's actually a really good question. You know, I don't know. Maybe because we all went to bed early the previous night? But if that was the case, then how did Tom, just, disappear like that, under our noses? Man, unless we just sort of *passed out* and woke up again. I wish I could *remember*.

Charlie's right: this is a sticking point. It could never be established by forensics, conclusively at least, whether Tom Jeffries left the centre alone or accompanied by someone else; there had been too much mud and rain. And, unfortunately, it's not like on TV: forensics cannot say what time he died.

I have a few more questions for Charlie.

—*Did anyone 'get with' each other that night – the night Tom vanished?*
—Not as far as I know. I didn't, anyway.

This is another interesting anomaly between the stories. When I spoke to Eva Bickers, she said she had been 'with' Brian Mings that night. She did not elaborate any further, but something tells me I shouldn't mention this to Charlie. I tread carefully.

—*Could something have happened that night?*
—You mean with me?
—*With anyone?*
—I dunno. It could have, it's hard to remember…
—*Could something have happened that made you storm off? Something with a girl?*
—Sometimes it drives me fucking mad, mate, you know? When

I can't remember stuff. I remember being mad – that fucking tight feeling at the back of my neck. I remember the darkness and the trees … I think I might have even climbed up one, just sat there, stuck my headphones in, had a smoke until I calmed down, I dunno. Maybe I wasn't even angry. Maybe I was hoping someone would wander out and find me there.

—*Someone like who?*

—Dunno mate. Just … someone…

—*I have to ask this, as I'm asking everyone else who was there: What do you think happened to Tom?*

—Wow … I mean … it's really hard, this. It's hard to speculate, because I just don't know; there's just no way I can say.

—*How about an educated guess … or a theory.*

—I just have no idea. I mean, it was just so *weird*. We all woke up and he was just *gone*. Maybe there was something, some noise that woke us; or some collective … I don't know … *knowledge* that he just wasn't there anymore.

A theory's really hard. I've gone through it so many times in my head, over and over – even now, even before I talked to you. It still sometimes come back, like a fucking recurring dream. Maybe it's just simple; maybe that's what's just so fucked-up about it: maybe he was just off his head, pissed and stoned, and he just *wandered off* … got lost, got disoriented and passed out or something…

—*You don't sound terribly convinced.*

—I'm not, I'm really not. But what else is there? What else could it have been? Nanna Wrack? Some mystery serial killer? I know it wasn't any of us; it just *couldn't* have been. Unless one of them – one of us – is hiding something.

—*I've still got two more people to talk to. But it's going to be tough – maybe impossible.*

—Yeah. Yeah, I guess so. Look, if you *do* happen to get in touch with Anyu, tell her … just tell her I said hi, OK?

—*OK.*

Charlie's theory doesn't sound convincing, does it? Yet that's the conclusion that the inquest came to. It's the explanation that everyone seems to be happy with, and it's the explanation that no one has challenged yet. The interviews with Charlie Armstrong have proved a little bit toothless, if I'm honest. I was expecting to glean more from him. However, there are a few things that stood out.

Charlie's home life. It was not alluded to by either Derek or Eva Bickers, which seems strange to me, if there was really something wrong at home. Maybe there was nothing; maybe Charlie, like he freely admits, was just full of pent-up teenage rage.

Then there is Tom and Charlie's relationship. Tom seemed to be usurping Charlie as alpha, or at least surreptitiously trying to. I honestly think Charlie simply did not know what to make of Tom Jeffries. He was sort of a friend and sort of not. What both Charlie and Eva mention is Tom's manipulative nature.

Then there is Tom and Charlie's sighting of 'Nanna Wrack'. I'm inclined to believe, and indeed, the evidence points to, some sort of hallucination – overactive imaginations fed with narcotic drugs. Or did they see Haris Novak up there on the fell, retrieving one of his animal corpses?

Finally, for this episode, what can we conclude from Charlie's account of what happened that day? It does seem that Charlie was far from the steady hand I imagined him to be. He was more than a little confused – thrust into his leadership of the group without really knowing why. More than anything, he felt like an outsider, an individual unable to find his place in the world. He seems more lost than any of them.

From an objective point of view, Charlie Armstrong could be seen as more capable of killing Tom Jeffries than the others. But I think it's a tenuous idea, based on a lot of assumptions; and is there really any motive, aside from, as Charlie himself might describe it, 'teenage shit'?

Next time, on the penultimate episode of Six Stories, *we will hear from one of the two remaining members of Rangers. It will be interesting to discover whether they can provide any more insights into the night that Tom disappeared.*

This has been Six Stories *with me, Scott King.*

This has been our fourth story.

Until next time…

Scarclaw Fell
2017

I leave Belkeld behind; go back the way I came, out onto the fell again.

My fell.

I walk against the grain, straying from the path and travelling upward. The grass is thicker this way and I am filled with a strange, forbidden thrill, despite the fact that this is Ramsay land. A part of me expects a shout with every step – someone asking me to come back; what the hell do I think I'm doing?

That voice never comes.

About a hundred metres up the slope of the fell, I'm out of breath; my thighs burn and my cheeks feel raw from the wind that has begun whipping its razor-edge around the upper reaches. Spots of gorse cling to Scarclaw, fewer and further between, the higher I go.

In my rucksack there's a walking pole that dad bought and never used. I loop the handle over my wrist and lean into it. After a while I fall into the shade of the fell's claw. The ground hisses at the touch of my boots and water rises through the grass.

That forbidden thrill again. I've crossed the boundary from the stark fell-side into the boggy shadow of the claw. Someone needs to tell me to stop, to come back. Someone needs to tell me it isn't safe.

I'm glad of the stick in my hand. Metal. Its end is sharp.

I press on through the upper marshlands. The air is decidedly cooler, here, almost thick with the iron scent of rain.

There was an opinion piece in last week's *Telegraph* about *Six Stories* – mainly about Scott King. I try not to read them, so I did so with one eye closed, waiting for some dismissive coda about me, about dad, about The Hunting Lodge. It never came. Instead, the article focussed on how clever the format of this series was, the impact on society that unearthing these old cases had. 'Digging up the Dead' was its title. Two paragraphs in and I was filled with a terrible guilt, my cheeks flushed, as if I still had something to disclose, as if I could have changed the way things went.

I could have told the police about the figure we were pursuing that night; but so could the others. I could have told Scott King about it, too. But to what end? Would it have made a difference or sent a hundred monster-hunters onto my father's land?

Tomo, Jus and I, we made a promise, a pact that we would not mention what we saw that night – not unless the outcome of the case depended on it.

The postscript of the *Telegraph* article spoke about how there might even be a full review of the Tom Jeffries case. I wonder how his mother and father feel about that. The Jeffries family have not spoken a word since *Six Stories* began. Scott King says his job is raking up old graves. When he says that I cannot detect a smile in between his words.

I manoeuvre back around the side of the fell; this way is shorter in distance, but the going is harder. I look out for rocks and skeletons of trees to hold on to. Between Belkeld and The Hunting Lodge, the fell holds this land. I am foolish to even consider being its owner.

I'm close now to my next stop on this tour of memories.

If it had been raining we would have stayed inside the Woodlands Centre, I'm sure of it. However, the downpour granted us respite, so we scrunched over the muddy gravel to Tomo's car. The light of the boot felt conspicuous and the dogs were going berserk. I was in charge of them and a few times genuinely expected to be pulled off my feet.

'They've caught the scent.' Tomo said, in control now, gun in hand, black North Face zipped under his chin.

His words were like a line from some film. The handles of the dog leads were cutting into my palms.

'I can't hold them much longer,' I said in a voice that was not my own.

In that moment I realised what was happening.

None of us had ever been in such a situation as this, not by ourselves; not without the guidance of some relation or other. We were reacting the way they react in films, on TV; the way writers who've never been in these situations write. We were saying everything we'd heard and never done.

'Let's go.'

Tomo and Jus held a lamp each and looked at me. In their faces, half hidden by the flickering shadows, I saw expectancy.

'Come on.' I said it more to the dogs.

One of them whined slightly as he pulled me on, desperate to breach the bulwark of thrashing vegetation. Desperate to reach his quarry.

I didn't tell them, I kept my mouth shut the deeper we drove into the woods, with the dogs snarling and throwing themselves off into the undergrowth and the lamps casting a terrible corpse-light, while the wind and the rain battered us. I didn't tell them about what Dad had told me the last time he came out here to work on the final plans for The Hunting Lodge. What he thought he saw on the fell.

I wanted to but the words would not come.

Sometimes I think that it was the first sign, they say family notice things are amiss; a change in routine, a face forgotten. But this, this wasn't like that. Dad wasn't a dreamer; he thrived on pure logic, sometimes infuriatingly so. What he said he saw skulking across Scarclaw Fell, I have told myself was the first sign of what was coming – the change in the air that animals can sense before an onslaught of weather. It was as if Dad's brain was battening down, preparing for a storm.

I reach the other side of the marsh faster than I expect to. This is not far from where they found the body … *we* found the body, or what remained of it. It's about a quarter of a mile downhill from here, at the edge of the trees. Along with the black shape at the window of the Woodlands Centre, and Dad's insistent story, I relegate these notions to the limits of imagination, speculation. The devil, a long, black man, Nanna Wrack, Alzheimer's. We like to give things names, personify our darkness. Maybe that's some innate human trait? If so, I wonder what purpose it serves.

I'm careful, picking my way through the thickest parts of the marsh-grass, its tube-like stems penetrating my trousers. It's like walking over the surface of a nettle. I don't worry that I might be sucked in, slip below the surface of the mud. I do worry, though, that the damp earth might suck at my feet hard enough to pitch me forward, make me twist an ankle. No one's out here to hear me scream.

I reach an alder that clings to the last of its life – its roots jut from the ground and I perch on top of one of them, holding hands with the last of the green catkins. Last time I stood here, I stared for a long time at the grinning green skull of a long-dead sheep. I imagined it caught out here in the marsh. Maybe its leg became tangled in the roots of this very tree and it tried to run, collapsed and died, its wool soaking with the foul water, its bleats fading into nothing.

I lean against the damp trunk of the tree and squint out. I can see what I'm looking for; it rises from the marshes like a single, skeletal digit, ensconced with moss and ivy. The remains of a wall and a single chimney – the engine house that was one day the beating, industrial heart of this land, pumping water from the mineshafts below.

'What's wrong with them?'

The rain had resumed, and the wind was hurling it down into the forest; it clattered against the leaves with such a volume that we had to shout.

Tomo shone his light off into the undergrowth. We couldn't see the dogs, but we could hear them yelping.

'They've found something!' Tomo shouted back.

He and Jus could not keep the lights still; like twin searchlights they rode the canopy before us.

'It went toward that ruin thing…' Tomo was pointing into the black distance. His words were just audible above the screech of the wind and the rattle of the trees.

The gun was in my hands now. I could not remember how or why, but I was holding it, my arms trembling with cold and the weapon's dead weight. I begged myself not to shoot the moment one of the dogs burst back out of the undergrowth.

'Fuck me!'

I nearly did it. I felt my nearly numb finger squeeze the trigger as one of the lurchers, its scant fur plastered to its wiry frame, bounded back into the clearing where we stood, eyes blazing.

'That's where it lives, that's where it…' Tomo was shouting.

But we weren't looking at him anymore.

He stopped, turned back. Followed our gaze to what the Lurcher had dropped from its jaws into the mud before us.

The animal wagged its tail and its tongue lolled.

We stared.

I never forgot that black shape. The one at the window of the Woodlands Centre nearly twenty years ago. But we didn't speak of it again; we didn't give it a name. And for that I will always be grateful. Of course, any one of us could have said something; we could have told the police that Tom Jeffries' murderer lured us out onto the fell, just as it had perhaps lured Tom himself. And then what? Would anyone have believed us? Believed any of it: a shadowy black ghoul leering through the window at three drunken toffs?

In the end, what mattered more than why we were out there in the first place was what we found. I'm sure Tom Jeffries' family would agree…

Episode 5: Qalupalik

—There was a French explorer, Jacques Cartier his name was –
he described it as … and these are his actual words by the way …
'desolate and depressing'. Nice, huh? Even Captain Cook said it was
'of incredible poverty', and that was before the fur traders and the mis-
sionaries came and *actually* ruined the place.

We have a saying here: *'God created Labrador in six days, and on
the seventh he threw stones at it.'*

It's certainly very different from the UK, but that's just the way
things work out, isn't it? I'm not wanting for anything. And, in fact,
the distance is almost like some sort of safety barrier. It's like I can
stand here and wave my arms, 'Look. Look! Here I am!' But no one's
coming.

*This is the voice of Anyu Kekkonen. Her mother, Eska, has retained
her maiden name of Noggasak after the two relocated back to Cart-
wright, a community on the southern coast of Labrador, Canada. Anyu's
heritage is Labrador Inuit on her mother's side and Finnish fisherman
stock on her late father's. Jari Kekkonen and Eska Noggasak emigrated
to the United Kingdom when Anyu was a toddler. Jari met and became
friends with Derek Bickers a year or so before his death. Anyu joined
Rangers when she was twelve.*

—I'm sort of adaptable, you see. Northern hemisphere genes. I'm
also pretty good at withstanding temperatures like this.

—*Just for the sake of people listening, I want to point out that it's
currently -10°c where you are right now.*

—Yeah. That's sort of normal, January weather here.

—*It's a long, long way away, Anyu.*

—Yeah. But it's kind of nice … pretty nice.

Welcome to Six Stories. *I'm Scott King.*

Over next six weeks, we are looking back at the Scarclaw Fell tragedy of 1996, from six different perspectives

In this, the penultimate episode, we will hear from possibly the most elusive member of the Rangers and the most difficult person I've had the pleasure to track down.

Anyu Kekkonen was, along with Charlie Armstrong, Eva Bickers and Brian Mings, on that trip to Scarclaw Fell Woodlands Centre in August 1996 when fifteen-year-old Tom Jeffries disappeared.

In the last four episodes we have talked to two of the four teenagers who were close to Tom Jeffries and were present the night he disappeared. From these interviews, we know a little about the dynamic of the group. Charlie Armstrong appeared to be the unofficial 'leader' of the clique, revered and looked up to by the others, especially by the 'lowest-ranked' member, Brian Mings. Tom Jeffries, while the same age as the others, joined the group later, and appeared to slot in on an almost equal footing with Charlie. Charlie and Eva have told me that Tom Jeffries was quite manipulative; that he had a way of getting to people, and was able to influence them. Both of them also did not think this was significant.

The other thing we know, and that could, perhaps, be seen as crucial, is that Eva Bickers slept with both Charlie Armstrong and Tom Jeffries at Scarclaw Fell – on different occasions. There appears to have been some attraction between Eva and Charlie, although Charlie says he saw Eva as a 'sister'. Eva Bickers was elated by her experience with Charlie and distraught by 'allowing' herself to have slept with Tom. Also, the night that Tom Jeffries disappeared, Eva has said she was 'with' Brian Mings.

Another thing we know is that Brian Mings, who held a torch for Anyu Kekkonen, was the victim of occasional bullying by Tom and Charlie. The night that Tom Jeffries disappeared from the Woodlands Centre, the teenagers had all been smoking cannabis and drinking. None of them left the immediate surroundings of the Woodlands Centre, save for Charlie, who claims he 'stormed off' in a huff at some point in the night, before returning shortly afterward.

All of them awoke at around six a.m. to find Tom Jeffries was missing.

Welcome to Six Stories. This is story number five.

According to accounts we've heard so far, Anyu Kekkonen is a bit of a passenger in the Tom Jeffries story. It is evident that she was thought highly of by the rest of the group, and was seen as a 'sensible head'. We also know that Brian Mings was attracted to her. However, her part in this story has still not really been established.

When I finally manage to track her down, Anyu is calm and unassuming; it's almost as if she knew that one day, this would happen. That I would track her down. Because of the descriptions the others have given of her, I am not surprised either by her manner, or that she is completely unfazed by my request to talk to her about the summer of 1996. She is polite and friendly when we talk over Skype.

Anyu is proud of her heritage and always has been. She feels grateful for the chance to have joined Rangers, a community that both she and her mother were accepted by when times were hard. I don't think Anyu's heritage is particularly relevant to what happened in 1996, but I do feel it is important to get a feel for how Anyu comes across.

—*There's so much I want to ask you, Anyu. I know loads about what happened in 1996 from the others, yet there's still so much I feel I don't know. So, if I'm completely honest, I'm having trouble working out where best to start.*

—Well, August 1996 is something that, personally, I haven't thought about too much since.

There's something intriguing about Anyu – the way she holds herself, perhaps? She has this ethereal quality to her – an other-worldly serenity.

She is certainly striking to look at, and I can understand why Brian Mings fell so hard for her. That 'otherness' is also evident in the way she speaks, too. It takes a little getting used to. Anyu doesn't err or umm or nod; she just watches you and waits for you to finish. At first, it's disconcerting. But when she smiles, her whole countenance ignites, betraying her years.

—When I've talked to the others, so far we've kind of started at the start – when they first joined Rangers – and then gone all the way up to that last night. And … well, that last night has always been the shortest part…

—I can understand that. Because maybe it was the least eventful part of everything that happened. It was the least exciting yet the most tragic. We drank, we smoked, we went to sleep, and in the morning, when we awoke, he had just … gone.

— That's exactly what both Eva and Charlie have said. Charlie said to say hi, by the way.

—Oh. OK. Hi, Charlie.

—You're blushing.

—I know. I've never hidden it. Even after all this time. I guess I should probably say something else: 'I'm sorry, Charlie.'

—I'm not sure I follow…

—Didn't he say? Bless him. It's nice if he didn't.

—Anyu, I'm sorry, I'm almost completely lost here.

—It's nothing. Nothing really. I liked him, that was all. I would have thought it was obvious to everyone.

—No one's said a thing. Honestly

—Oh. OK, then. Fine. Maybe he didn't know.

—That you liked him?

—That I liked him. All these years I've been blushing thinking of it, chastising myself for what a desperate little girl I must have seemed to him, and all this time he didn't even know. How disappointing.

As we talk, I find myself captivated, almost hypnotised by Anyu. Whatever she says, I can't help feeling that it is going to be seeped with some sort of exquisite wisdom. I'm not the first, Anyu tells me, when I admit this to her. It used to 'do her head in', or at least it used to when she lived in England. She says people either thought she was aloof or else some sort of queen. Back in Labrador, Anyu says that life moves slower, that people don't 'chatter'. I wonder if this is in some ways easier – more soothing for her.

—People at school thought I was rude or stuck-up. The teachers thought I was some sort of child prodigy. They used to call me 'Eskimo' – the kids, not the teachers.

—Yes, I...

—You know what that word means? It translates roughly as 'flesh-eater' or 'raw-meat eater'. When I was in year six, year seven, I used to come home crying about it to my mum. She was so calm about it, so serene. She used to say to me, what's wrong with that? We all eat flesh, don't we? Tuna, from a tin – that's raw, you know. Our ancestors no doubt ate raw seal flesh, to get vitamins. The word never bothered me after that. I know there's some who see it as an insult, a slight, but not me. I'm sort of proud. I'm proud of my heritage. They used to ask me if I lived in an igloo. I would ask them how I would make an igloo when there was no snow. After a while they just gave up. It stopped being funny to them.

I've talked to a few people who knew Anyu – teachers, family friends, other parents. They all speak of her in the same, almost awed tones: she's a quiet enigma. Anyu seems bemused when I tell her this. She shakes her head and flashes that smile at me.

—I think if we'd have stayed there, I probably would have changed, maybe become more adaptable. When I was younger I thought I was being a bit rebellious – drinking and smoking with the others. My mum, she never told me not to, you see; she told me to make my own choices, but that I could come to her if I wanted to know anything. I liked that way of doing it. More parents should be open with their children, especially in the West.

—*Doing this, Anyu, I've found out a lot about everyone – the people who were close to you and your friends; the people who were close to Tom Jeffries. I'd be really interested to hear your opinions of that trip to Scarclaw Fell, the dynamic in the group.*

—I'll tell you what I remember, although it was a long time ago now and my life is very different.

—*I appreciate that, Anyu.*

—So where do you want to start?

—*You were a friend of Eva Bickers?*

—That's right. Eva and I were good friends. She was a companion. We always felt *older* somehow than the others. It sounds a bit stuck up, but I think we felt *superior* to a lot of the other girls when we were growing up.

—*Why do you think that was?*

—Well, I think it was because we were under the assumption that all the other children just went home and watched TV, did homework, whereas we had those excursions, those weekends in the country.

—*It seems that Rangers felt like that for most of the group, or else a sort of escape.*

—I think it was that, too, for me anyway. After my father passed away, my mum, she sort of retracted back into her shell. We had come to England to start this new life and she just could never settle; her roots could never take to the soil.

—*She didn't mind you joining Rangers?*

—On the contrary, she was very much for it. She liked that they embraced the outside, the country, nature, that sort of thing.

—*But she never took part?*

—No. I think she did once, when I had just joined. She came for a walk; maybe it was to Scarclaw, maybe not, I don't remember. But I do remember her staring out over the land, just staring, and I could hear her clucking away to herself in Inuktitut, and I knew that she longed for home.

—*That can't have been easy for you.*

—How do you mean?

—*I mean that it seems you always knew you would be leaving.*

— Maybe. You know, I've never even thought of that, but it makes a lot of sense.

—*Would that explain why it never happened with you and Charlie, perhaps? Like, it was a subconscious thing; maybe you didn't push that extra inch to really … I dunno… make it happen?*

—That's interesting and probably true. In a way. I did a lot of listening when I was with Charlie; I sat with him, shared things with him – well, it was more like he shared things with me. I drank with him, though; smoked with him. But maybe it was not enough? Maybe I should have been more *bold* about how I felt; more confident.

It's easy to say that when you're not a teenager anymore, though, isn't it? When you're fifteen, you're just a bag of insecurities, terrified of saying or doing the wrong thing.

—*You and Charlie were undoubtedly close though, right? Do you think he would have judged you like that?*

—We were friends. I don't think he would have judged me, but that doesn't make it any easier – like I say, when you're young you're just so … I don't know. But, yeah, Charlie and I were close. We were close enough that he felt like he could tell me all that stuff about his sister. That was hard for him, I think.

—*His sister?*

—You know – his little sister?

—*I didn't even know he had a sister.*

—But surely, what with the inquest and the time it's been since then, people know? Doesn't everyone know?

—*I don't know about Charlie's sister. When did he mention it?*

—It was the time we went and did the insulating at Scarclaw; there were only a few of us: Eva and Charlie and Brian. We were helping Eva's dad – crawling under the centre and nailing polystyrene to the bottom of the floorboards to keep the place warm. We were excited because it meant we could come visit in the winter; without the insulation, the Woodlands Centre was an icebox. It also meant we were giving something back to a place that gave us all so much pleasure, you know? We were part of it somehow.

—*That makes sense.*

—Anyhow, Charlie. Charlie would sometimes just sort of *go off* – usually when he was drunk, and more when he was stoned. He'd just sort of *slip away*, just go and stand and *stare.* It reminded me of my mother – the way she used to do that. I always wanted to ask him what it was. I knew that there was something wrong and I also knew that telling someone else, it always lightens a burden; always.

—*And he told you something on that trip in 1995.*

—Was that when it was? Yeah, we were smoking at that special place – the entrance to one of the old mineshafts. No one else seemed to know about it but us and—

—*Haris Novak. We'll talk about him later on; just keep going for now.*

—So we were there; it was just me and Charlie. He was so full of anger and sadness, it was like he had this great cloud engulfing him, swirling around him. I was telling him a story and he just lost it.

—*What was the story you told him?*

—It's an old story my Aanak told my mother when she was a girl. It's about two boys – cousins – naughty boys who don't listen to the elders of the camp. They don't obey their parents; they go running off to the shore, where they're not allowed to go. Going beside the shore is naughty, it is forbidden. There's something in the water that waits for children who don't listen to their elders. Children like that make an easy target for Qalupalik.

—*Quaa-loo-pah-lick?*

—That's right. She lives underwater. She's a bit like a woman with long, tangled black hair and sharp fingernails. Her skin is rough like a shark's. You can sometimes hear her knocking beneath you on the ice.

That's right. I too have noticed the similarity between Anyu's grand-mother's story and Nanna Wrack. And I've discovered another local legend – about a creature that lives in Lake Blother, not far from Scarclaw: a witch-like entity with green skin that pulls children into the water if they get too close. It is interesting how these warnings transcend cultures. But back to Anyu's story.

—They say Qalupalik takes children in her hood. She takes them to live with her, to keep her young, to keep her skin green. So, in the story, she snatches one of the cousins – a boy called Angutii – and takes him away. The other cousin, he runs home and tells Angutii's father, who sails in his kayak for days and days and miles and miles until he finds his son.

Eventually they make the long journey home. When they get back everything returns to normal, but they all know Qalupalik is still waiting beneath the waters for children who do not obey their parents.

—*You say Charlie 'lost it' when he heard this story.*

—That's right: he began crying and shaking. I didn't know what to do. So I put my arm around him to comfort him and just listened. That was when he told me about his little sister, Lydia – how, when she was two and he was five, his parents had gone on an errand to the shop or something and left him to look after her. And she just wandered off. He couldn't remember what happened. He said it was a sunny day, that they were in a park. That one minute she was there and the next she wasn't.

—*Jesus Christ...*

—It was a terrible thing; a terrible thing. They never found her.

—*Poor kid...*

—Charlie says it broke his family, cleaved them into pieces. His parents stayed together for his sake, but there were whole days and nights of silence, no one speaking, just him playing on his own with his toys. He wished they had just broken up, that he always blamed himself for what happened; that he always felt they blamed him as well, but no one could say it.

What a horrible weight to carry for your whole life. What a terrible responsibility.

—*It sort of makes sense, doesn't it? The way he was. The way he acted.*

—I thought so. I always understood after that; understood why he did the things he did – the smoking, the drinking, the way he behaved, everything. He just wanted to be numb, I guess.

—*Charlie told your story, didn't he? He told it for everyone – changed Qalupalik to Nanna Wrack.*

—I didn't understand why at the time, but now it makes sense. In a strange way, Charlie was trying to come to terms with what happened, to almost take ownership of it. For me, every time he told that Nanna Wrack story, he was trying to heal himself, heal that scar in his life.

What Anyu is saying about Charlie fits. If the others knew about what happened to little Lydia Armstrong, they didn't mention it to me, nor did Charlie himself. I can understand that: it's a personal story. But now I know, I feel all of us have fresh insight into Charlie Armstrong's personality. But to what end? Are we building a case for Charlie to be involved somehow in Tom Jeffries' disappearance? If so, we still don't have a motive. Also, is it fair to do this? Charlie Armstrong was clearly the least stable of the group; but implicating him in a murder because of a lasting trauma in his life is a little presumptuous.

I ask Anyu about Tom Jeffries.

—Oh, I couldn't stand Tom; never could. As soon as he joined, my heart just sort of *sank*.

—*Eva felt much the same, initially.*

—Yeah, we talked about it – about him – but not much; just in the way that girls do. We both thought he was an idiot. A bully. He tried it on with me once, you know?

—*Really?*

—When he first joined – round the back of the church hall at one of the meetings. I was waiting for Eva and he gave me one of his cigarettes: Regals; he always smoked Regals, I thought they were horrible, but there was something about Tom – you couldn't show him weakness. If you did, he'd pounce. So we were stood there, smoking, and we weren't talking because, well, we didn't have anything in common. And he just came out with some innuendo about smoking and blow jobs – *sucking off*, that sort of thing. We were only about fourteen. I don't think I even knew what a blow job was then!

—*He tried it on?*

—He sort of leaned in to me, brushing up against my chest, said something about how no one was here, if I wanted to try it out, something like that. I wanted to be sick.

—*What did you do?*

—I just kept utterly po-faced, just raised my eyebrows. It's funny, because I think if someone said something like that to me now, I'd scream!

—*What was Tom's reaction?*

—It was weird because he looked really confused at first, as if he simply couldn't comprehend that I didn't want him. Then, when it dawned on him, he was really angry; for a few seconds I actually thought he was going to punch me or something.

—*Wow, really?*

—I think it was that no one had ever stood up to him like that before; especially not a girl.

—*That's…*

—It's pretty horrible, isn't it? After then we never spoke, I don't think; not a word to each other. I hated him.

—*What do you think happened to Tom, that night at Scarclaw?*

—I don't know. I have no idea, and in some terrible way, I feel he sort of deserved it.

—*That's a strong way of thinking, Anyu. Some might say harsh.*

—When he went missing and the appeals went out and everything, it made me so angry.

—*Really?*

—There was all this false sentiment flying around, about how he was a nice, well-liked young man who'd had his problems but at heart was a good guy. He wasn't at all a good guy. OK, so maybe I don't think he deserved to *die*, but he certainly didn't warrant the sentiment that was trotted out at the time.

—*Was he really that bad? The others don't seem to share the extremes of your hatred for Tom.*

—I understand that. But look where they are; look where I am. My position allows me to be a little removed. I'm guessing you heard about the incident with the homeless guy?

For clarity, this was the incident in 1993 when Tom and a couple of older boys were arrested for throwing coins at a homeless man. As far as I know, no charges were brought and Tom's young age was taken into consideration.

—He told us all about it at, I think, the second or third Rangers meeting – round the back of the church hall.

—*I know that Tom's mum sent him to Rangers to try and steer him away from some of the problems he was having.*

—Well, maybe so, but he didn't seem in any way repentant. It was pretty chilling, some of the things he told us. Him and those two older lads [names bleeped out – they have served their punishment and are not relevant to our story], there was a lot more going on than throwing coins.

—*What do you mean?*

—Tom was into fire. Him and those lads started out burning stuff on the streets, chucking fireworks into people's gardens, that sort of thing. Tom told us about a time they threw a lit banger through the window of a Chinese takeaway. Then it progressed. They started setting off bangers near sleeping homeless people and running away, just to give them a scare. Then it went on to trying to set their sleeping bags alight. He wasn't sorry or ashamed about this; if anything, he thought it was hilarious, he used to laugh himself stupid telling us about it.

I think I understand why it's taken this long to find this out about Tom Jeffries. This unpleasant little vignette is not something that would be widely known – if no charges were brought, there would be no official record; and who would tell? Certainly not Tom's mother. Tom, it seemed, was careful about who he bragged to.

Anyu and I discuss at length what it was about Tom that Charlie seemed to like so much. Anyu has drawn similar conclusions to me and is the third to remark that Jeffries had a manipulative streak about him, was able to exploit weakness. If anything, Anyu says, it was Charlie that looked up to Tom. All of this also explains, to an extent, why Eva was in no way forthcoming with any of this information. She doubtless knew all this, and slept with Tom despite it. She was young, drunk, stoned and we know she regretted it. The shame of sleeping with someone who had bragged about doing these sorts of things must have been immense. It clearly still is.

As for Charlie, why he didn't mention it to me, I'm not sure. It's certainly possible he forgot, and it's also possible there was shame surrounding his close association with Tom Jeffries. Yet, it still begs the question: Why did these four teenagers tolerate Tom's presence? I put this to Anyu.

—I think that was the whole problem. Just how tolerant we were. I think Tom knew fine well we weren't the sort of people to turn around and tell him to get lost, even though we probably should have. And Charlie – if anyone would have done, it would have been him. Looking back, I think Tom saw that immediately, and honed his charm offensive – fought hard to get on Charlie's good side.

Tom took advantage of us, so even when he told those stories, even when he told us about what he'd done, we – and this includes me, I'm not innocent – we all sort of just got on with it. None of us knew what to do about it. But that's how we were raised: to accept people, to forgive.

—*It sounds to me that this is something you've been wanting to say for a while.*

—It's been nearly twenty years. I still remember everything in the press about what a good kid Tom was, all this sentiment because he was dead. It left no place for any of these kinds of thoughts, did it? I couldn't exactly turn round and sell my story to the papers. I couldn't say, 'Actually, Tom Jeffries was a repulsive little bully and we hated him,' could I? We all know what would have happened then.

—*You would suddenly become a prime suspect.*

—Correct.

—*So … why now; why do you think you can say these things to me?*

—This is a podcast. I know you get hundreds of thousands of listeners, that you're popular, but still – and I don't mean any offence – it's hardly worldwide press attention.

—*No, it isn't. Not yet.*

—I feel like the time is right, that I want to say to people, 'Look what he was like.' I mean the way he picked on Brian for a start.

—*That's been mentioned by the others, but without a great deal of significance. It seems to me that it was gentle ribbing on Tom's part to help him establish himself in the pecking order. Would you agree?*

—No. Not at all. You see, the thing is, unless you've been on the other end of bullying, you don't really know how much these smaller things can affect you. People's perception of bullying is still so archaic or clichéd: the 'give us your dinner money' schoolyard stuff, or else the 'OMG you're so ugly' stuff online. Tom bullied Brian in a *professional* way.

—*'Professional'. I've never heard it called that before.*

—No. But when I was younger I was professionally bullied, too. It's the little things – the name-calling, the comments, the giggles when your back's turned. That's how the professionals do it. Like water-torture, or death by a thousand cuts. 'Professional' bullies crush your soul a sliver at a time.

—*That sounds … intense.*

—It is and already I feel like you think I'm exaggerating. I'm not. When I was younger, at school in England, I was made so *aware* of how different I was – not by anyone explicitly, but just hearing little comments, sniggers, the subtle way that children have of showing up difference. I heard it all.

—*And Tom Jeffries was this way to Brian Mings? It seems somewhat at odds with his personality. Surely he just would have come out with it.*

—That was the thing. Tom Jeffries knew that if he was too obvious, we *would* have turned on him. So he played the long game. Like I said, Tom Jeffries was a seasoned pro.

—*Tell me a bit about Brian. By all accounts, he's not really played a huge part in this story.*

—No, that doesn't surprise me. Brian wasn't exactly memorable.

—*Harsh!*

—Maybe. But at least I'm being honest. Look, I know Brian liked me; he always did. I knew from when he first joined. He looked at me *that* way.

—*And what did you think?*

—If I'm totally honest, at first, I was surprised; that was the overriding feeling. I suppose I'd been led to believe that my difference, my foreignness, wasn't endearing. Rangers helped with that; *Brian* helped with that. In his small way, his idolising of me, well, it made me.

—*Really?*

—Yes. But only after I realised what his affection had meant. How harsh is that? At the time I simply *didn't fancy him back*; that was the problem. He sent me a card on Valentine's Day; he must have got my address off Derek or something. This home-made card came through the post – all black paper and silver marker; it was lovely.

—*The others knew?*

—Not about the card. No way. I didn't say anything. They would have just teased him. Everyone knew how he felt about me, but no one minded. That was the nice thing about that group. Brian was never pushy; he never tried to corner me, to force me. He was just persistent, dogged. I could let him off for that; I cut him a lot of slack.

—*Did you two never talk about it?*

—No. I mean, I made it my business not ever to be alone with him – not in a creepy way, but just so the situation wouldn't arise, so that conversation would never happen. Brian wasn't predatory like Tom. He was just a bit sad.

—*But it was Charlie who you liked?*

—Yes. Poor Brian. I don't think he even knew; or if he did, he didn't say anything. It was that teenage thing of wanting the person who wasn't interested. It's funny, because I saw a lot of me in Brian, if you know what I mean – in his pursuit of me.

—*Did you ever send Charlie a card or anything?*

—No. I wasn't nearly brave enough. Some of those times when he'd go off, I just wanted to follow him, to hold him. In fact, I kind of respected Brian for having the guts to try all that with me. Fair play to him.

—*But you and Charlie never...*

—No. Never.

I contemplate giving Anyu Charlie's contact details, but think better of it. If they want to find each other again some day, they will. I refocus our conversation back on Brian Mings.

—*He was bullied? Brian, that is.*

—Yes – definitely by Tom and, I suppose to a lesser extent, Charlie.

—*Really?*

—I wish I could say no; I wish I could say it didn't happen. Maybe it was the thing that stopped me ever really attempting to get with Charlie, I don't know. But, yes, before Tom arrived on the scene, Charlie wasn't exactly what you'd call pleasant to Brian.

—*Why do you think that was?*

—I think it was because Brian was just so desperate for our friendship. Kids are awful like that, aren't they? The more desperate someone is to be your friend, the more you push them away. I have no idea why the hell that is, but that's just how it was. Brian was having a rough time at school; I think there was bullying there, too. He never said, but with someone like Brian, you just sort of *know*.

—*So what was it, do you think, that induced the same bullying in such a tolerant and accepting group like yours?*

— I think it's some sort of universal thing. It's hard to explain, but Brian managed to just wind people up. He didn't have any personality of his own. He borrowed everything – mostly from Charlie: his dress sense; his mannerisms; *everything*. It used to drive Charlie insane. I wished someone could have just told Brian that it was OK to just be *himself*, that people would have respected him then.

—*But no one did?*

—Again, when you're that age, you can't *see* things in that mature, analytical way; things are really black and white, even for a group like us, who would proclaim to be more tolerant and accepting.

—*So what were some of the things Brian had to endure at Rangers?*

—I remember Charlie used to call him a '*Thing*'.

—*A what?*

—Do you remember that old film *The Thing*? Of course you do, you're about my age. It was one of Charlie's favourites. The monster in it, the alien could take the shape of anything it liked. Charlie once said that Brian was a 'Thing' that took his shape. Brian was his 'Thing' and I was Eva's. I'll never forget him saying that – it hurt me more than anything anyone's ever said.

—*When was this?*

—Oh, this was early days. A long way back, when Brian and I first joined. I nearly didn't go back after that.

—*But that's all it was? Charlie just doing a bit of name-calling?*

—But what an apt name. I'm sure Charlie didn't think of it so deeply, but how appropriate – an alien that must hate its own form so much, it just mimics anything else. That was Brian all over; and me, to some extent.

—*But you weren't bullied at Rangers.*

—No. After that something inside me hardened. I thought, I'm not going to take that sort of crap, and I didn't. Brian, on the other hand…

—*He just took it.*

—It got worse when Tom joined. Brian didn't help himself, either.

—*There was an incident with a coat...*

—Oh god, I'd forgotten about that. Yes, it's all coming back. I think Brian had got so fed up with Charlie calling him 'Thing' that he'd finally attempted his own style. He came to a Rangers meeting in this sort of *bondage* coat, with all these straps that hung down off the arms and fastened across the back with these metal clips. God only knows where he got it from; it looked ridiculous.

So Charlie and Tom, they were all over him straight away; a pack of wolves. They started pulling all the straps off the coat, tying them around his wrists and ankles. They took his boots off and threw them out of a window as well, and it angered me *so much*.

—*Because it wasn't like them to act like that?*

—No, not just that, but because Brian just *stood there*. He just stood and *let* them do it. He just allowed himself to be humiliated. It was horrible, really horrible. I think Eva tried to have a word with him afterwards, but it made no difference because of course, Tom turned up. So there was no apology after that; there was just Brian sat there like an idiot with his hands tied up and his socks on – Tasmanian Devil socks; you know that old cartoon? My heart sort of crumpled because he just looked so *pathetic*, like a little kid.

This unpleasant story is the same as Eva's. It certainly doesn't seem like the sort of thing young people in a group like Rangers would do. But is it fair to say that it is all because of Tom Jeffries' influence? Brian Mings came under a lot of fire from both Charlie and Tom, Anyu explains. She remembers watching Brian's self-esteem crumble from ashes to nothing, and wonders why no one did anything about it.

It's important, Anyu tells me, to know that this bullying didn't happen all the time; it wasn't a constant barrage of abuse. Most of the time, Tom and Charlie simply ignored Brian. But it hadn't always been this way.

—No, Charlie and Brian were actually sort-of friends before Tom came along.

—*'Sort-of' friends?*

—I don't know – maybe that's pushing it. Charlie just sort of *tolerated* Brian. When Tom came on the scene, though, it all went out the window.

Anyu says she saw how all this was affecting Brian. He was getting more and more desperate to please Charlie and Tom, more and more desperate for them to accept him.

In the weeks leading up to Tom's disappearance, Tom and Charlie were spending more and more time off on their own. Again, like Eva, this irked Anyu.

—I'm not sure it was solely because of Brian. As I said, Brian was never that *forward*, he was just persistent. He never gave up. I think the reason for it was Tom; I think he wanted Charlie all to himself. They just smoked weed and listened to music in that mineshaft, the place Haris showed them.

—*I think now's a good time to talk about Haris Novak.*

—Yes, OK. Well, that was yet another thing that Tom spoiled.

—*So the first time you met Haris…*

— That was back in '95, when he showed us the place. I'll tell you now, and I'm not proud – I was a little scared of Haris.

—*Really?*

—I know; it's not politically correct, is it? But he was just so *strange*; so alien to what any of us knew. I know now, obviously, that he was on the autism spectrum, that he had a learning difficulty, but still. It was the way he talked – just like a sort of malfunctioning robot. I know, it sounds horrible, but that's what it reminded me of back then. I was *scared* of him.

—*Tom wasn't…*

—That's right. Tom was just *awful* to him; really bad. It was pure Tom Jeffries that; he saw a weakness and pounced, to establish his own dominance. But it was Brian who surprised me the most. That was one of the reasons I stopped having anything to do with him after what happened to Tom.

—*Brian?*

—Yes. We had a trip to Scarclaw in winter – '95 or '96.

—*The snowballs incident.*

—Right. Of course, you know about that.

—*What I've heard is that Tom gave Haris some cannabis, convinced him to eat it, then Charlie told that Nanna Wrack story, which scared him half to death, before Tom started pelting him with snowballs. Is that right?*

—Some of it. Some of it isn't.

This is interesting. Anyu and Eska moved back to Labrador not long after the ruling about Tom Jeffries' accidental death had been confirmed. As far as I am aware, neither of them stayed in touch with their former friends. Perhaps that was due to the remoteness of where they had moved. Or perhaps it was because of something else entirely…

—*So what did happen, Anyu? Start on the minibus on the way. Tom and Charlie got picked up together, didn't they?*

—They did. I remember being fed up because Tom just sort of *took over*. He was sitting next to Eva before they picked me up, so I had to sit at the back with Brian. I was trying to read a magazine – *Vox*, that old indie one – and he kept *peering* at it over my shoulder and trying to talk to me.

I was more annoyed with Eva, though; you could see then what Tom was doing – buttering her up. I remember thinking, 'Is that all it takes?' – some stupid bloke to come along and give you a bit of attention, and that's it?

—*Do you think Eva was attracted to Tom?*

—I don't think she was as such, but I think she allowed him to do what he was doing, if you know what I mean? She didn't put up much resistance.

—*She slept with Tom that night.*

—Yes. She did. It was unpleasant to say the least, but we were all in a state. Tom had made those 'lung' things to smoke weed with.

Brian kept asking me if he could give me a 'blowback', just like Tom was doing with Eva. I think he thought it was as close to kissing as we'd get.

—*There were other kids on that trip, weren't there? Younger ones. Did that not bother any of you?*

—Well, it worked in our favour. Derek and Sally and the other adults, they were preoccupied with hot chocolate and washing-up, that sort of thing. It left us with plenty of cover. We also had Brian's rucksack.

—*Go on...*

—Brian had this great long rucksack, like some sort of hiking bag. He brought it the first time we went to Scarclaw and Charlie had ribbed him so much, we'd not seen it again. But because it was waxy and waterproof, Tom and Charlie had convinced Brian to bring it this time.

—*What for?*

—It was to keep stuff in: like the booze and Tom's 'lungs'. Brian used to stash it under the centre. Because it was so heavy-duty, it could withstand the damp and the cold. If Derek or Sally had searched us, they would never have found it. Brian was so overjoyed at finally being some sort of use. Also, Tom was skinnier than the rest of us and he could sort of fold himself up and get inside it. That seemed to crack Brian up. He was so desperate. Eventually, one of them – probably Tom – gave that bag to Haris.

—*And the next day? The snowballs incident.*

—Oh, I was so pissed off with Eva after that night; so angry. I could barely even look at her. We got to the churchyard in Belkeld and Brian, he was so *overjoyed* because Tom and Charlie were sort of treating him as an equal. They made him carry all their stuff in that great big bag, but he didn't care. He was bouncing about like an excited dog!

—*So you went to the churchyard in Belkeld...*

—Yeah. They were all smoking joints, and it was like I wasn't even there. And then Haris came along. Great, I thought; oh great, more madness. But it was *Brian* – Brian in his stupid, overexcited state – who suggested Tom gave some of the weed to Haris. It was *Brian* who suggested Charlie tell him that Nanna Wrack story right then. I remember him saying, 'Wait. Wait for a bit. Wait till the weed starts kicking in!' It was Tom who threw the snowballs; Charlie who told the story, but it was all Brian's idea.

This is in direct contradiction to Eva Bickers' account of what happened. According to Eva, it was Tom who instigated giving the cannabis to Haris. I tell Anyu this and she shakes her head.

—Nope. Nope, that's what I think everyone would have *liked* to have happened. That would have fitted the bill. It wasn't what happened, though. And I know why – it was just Brian trying to impress. You should have seen his face when Tom and Charlie started laughing. I think, if I hadn't been so angry with Eva, we probably would have tried to stop them. I remember her looking at me, but I just turned away; just made myself feel invisible like I used to at school. Horrible, right? We should have done something about it, shouldn't we? We were fifteen; that's what I have to keep reminding myself when I think about that day. We were just stupid children.

There is a lot of detail here; a lot of 'what if's and 'looking back's. I personally think that teenagers get a great deal of bad press for the things they do and don't do. But there's always layers to peel back before we can fully understand.

Look at this incident with Haris Novak – a pivotal event that was never covered or discussed at the inquest – and why should it have been? The papers saw Haris as a suspect, but his alibi was solid. Desperate to impress, Brian Mings would have sold his own mother for an inkling of approval from Tom or Charlie. Whether it was Tom or Charlie whose idea it was to give a vulnerable man cannabis and throw snowballs at him, doesn't matter. What matters is that it happened. And whether it was Tom or Brian who started it, both had self-serving, rather than purely vindictive motives – for one it was a display of dominance; for the other a desperate attempt at validation. Haris Novak seemed not to matter here; he was simply a pawn – a victim of what anyone who hasn't talked to those involved will quite rightly see as an impulsive and unkind practical joke.

That isn't to say it should have happened, or that Brian, Tom or Charlie are blameless. Even the two girls have some guilt: why did they do nothing to stop it? Eva Bickers had been silenced by the shame of sleeping with Tom and Anyu was furious with her best friend about her actions the previous night.

All of these things are layers; they all impacted on the group's dynamic and subsequent behaviour. I believe it is layers like these we will have to pull back if we are to gain any understanding of what happened to Tom Jeffries the following summer.

There is something else I want to ask Anyu about that night; something that Eva told me. Eva and Charlie both confirm what happened to Haris Novak in December 1995. I am now in little doubt that this profoundly affected him and may have been the trigger for his Beast of Belkeld stories. It surprises me that Anyu claims it was Brian Mings' idea but, as much as I don't want to believe it, I think I do. It makes sense. But it is that evening in December that I want another viewpoint on.

—What about after that snowballs incident – that evening. Had anything changed?

—What, you mean in terms of the group? No, we had more or less forgotten about it. How terrible does that sound? After tea and washing-up, we just went back to the dorm and got drunk and stoned again. I don't remember a lot of it.

—There was an incident with Brian, the night that Tom disappeared, wasn't there? Putting something in your drink?

—No. Not possible. No way. Brian wouldn't have done that.

—*Tom apparently saw him do it.*

—Tom was full of shit. Brian would never have done that, not to me, I am sure of it.

—*Didn't Tom take delight in pointing it out?*

—Thing is, Tom was *always* saying stuff like that; trying to embarrass Brian whenever he did *anything*, especially when I was about. It got to the point where Brian got too nervous to say or do anything around me. I hated Tom for that.

I think so far, we've seen an unexpected side to Anyu Kekkonen. She still seems unhappy with the others, and is particularly annoyed with Eva, whom she thought was her friend, for sleeping with Tom Jeffries that night in December. I don't let on about what happened between Eva and Charlie. I'm only presuming that Anyu doesn't know.

However, it feels like we are still no closer to explaining what happened to Tom Jeffries that night in 1996. The story is encumbered with these little spats and details of teenagers, well, being teenagers, I suppose. We could say that, so far, all suspicions point to Brian Mings. But was he capable of murder? Surely his first instinct before killing Tom would be simply to leave and not return?

There are a few more creases that I need to try and iron out.

—*Did Charlie ever tell you that he and Tom thought they saw Nanna Wrack up on the fell?*

—No. No, he didn't.

There is a moment of awkwardness after I mention this. Anyu's entire demeanour changes and her body language becomes defensive.

—*He and Tom saw her, apparently, up at the mineshaft, after they had been—*

—That's just…

—*What?*

—That's just wrong; just not possible.

—Charlie believes that it was probably some kind of collective hal-lucination, overactive imaginations, something like that.

—You're joking. This is a joke.

—No, I—

—Seriously. Just stop. Just tell me the truth. It's a joke.

—It's not. At least, Charlie seemed to believe…

—Please, please, tell me you're making this up – *please*.

Anyu's loss of calm is alarming. The grace and serenity that she has exuded for our interview has slipped rather dramatically. To say I am slightly unnerved by this is an understatement.

—Just take your time, Anyu. There is no joke here…

—No … you don't understand. We … this is going to sound crazy … but me and Eva … we saw her, too…

—What?

—Yes. I … I didn't believe it. I *couldn't* believe it. Because … just … it just wasn't *possible*.

—When? Where was it you saw her?

—You remember I told you about Qalupalik – the story that I told Charlie?

—Then he told you about Lydia, his little sister.

—Yeah. It was such a weird day – so strange, just the two of us in the mineshaft. And after he told me about her we were so *quiet*, just staring out over the hills. And then something changed. It was like … you know when you're talking about ants or insects or something, and you can almost *feel* them on your skin? It was like that; just like that. Something in the air just sort of *changed*. Neither of us wanted to say it, but it was like we were being watched.

—That's creepy. Where were the others?

—I don't know. Maybe they *were* there. But Tom Jeffries wasn't in Rangers then, so … and I just don't think Eva or Brian would do that. I really don't. But, later on that afternoon, it was quiet. It was just me and Eva, we were just sort of sitting around in the centre.

Looking out of the window and I don't think either of us believed it at first, but we saw this … this *shape* just sort of *creeping* along the fell … with this sort of *mane* of hair. It was horrible, really horrible, and we both sort of convinced ourselves we hadn't seen it, that it was a *vision*, a *dream*. It makes me feel just *horrible* thinking about it – Charlie's story, my story…

Anyu is visibly upset recalling this particular memory and it makes me think of Charlie's description of the arachnid motion that had repulsed him so much.

During the inquest and, what I can only presume, the questioning of the teenagers, this Nanna Wrack sighting was not mentioned, or if it was, it was dismissed.

Let's say that they did see something   or someone – up there on the fell. The descriptions are similar: the mane of hair and the spider-like movement. But in Charlie's story Nanna Wrack has seaweed for hair; and Anyu's Qalupalik has bedraggled black hair. The visions and the stories seem to meld.

Anyu regains her pragmatism as we iron out the details of both sightings. I have to say I am perturbed by the similarities. I ask Anyu what she thinks it was.

—I think the collective hallucination thing is valid. Or else we created a Tulpa, us lot.

A Tulpa is a Buddhist concept; it is a being that is created solely by thought, or a collective belief. A modern example of something like this is 'Slender Man', a creature created on Photoshop as part of a competition. If you don't know who Slender Man is, take a moment to search him out online.

After Slender Man found his way into popular culture, it wasn't long before people were reporting sightings of him. Some even tried to kill for him.

—*Would you go so far as to say Tom's disappearance was because of this Tulpa … that you created Nanna Wrack between you and she took him?*

—Do *you* think that sounds like a legitimate theory? Really?

—*Well…*

—Clearly not. But do you have a better one? Do the police?

—*The official verdict was misadventure.*

—Do you believe that?

—*Do you?*

—No.

—*So what do you think happened to Tom Jeffries that night?*

—I don't know. Honestly. It's like I said to the police at the time: I don't think it was an accident.

—*Someone killed him.*

—Maybe.

—*Let's go back to that last night at Scarclaw Fell. You, just like the others said you drank, you smoked and then you went to bed. And in the morning, Tom Jeffries was gone.*

—That's how I remember it happening.

—*There's just something that doesn't add up. The five of you were the only people at Scarclaw Fell Woodlands Centre that night, along with Derek and Sally. Every time you had all been together there, you had partied, drunk, smoked, et cetera. Both Eva and Charlie say that the night Tom disappeared, you all went to bed early. None of you seem to have a clear memory of that night. Doesn't that seem strange?*

—In a way. Or does it just seem strange because that was the night Tom disappeared? The whole thing is a question that, if I knew the answer to, well, we wouldn't be talking now, would we?

—*I suppose not. So what do you remember?*

—I remember that the whole weekend was *odd*. Maybe that was because there were just a few of us. I think Derek and Sally had a hard time because they didn't really know what to do with us. I mean, we were still children, but we wanted to be treated like adults. I think they felt a bit tentative, like they wanted to give us our space, so they sort of stayed away from us. We *were* all in a funny sort of mood, to be fair. We did the things we normally do: we went up to Belkeld; smoked a bit in the mineshaft; we even saw Haris, just like usual.

—*What happened with Haris?*

—Nothing this time; he just came up and said hello. I think Tom was a bit fed up; so was Charlie. But Brian, he was still trying to impress them and he said something to Haris – something about that bag. That stupid black bag of his that he kept bringing.

—*Can you remember what exactly happened with that bag?*

—No. Brian had this stupid idea he was going on about, that they could leave stuff in his bag, in the mineshaft, and Haris would keep it safe for them. He told Haris some crap about Nanna Wrack and Haris went running off. I was sick of Brian by then. I couldn't be bothered with him. In fact, I was feeling like I couldn't be bothered with any of them. Maybe that's why that night was just so nothingy.

—*Was there anything that happened that night? Anything you can remember that might have triggered what happened to Tom?*

—Honestly. I remember so little about it. I know we had a bit of a drink, a bit of a smoke. Charlie and Tom were doing a lot of creeping about together and Brian kept trying to get everyone to drink quicker, to 'get wasted'. I think he felt he had to sort of take Charlie's place.

—*One of the other things is that you all seemed to wake up at around the same time and noticed Tom was gone.*

—That was strange. Maybe that was something to do with a collective consciousness? I don't know. Maybe we heard something, sensed something. I remember one thing though one thing that didn't make sense.

—*What…?*

—It could well have been a dream, but I doubt it. Dreams don't feel like that. It's hazy, but it's definitely a memory. I woke up – it was summer, but still pretty chilly, so maybe three, four a.m.? We slept in bunks. I always slept the furthest from the window, just because

Tom always slept next to the window and was in and out all night with Charlie, smoking and pissing around.

I remember waking. We were all a jumble of legs and clothes – half in, half out of bunks or on the floor. That was normal, we just sort of slept where we fell, as teenagers do. The room was full of heavy breathing, smelled sweaty and kind of sweet – you know, that alcohol, fermented sort of smell? But I remember so clearly, the smell of the fresh air, the smell of the outside, coming inside. Maybe that's what woke me up.

Anyway, I sort of sat up, my eyes all sort of fuzzy.

—*Go on.*

—Someone else was awake, too. I could just sense an … an *urgency* … a movement.

—*Who was it?*

—I'm pretty sure it was Brian. In fact, yeah, it *was* Brian. As I say, it was dark in the dormitory, so I could only make out his outline; a shadowy lump. But he was at the foot of the bunks – Eva's bunk, just sort of *scrabbling*.

—*Scrabbling?*

—Yeah, like a sort of hamster or something. Both hands, going through the piles of coats and bags.

—*Really? What could he have been doing?*

— My first thought was he was stealing. But then I thought it was *Brian* – Brian wouldn't do something like that; he just didn't have it in his nature. No, it was weird … different. More like he was putting something *back*.

—*Did he notice you'd noticed him?*

—It was odd, because when I woke up and watched him for a few seconds, he sort of seemed to *sense* me and stopped. He looked up, right at me. I couldn't see his face. And there was a moment – a second when one of us should have spoken. But neither did, and the moment just sort of passed.

—*Why didn't you say anything to the others?*

—Yeah, why didn't I? OK, so this reasoning might seem skewed or wrong, or whatever, but I couldn't stop thinking what would happen if Tom got wind of it. It'd be enough ammunition for him to destroy Brian. Like I say, I know what it's like to be bullied. Tom wouldn't have let it go.

—*Where did Brian go then?*

—I don't remember exactly; it was early. I was half asleep. He went back to bed, I presume.

—*His own bed?*

—Yes. I don't see why not…

—*It's just that Eva said…*

—Oh yeah. Of course, yeah. That makes sense. He ended up with Eva that night, didn't he?

—*According to Eva, yes. Anyu, you seem a bit…*

—I know. I'm sorry. It's stupid; it's been twenty years, hasn't it. But, you know, it still … I guess it still hurts a little bit…

—*What does?*

—It's stupid, but Brian liked *me*. He always did. And then to just go with Eva, it was like … oh, I don't know … it was just a bit like, 'What's wrong with me? What did I do wrong?'

—*But you didn't like Brian.*

—No. That's why it's just so *weird* – why it still bothers me. I think I'd sort of made up my mind about Eva and the others that night. Then, when we woke up later and Tom had gone, it was just – something changed, something between us. For me anyway. I remember suddenly looking at them all as if through different eyes. I saw them all in a totally different light and I just knew that there was no way we could be friends again … after that, anyway.

—*Was Tom gone when you woke and saw Brian scrabbling in the bags?*

—He could have been. I have no idea. I didn't even look. I was so tired, just woozy. I just fell asleep again. Charlie, Eva, they all could have gone … I wouldn't have noticed. That's what made the police so annoyed with me. But you just don't take stock of everyone like that; it's not natural. You're not checking in case someone inexplicably vanishes, are you?

—*Don't you think this thing with Brian at four a.m. implicates him as a suspect?*

—What? For killing Tom? You think Brian managed to make Tom get up and walk across the fell with him, then managed to overpower him and kill him before hiding his body and coming back? It's just impossible.

—*What was he doing then – at four a.m., scrabbling in a bag?*

—You know what I thought at the time – my immediate assumption?

—*What...?*

—I thought he was looking for a condom. Maybe I still do. That's logical, right? Something like that? What else could he have been doing?

So where does all this leave us as this episode ends and with one more story to go? Any further forward? I'm not sure. The conclusions that can be drawn so far are significantly more limited than I thought they'd be by now. The events surrounding the trip to Scarclaw Fell in 1996 are stories, myths, angst, unrequited love – all underpinned with a naivety dressed in boots and armour. Teenage life, red in tooth and claw.

So what do we really know?

Well, we've learned a lot about the dynamic of the group. It's some-thing I know I keep coming back to, but being able to understand the world of those involved might in some small way help us understand what happened that night.

So, peeling back the layers, we know that Tom Jeffries was, at best, only tolerated by the rest of the group. However, at the same time he clearly had a major influence over them. Specifically, he quickly managed to 'get in' with Charlie, by using his ability to get hold of drugs.

Was he consciously trying to gain dominance over this particular group of teens? I do believe Tom had a need to feel dominant. And, looking at Jeffries' past, he was no stranger to bad behaviour, or how to influence others. Was he mimicking older people's influence over him? Or maybe it was his warped way of trying to fit in.

My gut feeling is it was the latter. From what we know about Tom Jeffries, it seems likely that he wanted to influence those lower down the pecking order than him. Look at his comment, as recalled by Eva Bickers, when he first meets the others:

'Hippies, eh? I like hippies cos they smoke *the herb.*'

To me, that's not a normal thing to say when meeting a group of your peers for the first time. It reeks of contempt – as if he'll lower himself to their level because it will do something for him. He also said it in front of the adults; testing the waters to see how they would react.

Jeffries then entrenched his position, asserted some sort of power over the group by sleeping with Eva; something that only Charlie, their leader had done. This was all about power.

But was all this enough to warrant murder? Some might think so. But, if so, who was the killer? From my experiences of Charlie, Eva and Anyu, I doubt any of them would be capable of murder. Charlie has his problems, but he asserts that he never hated Tom, nor does he now. Eva and Anyu both found Tom repulsive, but was that repulsion enough to kill?

So, did anyone have a real motive to kill Tom Jeffries? Someone with a clear motive is Haris Novak. We've seen how Tom took advantage of him – asserted his dominance and utilised his innocence to his own ends. The boys scared the life out of Haris with their Nanna Wrack story. Did Haris finally snap and seek revenge? First off, Haris has an alibi for that night – a twisted ankle and … well … he simply doesn't have that sort of violence in him.

That leaves Brian Mings.

So far, we know that Brian was a follower, not disliked by the others, but not deemed particularly important. We also know that he would have done anything to impress them. Tom picked on him, as did Charlie. The incident with Brian's new coat is particularly unpleasant. But was all of that enough to make him kill Tom?

Brian Mings seems to be the elephant in the room. I get a sense that everyone I've spoken to wanted to say more about him, but, for some reason, didn't.

However – and it's a big however – Brian Mings had the safest alibi of all of the teenagers for the night Tom Jeffries vanished: Eva Bickers' bed.

So where does that leave us?

Next episode, in our final story, we will attempt to complete the circle; to fill in the gaps and review everything we've learned about the disappearance of Tom Jeffries.

Maybe there's a solution, a reason, or at least fresh insight, into what went wrong for him that night.

Next week, we talk to Brian Mings.

This has been Six Stories *with me, Scott King.*

This has been our fifth story.

Until next time…

An A road somewhere in Northern England. Establishing connection…
2017

Everyone is waiting for the final episode.

Everyone.

I actually heard some people discussing the thing in a service station Starbucks on my way here. I had to turn away before they saw me staring. *Six Stories* has found its way onto the nation's lips and wormed its way into the collective mind. It terrifies me. Maybe this is why I fled to Scarclaw Fell. Maybe it's why I'm fleeing now.

I've battened down the hatches; ignored the surge of web traffic to The Hunting Lodge; the questions, the requests. Sky Television has asked me if they can film some sort of reality show. The BBC want to send someone out to make a documentary.

I haven't given anyone an answer. I feel like I'm being lured out of the dark, and I won't be. I simply won't. For me, for Dad, for the Ramsay name.

I could pay for security – fences to enclose Scarclaw Fell, but what message would that send? People would ask what we were trying to enclose, what we don't want anyone to see. This Ramsay land is no longer Ramsay land; not since *Six Stories*. Scarclaw Fell belongs to the rest of the world now, and that's why I'm getting away from it. That's why I'm not going back.

There are barely any cars here – no services, no hard shoulder. It's as if the road is ushering me as quickly as it can away from Scarclaw Fell. I've put on the radio; one of the stations that won't be talking about *Six Stories*. I've tried to ignore the thrumming desire inside me that wants to stop, pull over and connect my phone to the Bluetooth; listen to those five episodes once more.

He's smart, Scott King, I'll give him that. It's been a few weeks now since episode five, but he's gone quiet, too. All under the advice of a newly acquired agent, I imagine. Probably trying to convince King to charge for the final episode. King wouldn't do that, would he? How am I to know? I know nothing of the man. Just how he likes it.

It's good advice, whoever's giving it to him: keep them waiting; build the tension. The internet is bristling with theories. I'm told there's a *Six Stories* SubReddit; someone sent me a link to the 'Top Ten Reasons that Charlie Armstrong Killed Tom Jeffries' on Buzzfeed. Vice went with 'I went on a *Six Stories*-style 90s camp with some old school friends'. Some guy called @tomjeffries on Twitter has just closed down his account.

It's a mess.

To add some poetic sentiment to my own feelings, I'd like to say that, as I get further and further away, I can still feel Scarclaw Fell behind me, rearing up from the land, watching me as my car twists along this endless grey artery through the English countryside, as inscrutable as it ever was.

But I can't say it. Because I don't feel that.

All I do feel, if anything, is a twinge of sadness that I won't be coming back here again. Sadness for when this land was mine. Now, all that's left of Scarclaw Fell is the feeling of the knot that tightened inside me when I closed the door to my car and heard the crunch of the gravel beneath the tyres.

I look out at the woods that pulse by me on the left and I wonder what their name is, who owns them; how are they maintained?

There was a time when a part of me believed I had tamed Scarclaw Fell, calmed the residual memories that haunt its hills. But that time has gone. What is wild should stay wild. Even with all the fences and walls and stories and warnings; you cannot tame a place like Scarclaw Fell.

Rain has begun to fall; great big slugs of it streaking my windscreen. A lorry shudders past, its backdraught making me clutch the steering wheel a little tighter, leaving this land with a question that rises up like a vast menhir, higher than the fell; a question that my ownership of this land cannot answer.

It is, of course, about what we saw that night we found the body of the boy. There have been times when I've walked the forest floor and heard things. I have heard the birds stop mid-song, and the presence of something terrible begin to fill the silent, green places. It calls to mind an old story, a dusty book from Dad's library. A troop of men out in the wilds, hunting. One of them is called by the voice of some terrible, unseen presence.

'For the voice, they say, resembles all the minor sounds of the Bush – wind, falling water, cries of animals and so forth. And once the victim hears that – he's off for good of course!'

On his return to camp, the man is changed, broken. He has seen something he dare not speak of – some rustic leviathan whose myth winds deep into the roots and soils of the forest.

When I feel that presence in the woods, I wait it out, stand trembling and allow it to pass.

It always does.

Because perhaps it is only a part of me that, in the silence of the forest, I can hear; a part of me I can't hear anywhere else.

'What the fuck is that?' Tomo stood, pointing at the cream-coloured pile that lay in the muck before us.

We, all three of us knew what it was. It curled in on itself like a dead insect. Tendons hung from the wrist like thick, brown wires, and the remnants of flesh were grey and limp. But none of us wanted to say it. We could smell it, a foul reek that wound its way into your very soul, it seemed.

I wanted it to be a joke. I wanted Jus or Tomo to start snorting, apologising; the other one furious at him for breaking the spell. I wanted to see the flickering lamplight reflected in the lens of a camcorder.

But there was only the stench of old flesh and the rain.

The lurchers were tied to a tree. Jus and I helped Tomo do it, the leads burning our hands as the animals strained to claim their prize.

None of us dared to follow their trail. Our feet were numb and all of us were shaking with cold and adrenaline. As we tied the dogs up, eyes fixed on each other instead of the grisly trophy a few feet away, we began to confer.

'We were lamping deer,' Tomo said. His eyes were wide and desperate. 'OK guys? … OK?'

Jus and I nodded.

'Say it,' Tomo said.

'What?'

'Say it out loud. Say we were lamping deer.'

Like children greeting their headmaster at assembly, Jus and I said it out loud. Accompanied by the rain and the wind and the panting of the dogs and the reek of rotten flesh, we said it.

'We were lamping deer.'

It didn't need to be spoken, none of the rest – the questions that would come about what were we really doing out here; what were we hunting with the lights and the gun. What would we have said? The black shape we all thought we saw became suddenly shrouded in doubt.

'Say it again,' Tomo said.

We did.

And like some arcane chant, like some invocation, we said it over and over again. And with every breath, that black figure at the window became less and less real.

Became more like a dream.

Or some figment of a child's imagination.

I am going to stop at the next service station – it's in twenty miles, according to a sign that slips by. I'll buy a bag of sweets; toffees, fill my mouth with them like I did when I was a boy, allow the buttery, brown liquid to run down my chin as I drive. The sound of the toffee between my teeth, the ache in my jaw, will block out the rest of this journey.

There's nothing more I can do out here. I feel if I stay and try to answer what, if anything, walks Scarclaw Fell, I will become that man from the story. The one that came face to face with what was out there. Or else, I will stand and watch all the others seeking the devil in the woods of Scarclaw Fell.

I can't build more fences, because they'll just ask me what I'm trying to contain. So, maybe I should just let them – let people search Scarclaw for their own Devil, Wendigo, Nanna Wrack or Qalupalik. Let this land become a monument to a mystery.

Which leads me to another question that I cannot answer now. It's not the one that is on the lips of everyone else; it is not about who or what killed Tom Jeffries.

It's, will this story ever rest?

For me, *Six Stories* is over. But something tells me, that for other people, It will continue.

A buzz from my phone startles me, breaking through the tattoo of the rain and the squeak of my windscreen wipers. The road twists, so I do not look away from the blind corners. With a glance, I think I see the name on the screen but I want to concentrate on the road. Let the buzzing subside.

'They'll call us mad. They'll fucking implicate us in this somehow!' Tomo pointed, without looking, to the coil of bone in the muck beside us.

Jus and I nod.

'WE know what we saw, and that's what matters, OK?'

I think of the rhyme that Tomo recited before some relic from the silt-choked lake we all have in the backs of our minds; the place where we keep the bad stuff; the scary stuff.

'Mother, is that father's form at the door?

It's taller and longer than ever before,

His face is all white, coat black like a loon,

His teeth glow like blades in the light of the moon.'

'And that's where we'll keep it,' I said, pointing into the blackness of the trees. 'That's where it'll stay.'

The others nodded.

The rain dripped down our faces like tears.

I'm still not comfortable with talking, as I drive, even with hands-free. So I pull into the space in front of a gate and look at the screen. A sinking feeling fills me: it's the name I thought I saw.

By the time the police arrived, Jus had gone back to the Woodlands Centre to pick up our clothes. We were all shaking, our teeth chattering. I don't remember who called them. Maybe it was me?

All I knew when they arrived was that I wanted my dad.

'Harry?'

'Yes, speaking.'

'I'm sorry, but I need to talk to you again.'

'What? Why? I thought you said…'

'I know. I did say. I'm sorry. There's … something's come up.'

'Your voice sounds…'

'Different? I know. I'm sorry. Look, is it OK if we talk? One last time? I mean, if you say no, I'll understand.'

'We can talk.'

After we've finished on the phone, I put my car in gear and pull away from the gate. The roads get straighter as I move toward the city. I can see buildings on the horizon and more vehicles begin to pass me on the other side. Through the rain, their headlights are glowing eyes; their engines are growls.

Behind me the trees wave in the wind as if bidding me farewell.

I don't look back.

Episode 6: The Sixth Story

Hi.

Before we proceed, I'd like to introduce myself.

Properly.

My name, as you know by now, is Scott King.

Except it isn't, not really. Scott King is simply two words – generic first and surnames put together. It's not me.

Not really.

Scott King is my professional name; the name I chose in order to protect my real identity. Who I actually am doesn't matter. It never has.

I'm not a journalist. I used to be, but that was a long time ago now. These days I devote my life to this, what you're listening to now: my podcasts.

It's far from an original concept, this thing I do – shining a light on past darkness, picking through the settled dust of a cold case. Raking through the earth of old graves.

My podcasts make money … at least they do now. After my first series, I very nearly lost everything. I was down to the few coins I had in my pocket, and that's no exaggeration.

That was before the donations started coming in; before you listeners, through the kindness of your hearts, pledged me as much as you could afford – a dollar here, a pound there. I never asked for much, but it's because of you that I can do what I do.

That's why I want to be straight with you now.

That's why I want to tell the truth.

So here's the thing. I am careful to seek agreement from everyone I speak to. I am not here to pick at old sores, nor to stare into forbidden places. I make these podcasts with the full permission of everyone involved, and I draw no conclusions of my own. That part is for you, the listener.

As regular listeners of my podcasts know, I do not have a 'brand' as such, a USP. However, the type of cases I look at are similar, inasmuch as each case has a sense of something unresolved, a question that rises again and again to its surface, impossible to ignore. I do not seek justice. I do not push for the freedom of incarcerated people. I only look at the facts. That's the way it always has been; the way it always will be.

The case of Tom Jeffries in 1996 was, I will admit, completely unknown to me until very recently. I do not give out an email address; I do not use social media. Yet somehow, about a year ago, an anonymous listener got in touch and pointed me in the direction of Scarclaw Fell and Tom Jeffries.

It was perfect for me and they knew it.

Like any of the podcasts I create, a lot of leg-work and research has to be done before I can start recording. So imagine my surprise when I started contacting those involved in the disappearance of Tom Jeffries. They all told me they didn't want to hear from me again, that, for them, it had been enough, it was over.

Even more troubling, each of them claimed I had told them that neither I nor my production team would be back in touch. They were furious: how dare I break my promise? They felt betrayed.

It felt like a terrible dream. It couldn't be true, could it?

Only one of the people involved agreed to speak to me again. For that, I will always be grateful. Without them, I think perhaps you wouldn't be listening right now.

That person is the one whose voice you heard at the start of episode one: Harry Saint Clement-Ramsay. He was the only one who was willing to explain to me what on earth was going on. He will join me later. Don't get me wrong, I hold nothing against Eva, Charlie, Anyu, Derek and the others. But I wish I could have had the chance to explain myself to them. Harry is one step removed from what happened in 1996, so maybe it was this that allowed him to feel comfortable enough to speak one last time.

Harry told me that he had been contacted by my 'researcher' six months ago to arrange an interview about Scarclaw Fell. He was unaware of me and what I do and thought it sounded a bit shady, which, to be fair, it does.

Harry agreed, however, to the interview, so long as there were certain parameters and restrictions in place; i.e., there were things he did not want to talk about for legal reasons and for the sake of his father. The interview itself was conducted in a car with a man that Harry had been corresponding with for a number of weeks.

Me.

Or someone he thought was me.

This person – this 'other' Scott King had enough of the right credentials – the paperwork and knowledge of the case – to seem legit. However, in retrospect, Harry says that there was something not quite right about the man; that when the interview was over, he was filled with a troubling sense of relief, which, Harry felt, had nothing to do with the subject matter.

What was going on?

Eva Bickers, a big fan of my previous podcasts said something in episode three that has stayed with me and will help you to understand what has happened.

'The thing is, Scarclaw Fell – it's exactly the sort of case that you would cover.'

She is right.

And I did. Sort of.

I'm Scott King. Welcome to Six Stories.

For the last time.

I heard about this particular series at the same time the majority of you did: the day episode one was released.

In actual fact, I was out of town for a weekend and came back to a plethora of text messages, voicemails and emails from iTunes, congratulating me for episode one's fantastic chart position, despite the complete lack of any promotion. As you well know, my series run predominantly on reputation, but I am not above employing the services of promoters to assist in making the public aware of the thing I have created. However, Six Stories *did none of that; it just appeared, as if from nowhere.*

The entire concept of this series was brand new to me. This isn't how I usually do things. This series felt like a drama, a captivating one. I was as compelled as you, constant listener.

So I sat down and listened.

I listened to episode one twice in a row; heard the voice of the presenter, his lexical choices and mannerisms identical to my own. Did I feel invaded, violated, robbed? Was I furious at this copycat who, as I would find out, had used my own identity to catfish the people involved with the Tom Jeffries case to come forward and reveal themselves?

I know I should have done. But I didn't. You know what my overriding emotion was?

Jealousy.

That's right; a burning black jealousy. Like Eva Bickers said, the Tom Jeffries case was exactly the sort of case I would cover in one of my podcasts. The extent to which this case has been researched, the attention to detail and the care that has been shown to the interviewees has been nothing less than professional.

Also, Six Stories *is very, very good.*

—I mean, it was weird. But I just thought it was another *thing* — some pop culture teenager craze that I wasn't aware of. I had no idea of the name Scott King or anything.

Why did I do it? You … *he* … sorry – it's still so bizarre – *he* just sort of convinced me. He just made it sound so … good.

This is the first voice you heard in episode one – Harry Saint Clement-Ramsay. He tells me about the interview that he agreed to do with 'me'.

—I had a few of the guys, yeah? Just sort of *watching*. You – he – told me I had to come alone, which was already a bit suspect. Why would I have to come alone?

—*But you did?*

—Yeah. As I say, he was really convincing. He told me all about the other podcasts and stuff. I searched the name online, did a bit of digging. It all seemed legit.

So, when the day of the interview came, I had a few of my guys sort of *hiding,* nearby. They had their guns, just for protection; none of us ever thought we were going to use them. But you can appreciate, it's not every day you are asked to do an interview about a kid that died nearly twenty years ago – in a car, in my dad's driveway, with a guy wearing that … that *mask.*

Just to clarify, I sometimes wear a mask when I interview people for the podcasts. It's just a plain, blank-faced thing which, I admit, can be a little unnerving for some.

I've got nothing to hide, but I want the show to focus on the case itself, rather than me. So it's better that people don't know who I am. That way, if our paths cross again, there's no awkwardness. I know some people find this strange, it makes them uncomfortable; it makes them think that I am hiding something, but there you go. For this final episode, my face is bare.

—If I think about it, yeah, his voice was probably a bit different to yours. But you don't notice these things at first, do you? His eyes were … I don't know … were they different? Again, unless someone's got really distinctive eyes or something, well, you just kind of relegate them to the back of your brain, don't you?

I ask Harry if he ever explained what he and his friends were doing in Scarclaw Wood, the night that they found Tom Jeffries' corpse. This is something that's been troubling me as I've listened to these podcasts.

—*Did any of you, or anyone you know, ever see* something *out there?*

—What do you mean, 'something'?

—*Like, something that shouldn't have been there: a figure, a person, an animal. Or were you looking for a body?*

Harry pauses for a long time and stares beyond me. It's as if he's battling with something. And in this moment I want to thank him – not just for agreeing to talk to me today, for being the only one who has – but for being honest. What happened to Tom Jeffries was nothing to do with him or his father, but Harry is fully aware of the impact that this podcast may have on his father and his family's reputation.

—Look, we weren't looking for a body. We were looking for … something else.

—*You had your lamps and guns with you.*

—Right. We weren't hunting deer, though. Look, it sounds so ridiculous, I almost don't want to tell you but…

—*Go on.*

—Dad had … Dad had seen something out there. I know – he's an old man, probably in the first stages of senility. But I know my dad, and I know when he's talking cod and when he isn't.

I'll freely admit, after listening to the five episodes of Six Stories, *it was not without trepidation that I asked Harry about what his father saw. I was hoping it wasn't what I – and, I imagine you are thinking…*

—He said it was some … some gangrel thing, some phantom. At first I thought he was joking. He's got an odd sense of humour sometimes. But he wasn't – not at all; he was really scared. And my father doesn't get scared.

This was just what I didn't want to hear. Lord Ramsay had allegedly seen something akin to the creature Charlie Armstrong and Tom Jeffries claimed to have seen that day in 1996. Harry reiterates that, yes, he's heard a whisper about the Belkeld Beast, but always put it down to some old story or an escaped wild animal. Harry says the old man paled as he spoke, and that he was unable to describe the thing in detail, only spoke of its strange, unnatural movement – long limbs dragging themselves across the land.

—*And did you or your friends ever see it, too? Do* you *think there was anything there?*

—Well, that's the thing. The dogs *were* following a trail; but whether it was the scent of that boy's body or ... whatever the other thing was or is ... we'll never know.

—*What do you think was there, in your heart of hearts? What do you think your father saw?*

—If I knew, well, we probably wouldn't be talking now, would we?

It would be pointless for Harry and I to speculate about Charlie Armstrong's 'Nanna Wrack', or Anyu Kekkonen's 'Qalupalik'. These creatures are naught but myths. Perhaps it's something inherent in Scarclaw Fell itself, with its wild forest and hooked peak. Maybe it's a place that conjures monsters from the mind.

Still something bothers me, though; something my mystery imposter never really investigated. That is, how was it possible that the body of Tom Jeffries had lain undisturbed for a year? One theory at the time was that he had sunk so deep into the bogs, the sniffer dogs and search parties at the time were not able to find a scent. And then, subsidence, caused by the ever-churning mineshafts beneath the land, spat him back out a year later. The figure that Lord Ramsay saw was never investigated, as far as I'm aware.

So what stopped the other Scott King following up this question? Was it the same fear that rendered Lord Ramsay silent for all this time?

Or does my doppelganger know something we don't?

So where do we go now? The rest of the Rangers will not speak to me; and I don't blame them for that.

I've followed each story like you have done; read the web forums, the Reddit thread that has sprung up around the case. Through episode two, episode three, I remain silent, simply accepting the praise that comes my way.

Should I have worried that this mystery impersonator had a vendetta against me? That something terrible would unfold, that my identity would be revealed, that he would heave away my shell, leaving me soft and exposed, like the underside of a limpet?

No. Because I realised as I listened, that this was not about me.

This really was the story of Tom Jeffries and the Rangers; this is the story of what happened on the 24th of August 1996 at Scarclaw Fell.

The day that episode five appeared on iTunes, I received an email from an encrypted IP address. The email contained an audio file and an address.

The audio file had a title: 'The Sixth Story'.

I have not edited that audio file in any way, save for adding this rather lengthy introduction, a few asides and some words at the end. I'm sure that there are things you want to know and I can say now that the following audio answers those things.

Yes, we will find out what happened to Tom Jeffries that night.

Yes, we will find out who 'Scott King' – the other 'Scott King' is.

—Welcome to *Six Stories* for the last time. This story is mine.

I hope it doesn't disappoint. Unlike everything else I have ever done in my life, I can say with some certainty that it won't.

—My name is Brian Mings.

I can't remember how old I was when I knew I'd be famous. I just knew it, man; I just *knew it.* You know when you just … *know?*

I'd aced grade two piano by the time I was eight or nine: not bad for someone like me. Someone like me? Short-arse, speccy. I wore those horrible orange NHS things all the way up to year seven, you know?

It's amazing what such a small thing can do for you; the furore it invokes in your fellow children. The cruelty.

But back to the piano. It was a battle, it was always a battle; I never felt like … natural, you know, like some of them do, giving it their whole 'oh, it just comes to me from somewhere' bullshit. Helen Stocksfield, she used to say stuff like that. I think she was the first girl I ever loved, was Helen.

She lived down the road at [street removed], and Mum used to make me call for her in the mornings on the way to school. I can't remember if we talked or anything. Think of that: a boy and a girl walking to school together. A fat, speccy boy and an awkward, skinny girl. I knew her from piano; that's what I used to say when they took the piss: I know her from piano and my mum *makes* me walk her to school.

They still took the piss. 'Speccy-four-eyes and Fuzzy (a reference to the cloud of wiry, blonde straw that surrounded her head) K-I-S-S I N-G!' We weren't either of us worth a well-constructed rhyme.

When I used to call for Helen, her mum used to poke her head round the door. She had the exact same hair – like a toilet brush on top of her head; but hers was grey.

'Will you walk our Helen to school, Brian?' she used to say, every fucking time; as if I'd just knocked on the door to wash the windows or something.

Dad left about the time I did grade two piano.

I never played it after that.

I never called for Helen again.

Hi again, it's Scott King – the real one. Of course, we're going to hear the recording in full. As you've heard, I've edited out the place names. Other than that, I haven't edited any of Brian's recording.

What I have done is researched some of the people mentioned. First off, Helen Stocksfield, now Helen Morris, mother of three, tells me about her former school-run companion.

—Yeah, Brian Mings was an oddball alright. We shared the same piano teacher: Mr Karlsson. He was a disaster as well; he always

stank of fags and drink and would stop your lesson halfway through
to go outside and cough up a lung!

Helen is unaware of Six Stories *and doesn't remember the Tom Jeffries disappearance back in '96.*

—Because I would have recognised the name, wouldn't I?

Brian Mings … I always wondered what became of him, you
know. We used to walk to school, when we were little, like in year
five and that. I don't really remember what we talked about, to be
honest. Probably nothing much; we were just at that awkward age
… boys and girls and that. I do remember some stuff from school
that was weird, though. There was something that happened in year
six … they did a really rubbish job of keeping it quiet, the teachers.
They'd found something in Brian's bag. I didn't see it but everyone
was saying that it was a jam jar with a … a poo in it … like *his* poo.
Like, he was just carrying it round with him.

But his mum and dad had broken up and that was sort of
the 'explanation' for it. It was, like, the late eighties, and people's
mums and dads didn't really break up, not around [name removed]
anyway! I think that singled out Brian quite a lot, anyway, in school
and that. His dad was a massive alchy, wasn't he? We all knew who
he was: you'd see him after school up against the wall of The Swan,
his hands all yellow from his fags, or asleep on the bench next to
the fountain.

—*What about his mum?*

—Yeah, I don't remember her much. She and my mum were
friends, but when they got divorced she just … she just … I think
she was concentrating on Brian, making sure he was OK and that.

*According to others I've spoke to who knew Brian Mings, there were
more peculiar behaviours. Schoolmates of Brian's say he was an atten-
tion-seeker, always doing something to get everyone to laugh. But they
were pretty extreme things he did, though: drawing all over his own face*

with black pen, or holding the pipes of the old radiators until he burned his hand, then proudly displaying the blisters before bursting them.

A number of people say it was hard to feel sorry for Brian Mings, because a lot of the bullying he received in those early school years, he brought on himself. Another schoolmate, who asked not to be identified, says Brian used to lie on the classroom floors, trying to look up the girls' skirts, but it was only when he did this to his teacher that he was reprimanded.

Helen Morris tells me one more story about Brian that I feel is significant.

—He had this sketch book that he used to carry round and he used to write these *stories*. He did the drawings and that as well. They were always about, like, a little prince who killed, like, a dragon; but there was no *story*, it was just pages and pages of how he cut off the dragon's finger, then its other finger and stuck a burning sword into its mouth, and cut out its eyes. He just used to go on and on…

It wasn't just Helen who Brian showed these obsessive stories to. In fact, everyone I spoke to about Brian remembers that notebook. Its content became a bit of a craze in the primary school and always the stories involved defecation, urine, blood. This moves us onto the next part of Brian's recording:

—Helen's mum was … well, she thought I was a psycho because I had a bit of an *imagination*, more imagination than the others. I used to write stories. The other kids *loved* them; they used to crowd round in the yard to see the drawings. Honestly, I've never felt so popular. I don't think anyone's listened to me like that since … well … until now!

So that's when I realised it wasn't going to be piano that'd make me famous. Not that out-of-tune piano I used to clonk away on night after night after night, with mum wailing away up in her bedroom. It was stories … I was going to tell stories. Even as a kid, I knew that's what I was going to be known for. But then school just … just *fucked everything up*. The teacher, she got my notebook, all my stories, and called my mum in. And that was that, it was over. No more stories. Thanks, school, yeah, cheers for that.

As Helen Morris makes clear in our interview, things at home can't have been easy for Brian.

—Did you ever meet Brian's dad? When you two were growing up?
—Nah. I mean, like, I never *met* met him. I knew who he was; everyone knew who he was.

From what I have gathered, Stanley Mings was known in the area, more as a sort of local eccentric than anything else. He was an alcoholic who sometimes slept rough, or else crashed at the houses of various other alcoholics in the area. Mrs Mings was at the end of her tether with him and wouldn't let him stay in the house. He would flit into Brian's life, make a load of promises about how he'd change and then, within a week, he'd be passed out outside the supermarket in the precinct in a pool of his own vomit.
What is significant is that both Helen and Brian's former teacher in high school both assert that, at some point, Brian tried to help his father – even trying to assist him in finding some help and a place to live. However, Brian gave up when Stanley made it clear that his priority – the thing he put before his wife and son – was drinking. The effect that would have had on a young boy like Brian, going through his formative teenage years, must have been deeply wounding.
Let's go back to Brian's recording for a moment:

—So what I started doing, right, was doing other people's home-work for them. I just sort of copied their *style* and wrote my own stories in their books. I had new notebooks now. But I kept them secret from everyone.

Brian Mings' secret notebooks were his refuge. By the time he joined [name of school removed] High in year seven, he was already being picked on. Friendless and ostracised, I cannot imagine the outpourings of rejection and anger that filled the pages.

—Mum ended up on these tablets, for her sleep. She would take them after tea and get all dozy. She never really understood what was going on with me. I'd tell her what was happening; show her my bruises; my specs that had been broken again; and she'd just say, '*Whaaaa*' in this fucking stupid way. Like she was retarded or something. So I used to play away on the piano, loud as I could, scales and songs. And I used to ask her why she never tuned it, how I was ever going to get my grade three if it was all out of tune. Bing, bang *bong*, and she would say, '*Whaaaa?*' like a zombie.

From the interviews with Derek Bickers and the others in the previous episodes of Six Stories, *it is more or less clear that this secret life of Brian's mother was not known – that she managed to hide it from her peers. It is either this or else clever editing on Brian's part, assuming that Brian is, indeed, the creator of* Six Stories.

I can't help feeling sorrow for the poor little boy left playing away on the piano, trying to please his mother. There appear to have been a few concerns about Brian at school; Mrs Mings was called to several meetings. Yet nothing was followed up. It is a tragedy that someone like Brian was allowed to slip through the net so easily.

Before we start condemning the district's overworked and underappreciated children's services, we need to remember that Brian Mings lived in a nice house in a well-to-do area. Brian was never violent – at least not in reality – and there were no outward signs of neglect. And you can also understand Mrs Mings' adeptness at concealing things, the shame of her husband hanging over her at every step. It is hard enough for our services to intervene in the families of the most needy, the most deprived. It is easy to see how the Mings may have been overlooked.

It seems that things really began to get bad during Brian's years at secondary school. Brian discusses this next.

—By the time I was in year eight, oh *man*, I was getting kicked to shit most days. I lost my glasses in the end. Keiran Thompson stamped on them in the changing rooms. They were held together with sellotape, anyway, and this time they just … well, I didn't wear them anymore, let's put it that way. Mum didn't even notice … I think she forgot I even had to wear them. She was taking lots of those pills by then and sometimes just stayed in bed all day.

Then something happened to Dad; he just … he wasn't there anymore. Sometimes I'd sneak in the back door of The Swan and he would buy me a bag of crisps; him and his mate at the back carrying on, smoking their fags and laughing. I don't know where he got the money from.

Then one day he just wasn't there and his mate – that Mick with the smashed teeth and the blue spiderweb on his cheek – he says that some lads were chasing him, chucking bangers at him, and well … he was in the Falklands, my dad was, and I think … well, I know *now* about stuff like PTSD. I didn't then…

Ladies and gents, it's not for me to point out the obvious here, but I think we finally have a motive.

It's an unexpected one. And, just like every revelatory fact has done so far in this series, this new piece of information has created more questions than it's answered. Notably, how on earth did no one know that it was Stanley Mings, a traumatised war veteran, who Tom Jeffries and his friends terrorised, and drove away from where he slept, with fireworks?

I have a theory.

First, the focus was not on Stanley himself, who, as I am led to believe, suffered no lasting physical injury as a result of Jeffries' attack. Second, the media coverage at the time was limited to the local press. What Jeffries and his friends did was not seen as particularly newsworthy. The Eurostar had made its maiden train journey through the Channel Tunnel that very same day, and what was seen by many as a simple prank pulled by some wayward teenage boys in a predominantly middle-class area, with no fatality or even a good third-degree burn to take a photograph of, was quickly dismissed.

With the problems the Mings family had, it is not clear how Brian's father's state was not seen as a bit of a local scandal. How Derek Bickers and the rest of the adults didn't know about it is a mystery. And if they did know, why didn't they offer to help?

Stanley Mings seems to have disappeared off the radar after that. A cynic might argue that, secretly, behind the closed doors of the middle classes, some were glad to see the back of him. Tom Jeffries had performed a welcome service.

Just like I've always done, however, I draw no concrete conclusions; I only make my listeners aware of the possibilities.

One person who did know, though – about everything – was Brian himself.

—Dad never came back. He was like a witch or a monster from an old story – driven from the village by flames and pitchforks. We all knew who'd done it, everyone at school, but no one dared say anything. Tom Jeffries knocked about with Jonny Wagstaff: *You looking at me or chewing a brick? Either way you'll lose your teeth!* So no one said nothing.

I kept out of Jeffries' way. I kept my head down because if he knew it was my dad, things would just get worse. I used to have this little fantasy, just before I went to sleep: I imagined I was in assembly, and it's that weird silence when the head stands up there and he stares out and you feel yourself sort of shrivel inside cos you're hoping his eyes don't land on you. But I've got no reason to be scared, because I know he's going to say my name and I'm going to be called up there in front of everyone. I'm going to get a medal for bravery, cos I saved him. I saved my dad from Tom Jeffries and Jonny Wagstaff. I 'laid my life on the line'. And everyone will be clapping and cheering and they'll be waving their scarves and Miss McCluskey will hold me tight to her…

'Well done, son,' she'll say. 'Well done. You're a hero. You're *my* hero.' And she'll hold me and she'll be wearing that silky white shirt she wears; the one where you can see her bra.

I never wrote that story down, never. It was too delicate, too *sacred*. It would change every time as well. Sometimes I'd be waiting under the bridge, just hanging up in the arches like batman, and I'd swoop down on them: Wagstaff and Jeffries and them.

Sometimes I'd be a sniper; waiting for days, for weeks, hidden away, my scope focussed on the back of their heads. I'd pull the trigger gently *gently*, and watch, *pfft*, as their heads would explode in a sea of skull and brains and blood.

Sometimes I'd find dad wounded by the river; sometimes he'd die in my arms and I would swear vengeance, the camera panning away from us and up into the moonlight. Sometimes we would stagger back to Mum's, his arm around my shoulders and his voice a dying breath: 'Thank you son, thank you.'

All fantasy; all of it. Even the simple little dreams I had. After I walked home from school in the autumn dark, the wind biting through my blazer and the stink of rotten leaves and rain, when I opened the front door, I used to close my eyes, praying that he'd be there, that he'd be standing in the kitchen, sipping a cup of tea.

'C'mere son,' he'd say and I'd run to him, a little boy again. 'I'm sorry,' he'd say, 'for leaving, for doing it all wrong. But I'm back. I'm back to be your dad now.'

Of course, that never happened.

After school, the house was as cold as the street; sometimes it felt colder. Mum would be tucked up under the duvet, dribble in her hair. I'd turn the heating on, get the oven going, fingers frozen, radio on loud, stories whirring around my head, blocking out the day.

It's difficult to follow Brian's timeline. I can only assume he's talking generally about life before he joined Rangers. It is clear he has a vivid imagination. It is also clear that life at home with his mother was not particularly happy.

That's an understatement.

However, I do have my doubts. Mrs Mings' addiction was either hidden, or gone by the time he joined Rangers. Or else imagined completely. Maybe it's the cynic in me that thinks Brian is perhaps exaggerating just how bad things were. I wish there was some way of knowing. Mrs Mings seemed compos mentis *enough to have sought out the Rangers group for her son, and was able to see that he was having trouble with his peers at school. But what does this say about how things really were? Perhaps we'll never know.*

Derek Bickers, in episode one, said that Mrs Mings would drop Brian off on a Wednesday night at the church hall for the meetings. That's all we have to go on.

Let's hear more from Brian.

—It all got a little better when I joined Rangers. That lot gave me hope. Charlie, Eva, Anyu – they were the best friends I ever had; they were the best people I ever knew. I'd never seen people like that before. They seemed aeons older than me – like adults, like proper *people*. That's when I knew I'd found my *tribe*, people like me. Especially Charlie. In him, I saw a potential best friend; someone I could tell about Mum, about what happened with Dad.

This part ties a knot in my throat. A part of me wants to phone Charlie Armstrong again; play him those last few sentences down the phone. But really, what good would that do? What would it change?

—That's when I started buying my clothes from the army shop; one of those big parkas with a furry hood like Anyu's; some of those boots like Charlie's. It took a while, because they didn't like me at first. Charlie used to call me a 'Thing', but none of that hurt anymore; I could take it easy. I just kept going, just kept on until they liked me. That's what you have to do when you're someone like me.

Right here, I'm starting to feel a lot of sympathy for Brian Mings.

Shunned by his peers at school, lonely at home, Brian would have taken anything from Charlie and the others, so long as they accepted him. And by now, Brian appears to have found a way to cut himself off. He'd built a shell to protect himself. So the treatment he received at the hands of the other Rangers presumably did not even contend with what he had already endured.

—But then the day came when *he* arrived. *Him*, there, in the church hall with *my* friends, *my* people. I wanted to get up that second, to shout; to tell all of them what he was, what he had done. But ... I just *couldn't*.

At first I thought they'd see what he was. I was looking forward to Charlie tripping Tom up – giving him a dead leg and calling him a 'Thing' instead of me. I couldn't sleep the next Tuesday night, and all Wednesday my stomach was jittering away just waiting for it. Maybe Charlie would get his fingers in that finger-lock he got mine in some-times. I'd got it to the point where he could bend them back almost to the back of my hand and I didn't cry out. I forced all the pain down into my boots. 'Look at this! Look at this!' Charlie would say to the others. And they'd all say, 'That's sick; that's mint.' I couldn't wait for him to do that to Tom.

But that night, for some reason it all just went wrong somehow. It was my fault; I arrived way too early and I'd worn my new coat – the one with the straps; the one that I knew Charlie wanted, that he'd been looking at in that magazine. I'd asked him if I could borrow it, just to read about some of the bands – Cannibal Corpse, Obituary, Morbid Angel. I liked them, too; I liked them cos Charlie had got me into them. That's what I told everyone.

So I wore the coat and I arrived early. Derek wasn't there yet and I stood around outside for a bit. I was scared in case I saw anyone from school. In my heart, I knew Tom would tell everyone anyway about what he did to my dad; that next week he'd probably break Jonny Wagstaff out of that young offenders unit and bring him along. But, still, I wanted Charlie to see my coat; I wanted Anyu to see I wasn't being a 'Thing' anymore. Darren Michaels had ripped the hood half off my parka anyway at school, called me a 'fucking hippy queer'. Now the hood hung down my back like a dead thing.

And then I saw they were all smoking round the back.

With Tom.

I went inside with all this sadness running through me, and I thought Anyu might have seen me; that she might come in after me and ask what was wrong, and I'd say:

'Why the fuck's Charlie friends with Tom Jeffries all of a sudden?'

And then I'd tell her about him. I'd tell her how at school he went round writing his name all over everything with his pen; that he called people 'hippy cunts' and threw fireworks at people. That he tried to set fire to them and everyone just thought it was *funny*. I'd tell her about how mum slept with all dribble down her chin and that my dad was still missing; that my dad still hadn't come back and it was *his* fault. I'd say there was no way he was going to fit in here; that we should get rid of him. And she'd understand and she'd tell Charlie and everything would just go back to the way it was.

But no one came in. I was just stood there on my own.

Then they all filled the doorway, started laughing at something *he* said and I felt this fucking *weight* in my stomach, like a fucking *landslide*, a wave of shattered slate just pouring inwards. And I knew then that I should have turned and run and never come back. But Tom and Charlie were all over me, and I let them take the straps of the coat and tie me up with them – because it was just a laugh, just a joke, and I wasn't being a 'Thing', was I? If I let them look at my coat they'd see that that I was my own person, and Charlie would ask if he could borrow it and I'd say I'd think about it. And he'd get Tom in that finger-lock and make *him* scream this time.

But it wasn't happening, they were still just standing around me, and it was like I was frozen, just *waiting*. I couldn't even speak.

I looked down and saw Tom was wearing that stupid cap of his and a little light feeling began in my stomach, because this was it;

this was when the tide turned. I kept looking at them and *willing* Charlie to just start – to start calling Tom a *charver*. He always used to tell me about the charvers with their *Spliffy* jeans and their *NafNaf* jackets and how he used to fight them if they called him 'hippy'.

I remembered when Tom had called us lot hippies and no one did anything.

Sometimes, when we were smoking behind the church hall, I used to tell Charlie about the charvers in my school, too. And those moments, when me and Charlie were laughing at the charvers with their shaved heads and their *NafNaf* jackets, those moments were the fucking *best*. Those were the moments of us nearly being friends. But, right then, that night, Charlie said nothing about Tom's jeans; he just started tying me up with the straps from my coat. And then my boots were out the window, and Charlie was calling me a 'Thing', and they were all laughing.

I realised then that everything was different, that if only Anyu Kekkonen had followed me into the hall, and I had told her about Tom Jeffries, maybe then things wouldn't be like this now. But that hadn't happened. Instead I was outside round the back, all the fag butts like little orange shotgun shells in the soil. It stank out there – like leaves and mud and night, and my cheeks were burning hot and my toes were wet and my boots were hanging half in and half out of a rose bush. And I wondered, if dad was there, too, what he would think if he saw me here, blubbing away like a little girl, crying round the back of a church hall when he'd fought for his country.

And then I saw him, hiding down there under the rosebushes. His face black as mud and his breath like the smell of Tom Jeffries' Regal King Size.

'C'mere son,' he said, and I bent down and knelt in the mud. Dad's face was all thorns, and he told me that I didn't have to take this anymore, that if I wanted him to come back, I had to stop being such a sissy and stand up for myself.

That's when we came up with the plan. Me and Dad sat down there, under the rosebushes, with wet jeans and the straps of my coat hanging around us like garlands. That's when we came up with the plan.

This incident with the coat has been mentioned by a few of the others and it is interesting and distressing to hear Brian's take on it. To me, it seems a defining moment for Brian Mings. For want of a less flippant phrase, possibly it was the moment he 'snapped'.

Next, Brian moves on to the summer visit to Scarclaw in 1995, when Tom was not present. From what he now says, it seems his psychosis was now in full flight. Either that or, a bit like Haris Novak, he is re-imagining what happened.

We'll never know.

—Me and Dad finalised the plan not long after we'd been up to Scarclaw doing the insulation. It was only going to be me, Anyu, Charlie and Eva. It was a good to get away from home.

Charlie and me had been smoking together in the mineshaft. He'd given me a cigarette. I remember taking it, hoping my fingers weren't going to shake, thinking that I was going to blow the smoke out through my nose. That's what I was going to do.

'Let's take one draw each then throw it away,' he said, and we did.

That's why I thought we must be friends by now. He was talking properly to me that weekend, like I wasn't a 'Thing', that, even with my boots that were just like his, and my Walkman full of tapes like Cannibal Corpse and Morbid Angel, that I was his friend. We spent an afternoon, just me and Charlie, listening to 'Where the Slime Live' and 'Lord of Emptiness' until the batteries on his little radio ran down. We melted candles from the centre into the walls and smoked more of the cigarettes he'd nicked from his mum. Dad was there, too, hidden in the back of the cave, his eyes glowing red like the ends of our fags, and he was nodding saying, 'Go on son, that's right.'

I thought we were friends then, me and Charlie.

When Haris showed us the mineshaft, I said that this could be, like, our place. I nearly said clubhouse, some word from the Famous fucking Five. But I felt Dad prodding me in the back so I stayed quiet. I said we could leave booze and fags down here, cos I had that bag – that massive wax army bag of Dad's. We could leave it in there, but they were all worried in case Haris took it and drank the booze and we'd get in trouble.

Charlie told the Nanna Wrack story, down in the dark with the candles and Morbid Angel going slower and slower, *grunt-grunt-grunt*, like it was music for slugs and snails and fat soft things that live below the ground.

Me and Dad went to look for her in the night after the others were all asleep. Me and Dad, up on the fell looking for Nanna Wrack with our guns and he said, 'That's right, son. That's right.'

We remembered that day when Dad came back; me and Dad behind the church hall, in the mud and the roses; my soaked socks and the echoes of their laughter in our ears.

Me and Dad, we had a few months of planning it: stockpiling Mum's tablets and trying them out. I didn't write stories in my note-books anymore – they became actual notes. I made notes: which tablets did what and for how long. It was better than school; school didn't matter anymore, Dad said, because we had the plan.

What I have discovered after hearing this, is that, indeed, Brian Mings had a lengthy absence from school between October and November 1995, attending sporadically, with absence notes, which the teachers suspected he forged. Like so much in this story, however, nothing was followed up when Brian made a reappearance in New Year 1996, apparently all well again.

Speaking to Brian's old classmates is not as easy. The ones I've spoken to simply don't remember anything particularly significant about him. It seems he just flitted along like a little ghost.

We will continue to listen to how Brian's plan panned out. He talks now about the winter of 1995 – Tom Jeffries' first visit to Scarclaw Fell.

—The plan took another step forward when we went to Scarclaw in the snow. Dad rode in the bus with us all the way there, sitting in the back beneath the bags. I could just see the little orange pinpricks of his eyes. I sat with Anyu and tried to tell her about Nanna Wrack, about how we'd found her up there on the fell, me and Dad on one of our walks. She wasn't even listening. I could hear Dad muttering from the back: '1/4 diazepam, four hours.' I had to hold my mouth closed to stop laughing in her face.

It was a good time, a great time. Just Dad and me in the snow, trekking over the fell while the others hung about in the mine.

None of the others have mentioned Brian Mings going off by himself like this. Maybe it's because they didn't even notice his absence. I hope that's not the case.

—That's when we found the marshes – the big tree that sticks out of there, black, like it's been hit with lightning. The wind whistles up there, like a long, cold, lonely song.

Up there's where Nanna Wrack lives; up there where the water is frozen over, the broken-down house with its great black eyes staring out at you through the snow. We had to creep over the marsh using sticks – big branches like spiders' legs. I had my parka on and it had got soaked, the furry hood hanging all down my back. That's where she slept, her hair sticking up through the ice. Her green fingers. We lay down, Dad and I, like best friends. And we whispered into the snow to Nanna Wrack, told her about the plan.

Brian doesn't mention any more about the trip to Scarclaw in the winter of 1995, when the incident with the snowballs occurred, and which he, according to Anyu Kekkonen, instigated. Perhaps it wasn't significant to him? Perhaps, by then, his psychosis had already consumed him; or else it's been sufficiently covered in the previous episodes.

Perhaps now, we can attach new significance to whether it was indeed Brian who initiated the attack on Haris Novak, encouraging Tom Jeffries to give him cannabis to eat. My initial idea was that Brian had done it to show off to the others, to fit in. What appears to be his reasoning instead, is something to do with his plan – to expose Tom Jeffries for what he was, or to turn the tide of feeling against Tom. It certainly assisted in creating suspicion around Haris Novak – another deeply unsettling act of manipulation on the part of Brian Mings.

What is deeply unsettling is the callousness with which Brian discusses Anyu and the others. Throughout this series we have been led to believe that Brian had a fierce attraction to Anyu Kekkonen. But now, as this episode unfolds, it seems increasingly likely that this could well have been a front, a way to carry out his plan. What is apparent, however, is Brian's hero-worship of Charlie Armstrong. It is, of course, possible that Brian associated losing Charlie as a friend with his father's disappearance. It is also possible that Brian was attracted to Charlie, but couldn't express it. By now, though, I doubt Brian Mings was capable of what we know as love.

—The last day of the summer holidays, Dad was waiting for me in the house when I got in. Mum was asleep on the sofa, mouth open, catching flies.

'C'mere son, c'mere,' he said, and he ruffled my hair.

We both looked at Mum for a bit and I could feel a strange feeling building up; like a cross between anger and wanting to cry.

'Shhhhh,' Dad said, and he put his arm around me.

I wanted to tell him about Damien Wright, who'd smashed up his biro and stuck it down my back. But Dad got the notebook out and had all the charts going: the pills and times and doses. His hair was all brambles and he left a great soil mark where he sat; blue curls of smoke coming off him.

'Will you come with me?' I asked, and his laughter was the rustle of leaves and the *crick-crick* of a magpie.

He showed me the graphs and the figures and the list of names. We were all set. Derek would be bringing the big bus round in a couple of hours and we knew we had to get Mum up in time for that; give her some coffee and brush her hair.

The first night we were at the centre I was scared in case it didn't work. Every time we went outside, I could feel Nanna Wrack looking at us from the fell, from her home beneath the mud, between the roots of that black tree. The ice had melted, of course, and she was hungry. My dreams that first night were all fingers and teeth rising up from the marsh.

When we ate breakfast, I thought of me and Dad and Charlie flying a kite on the fell, listening to 'Where the Slime Live', the three of us smoking cigarettes and singing along.

And it was easy, just so easy; easier than last time, in the winter, the trial run, when Tom saw me slipping Mum's pills into Anyu's vodka. No one believed him, anyway, just like Dad said they wouldn't.

I remember lying there on my bunk on my back. I'd been there for the last few hours and none of them had noticed. I was getting good at being invisible, Dad told me from beneath the bed. I lay there for a few hours, watching them all start to get drowsy; start to lie down on their beds. I had all the booze in Dad's big army bag, with my notebook in the secret pocket with the doses and the charts. I knew exactly who was getting what and how long it would take them to go to sleep.

Tom was all pissed off, staggering about, telling Charlie to stop being such a *gayboy*, but Charlie fell asleep first. Then Eva. Then Anyu last. I could never quite get it right with her. I told Tom I was still up if he wanted to have a smoke, and he told me to keep wanking with my *nob this big* and I was laughing until he shouted at me to fuck off.

That's when I waited. Those hours went by like a dream. I could hear Dad slithering about under the centre, and Nanna Wrack rumbling away on the fell. When the daylight started coming in, that's when I waited for the signal. Nanna Wrack would send a bird – one of the big black carrion crows – and that's when it would be time.

I took a last look at him, lying there in his sleeping bag, and I wondered what he was like as a baby – whether he was a nasty little boy who took people's toys, or if he was kind. I looked in his face and it just looked like he was made out of wax, as if someone had slipped in and swapped Tom for a wax dummy. I was starting to get scared, so I poked him in the face, prodded him hard, just to see if he really was wax.

'Come on son, come on!' said Dad. And there was a big ragged crow outside and I got up from my bunk.

I was starting to get too excited and my stomach was rolling around. I nearly got it all wrong and forgot to get one of Eva's bras from her bag. I wanted it for proof – in case anyone ever wondered why someone like Eva had lowered herself to go with someone like me. I had to be quick, trying to find it but my hands were shaking and I suddenly thought that maybe what I was about to do wasn't right. But she'd slept with him; she'd *slept* with Tom fucking *Jeffries*, hadn't she? If that wasn't punishment enough!

So that's why I climbed into her bunk, because Anyu woke up and stared out at me, and for a moment I thought she was going to start screaming. So doing the best quick-thinking I'd ever done, I climbed into Eva's bunk before I went to get Tom.

This is chilling. The tone of Brian's voice betrays a relish for what happened that night. He speeds up and he lingers on the finer details. It is at this point that I wonder about Brian Mings' psychosis – wonder whether it isn't just a convenient cover story for the spurned boy with the huge imagination.

—'What, what?' Tom was saying.

His eyes were all bloodshot and his limbs were all floppy. The others were asleep, but every move I made was huge and loud. Tom was heavier than I thought, as well. As I lifted him, he started waking up more. 'Fuck off Brian, man,' he mumbled. 'Fuck off; go back to bed. What are you doing, you queer? You fucking little gay.'

I told him to shut his fucking mouth, but he did that face – that fucking face, which is a bit like a wink and a bit like a sneer. And I felt my fists against his mouth and he shouted then and I thought, this is it, that the game was up.

He started to get to his feet, but his legs were like a baby deer's, all wobbly. I could see he was just about to start shouting, to start screaming, and if that didn't wake up the others, it'd wake up Derek in the room down the hall. That was when I pulled out the knife, the big one from the kitchen with the black handle. Suddenly Tom wasn't so hard.

'I'll shout out; I'll wake up the whole place,' he said, as if he could read my thoughts. I just laughed at him and kicked Charlie, who was lying right there. He didn't even budge.

'Go on then,' I said. 'Go on, then, Tom. Why don't you just cry out and then I'll stab you up.'

At first I thought he was going to laugh. I saw his face twitch, and I swear down, I would have done it – stuck that knife right in his belly. I think he knew that, so he shut up.

I'd never felt so brave in all my life, and I could see Dad skulking around outside, the wind pressing dead leaves against his ribs. And I could hear Nanna Wrack – her stomach rumbling; the sound of worms writhing in the earth.

'Get out of here and get the bag,' I said.

Tom tried to make a run for it when we got out the window, but I was too quick, and it was in that moment I realised how much taller I was than him; that he was really small, like a little kid.

'Get up there,' I said.

'Where are we going? Where are we going?' he kept saying. But I wasn't listening because it was getting light and I could see Nanna Wrack up there on the fell, and her hair was black and green, and her mouth was full of gorse. I pushed Tom forward, and he was saying, *'Sorry, sorry, I promise, I promise.'* But I wasn't listening to that, either, cos Dad was beside me and he was saying, 'Go on son. Go on,' with his voice that pushed us further up the fell.

When we got to Nanna Wrack's house, I think Tom knew he was going to die, because he started crying and telling me about his mum and his dad, and how he wouldn't say anything to anyone about all this, and how we could be friends.

We stood there on the fell with the new day shining behind us. He was crying, and right then he looked like a little kid, and I nearly fell for it, I nearly fell for his lies.

'Please, Brian, I'm sorry.'

'What are you sorry for, Tom?' I asked. If he'd said he was sorry to Dad, if he'd got down right then and said sorry to Dad, said he didn't mean to drive him away like that, and that he would help us be a family again, I might have let him go. I might have.

But as I was thinking all this and Tom was crying, I lowered the knife and he kicked out at my hand. It stung like a wasp and I heard Nanna Wrack give out a great big scream, a scream like there was a hole in the world.

Tom started running then, shouting out. But he didn't know the fell; he didn't know what I knew. I scrabbled around on the ground for a second, found the knife and started chasing him.

I could see Dad, this shadowy figure running at Tom. I was screaming to Nanna Wrack: *Have him! Have him now!* And soon Tom was in the marsh, mud all over him, screaming and screaming. He was sloshing about, up to his knees in water, and his voice was bouncing off the fell, crying for his mum, his dad, the police.

He was quicker than me, so quick and I thought it was over, that we wouldn't catch him. But then I smelled fags and Dad was beside me.

'Go on, son,' he said, and handed me a big flat stone. I threw it at Tom.

Nanna Wrack and Dad cheered because it was a direct hit. It made a crack sound and I saw a bit of blood. Tom just fell on his face in the mud.

Nanna Wrack was rising up out of the marsh behind him, and it was either him or me. So I pushed him down. He was strong for a little kid, but the three of us – me and Dad and Nanna Wrack – we held him down there until he was still, and his screaming was gone, and all I could hear was the sound of my heart beating and the sound of Nanna Wrack feeding.

Of course, no one thought to look at the toxicology of anyone's blood that night. The teenagers were fully compliant with the police, admitting that they had drunk alcohol and taken drugs, so presumably, that sort of detail wasn't necessary during the inquest. There was no reason, of course, for the investigating officers not to believe Brian's story. He, like the others, had simply fallen asleep and woken up to Tom Jeffries missing. The mud on his boots could have been easily attributed to that day's walking on the fell to Belkeld. And, of course, he had Eva Bickers' bra.

Supposing what Brian says is all true – that he drugged the others and forced Tom outside onto the fell; supposing that's how it happened, how was Tom Jeffries' body not discovered for nearly an entire year after he went missing?

Let's hear why.

—We waited until he stopped moving, waited for Nanna Wrack to have her fill. We stood there in the blue light of the dawn. I wanted to feel happy, to scream and cheer, but I felt Dad's gun in my back and he said, 'We're not finished yet, son; remember the plan.'

'Aye, aye, sir,' I said, and we pulled Tom's body out of the marsh. His face was all covered in slime and mud, and his mouth was open.

With the mud and the marsh it seemed to take hours, but we used the knife and we got him into that black bag, the one he used to get into. I was saying, 'Why don't you want to go in the bag, Tom? What's wrong with it? It used to make me laugh so hard, Tom, you getting in the bag.' But he was saying nothing. We zipped it up and dragged it all the way across the fell to Haris Novak's place. Shoved it in the coal scuttle. It smelled like the dead in there – Haris' dead animal tomb.

That's when I went back and had a shower, waited for the rest of them to wake up. All the time I could hear Nanna Wrack whispering, '*Thank you, thank you.*' And Dad's hand in my hair: 'Well done, son. That's showed him; that's showed him at last.'

Of course, the other victim in the wake of all this, was Haris Novak. He'd been the one who'd agreed to keep hold of the bag for the teenagers, promising not to tell anyone about it on pain of terror from the Beast of Belkeld. Remember, it was Brian Mings that insisted Haris do this.

As I was rendering this audio, I realised that Brian Mings must have returned to Belkeld nearly a year after he'd murdered Tom Jeffries and moved the body back, for Harry and his friends to find. By then, of course, Haris' old house was empty. No one had thought to check the disused coal scuttle around the back. And Haris himself was probably completely oblivious to what was in there.

If we recall, Brian knew that Haris dragged animal corpses from the fell and buried them in his mother's garden. Was part of his plan to implicate Haris in Tom's death? There is even, of course, the possibility that Haris, in a panic, did find Tom's corpse in the coal scuttle, and buried it. I find this is unlikely, though.

There is another huge question here. Was it Brian that Harry and his friends saw, creeping around Scarclaw Fell that night? Did seeing him prompt them to take out the dogs and search for the Belkeld Beast?

Possibly. The stench from the decomposed body of Tom Jeffries would certainly have attracted Harry's dogs – perhaps masking Brian's scent as he escaped over the fell.

From the research I've done into Brian Mings, he was very good at keeping himself hidden. There is no social media account and his employment records show he worked for several telesales companies in his home town.

So what prompted him to exhibit the body of Tom Jeffries? Why risk exposing himself a year after murder.

And why now does he tell his story, twenty years later?

Brian Mings has clearly spent much of his time following my career, learning about the way I operate and being able to fool enough people

into believing he was me in order to create this series. I will allow him to
complete the postscript to his own story.

—The thing is, I always knew I was going to be famous. At first
I thought it was the music; maybe it would have been if Mum had
bothered to tune that piano instead of taking pills all day. Then I
thought it was the stories; but school spoiled all of that, with their
rules and their ideas about what sort of stories are acceptable and
what sort of stories aren't.

People like Charlie, people like Anyu – they're the sort of people who
are going to be famous for something. Their names are the ones that will
be in the papers for the things they've achieved. Not people like me.

That's what I always thought.

But when they ruled that Tom was killed by accident, that it was
'misadventure', that he had just wandered off because he was pissed,
that I had just got away with it so easily, I realised that, yes, there was
something I *could* be famous for after all.

We've been up there a few times – in the snow and the rain and
the wind; me and Dad and Nanna Wrack. There are stories, we've
decided, that need to be told. Despite schools and rules, and Mum,
and the Tom Jeffries of this world, there are stories that need to be
seen from different perspectives in order to make sense.

But who would listen to someone like me?

Who cares about my story?

You would. All you, who've been waiting with baited breath for
this final episode. I don't blame you. It's in our nature as people to
want to know the end, to find a conclusion amidst the mud and the
reeds and the leaves.

You're probably wondering how they'll catch us. You're wondering
how the police will track us down – me and Dad and Nanna Wrack.
And what if I even told you there was more to come? There'd be a
little piece of you that would want to hear it, wouldn't there? There'd
be a little part of you that would hope that we'd be able to tell more
stories just like this one.

And isn't there another little part of you – a little Tom Jeffries-shaped part of your heart – that wonders whether someone like me is just telling a story, that someone like me isn't capable of doing what I've done? That it's all just a tale to keep you amused on your way to work.

After all, that's what I'm famous for, isn't it?

And finally, don't you really want to know … about me?

There is no more.

That is the end, this confession of sorts.

Here we have what allegedly happened to Tom Jeffries, according to his alleged killer. Little is known about Brian Mings, save for the anecdotal evidence I have collected while researching this episode.

Maybe there is more, as Brian says. However, I decided, if Six Stories *was to be concluded by anyone, it had to be me.*

I have to at least try and convince you that I, Scott King, am not, in fact, Brian Mings. I have to try and do that – for my own sake, if not for anyone else's.

Obviously, I can make promises, I can promise that this recording will be turned over to the police and there is a possibility that I may be in trouble for releasing what could be crucial evidence in the case of Tom Jeffries.

There is a possibility I may be arrested, charged and tried for Tom Jeffries' murder.

I can guarantee there will be an exhumation of Tom's body. Derek, Eva, Charlie and Anyu will all be spoken to again and this old wound will be reopened for a third time, causing untold grief to the Jeffries family and untold agony to those who were involved. But maybe that is the intention?

Maybe it is wrong for me to do this, to put this podcast out? That's for you to decide. But for me, I think that the story of Brian Mings and Tom Jeffries is a story that, however abhorrent it may be, would have never been told otherwise.

Is that a good thing?

It certainly makes us think what side we take on this whole matter.

Is this a lesson? In some ways, I suppose it is. Tom Jeffries was clearly an unpleasant character whose actions went largely unpunished. A group of teenagers who were allowed softer boundaries than most, raised to be accepting and tolerant, yet still allowed one of their members to feel victimised.

Maybe that's it? Maybe that's the point?

Personally, I believe it's a combination of both, blended in the crucible of a damaged mind. I believe the story here has to be taken in many ways and there is no definite conclusion. In true crime, this is often the case.

However, I do believe, like Brian, that some stories do need to be told. Even this one.

I have been, I assure you, Scott King.

This has been our sixth and last story.

Farewell.

THE END

Acknowledgements

I would like to thank everyone who has, in small, large and sometimes oblivious ways, contributed to the writing of *Six Stories*:

Nick and Amy at New Writing North, who first told me about *Serial*; Laura at New Writing North for giving me such amazing opportunities to work with talented young writers at the weekends, and Claire at New Writing North for pulling strings she didn't have to pull.

Peter Mortimer at Iron Press, for his belief, which is as fearsome as his constructive criticism. Shelley Day for her exquisite company and huge writing talent. Paul Clark and the Disley family, for enthusing about my work, even when I was writing bad short stories about monsters; you lot kept me going in some dark times. My sister from another mister; Max Halls, Jex Collyer and Andy Bain; my Lancaster buddies. Benjamin Bee and Richard Dawson, my stupidly talented Newcastle friends who always told me I would get here even when I didn't believe it. Steve, Megan, Leah, the board game massive and the inimitable Dr Sarah Farmer.

Kati Heikkapelto, Amanda Jennings, Yrsa Sigurðadottir and Antti Tuomainen, for being not only hugely influential in terms of writing but lovely people who indulged me as a fanboy of their talent.

My family: Jill, for putting up with me for so many years; Mum, Dad, Chet, Joe, Katie, Gloria, Derrick and my incredible sister, Nina, who is not just a sibling but a sterling critic of my work, as well as a phenomenal friend. All that from a test tube, eh?

My son, Harry, for being the driving force behind all I do.

Huge gratitude goes to my publisher, Karen Sullivan, who plucked me from obscurity and gave me a chance – for your relentless support, your unwavering belief and the free books I thank you; you are truly an outstanding creature.

My magnificent editor, West Camel, for his help in honing my work into what it has become, and Mark Swan for the phenomenal cover artwork.

And, of course, if you got all the way here, you, dear reader; you're one of the good 'uns!

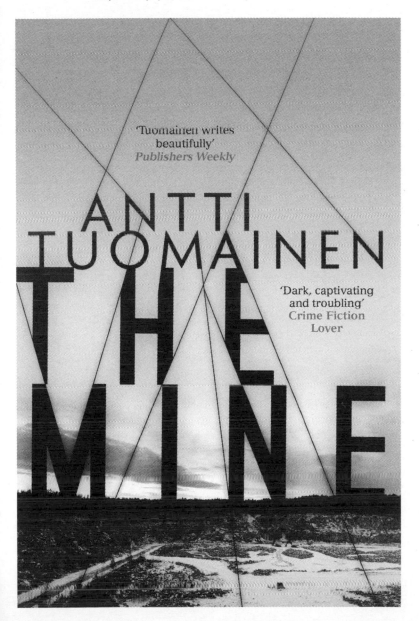

'Tuomainen writes
beautifully'
Publishers Weekly

ANTTI
TUOMAINEN

THE
MINE

'Dark, captivating
and troubling'
Crime Fiction
Lover

WINNER
ENGLISH PEN
AWARD

'Chilling, atmospheric and hauntingly
beautiful ... I was transfixed'
AMANDA JENNINGS

THE BIRD
TRIBUNAL

'Intriguing ...
enrapturing'
SARAH HILARY

AGNES
RAVATN

AS HEARD ON BBC RADIO 4'S BOOK AT BEDTIME